Cliff's Edge

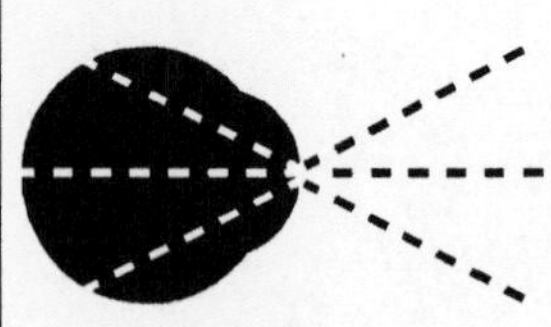

Cliff's Edge

Meg Tilly

WHEELER PUBLISHING
A part of Gale, a Cengage Company

Farmington Hills, Mich • San Francisco • New York • Waterville, Maine
Meriden, Conn • Mason, Ohio • Chicago

Solace Island Series.
Wheeler Publishing, a part of Gale, a Cengage Company.

Wheeler Publishing Large Print Hardcover.
The text of this Large Print edition is unabridged.
Other aspects of the book may vary from the original edition.
Set in 16 pt. Plantin.

LIBRARY OF CONGRESS CIP DATA ON FILE.
CATALOGUING IN PUBLICATION FOR THIS BOOK
IS AVAILABLE FROM THE LIBRARY OF CONGRESS

ISBN-13: 978-1-4328-6670-9 (hardcover alk. paper)

Published in 2019 by arrangement with Berkley, an imprint of Penguin Publishing Group, a division of Penguin Random House LLC

Printed in Mexico
1 2 3 4 5 6 7 23 22 21 20 19

To Jayne Ann Krentz

Your books delighted and enthralled me. Got me through difficult, lonely times. What an absolute joy to discover that the fierce intelligence, kindness, and generosity of spirit lives not only in your heroines but in yourself as well.

Prologue

He caught sight of her as the wedding party swooped past him and entered the church. Her arm was linked with the bride's, both of them laughing in the late-afternoon sun. Her head was thrown back, causing her long ebony hair to tumble down her back in glorious abandon.

Mine, the man thought with a fierceness that shocked him to the core.

He quickly parked, grabbed his phone, snapped a hasty photo through the windshield, then exited his vehicle. The path of his life had just veered to the left, and he had no choice but to follow where it led him.

He crossed the road and melded into the edges of a large group entering the church. Nervous sweat was starting to congregate in his armpits. He could feel it sticking his shirt to his back as he slipped past the ushers standing guard at the vestibule's arched doors leading into the nave.

He sat in the rear of the church and waited for her to reappear. And when she did, he bathed in her beauty, the gracefulness of her form.

The ceremony was finished, the bride was kissed, and everyone stood hurling flower petals as the newly married couple headed down the aisle. Only a few more minutes before they would pass the back pews and the crowd would disperse.

He tapped the lacy arm of the matron beside him. "Who is she?" he asked. He thought he had put his socially acceptable expression of bored interest on. But apparently a flare of the passion coursing through him had slipped past the mask, for the woman's eyes widened as she took a slight step back.

"The bride?" she asked, her dimpled hands fluttering up to her neck.

"No, her," he said, smoothing his face into benign kindness and tipping it toward the mystery goddess. "The maid of honor."

The woman's skittishness subsided, and an affectionate smile took its place. "That's the bride's sister, Eve Harris. Quite the beauty, isn't she?"

"I hadn't noticed," he lied. "She looked

familiar, and I was wondering how I knew her."

"She and her sister are co-owners of the Intrepid Café. It's a pretty recent addition to our town, but it's been quite the smash hit, let me tell you! My friends and I meet every Wednesday for our afternoon social and, oh my, do we enjoy their baked goods." She glanced over her shoulder and noticed that her friends had moved on. "Excuse me," she said, hurrying after them.

Dazed, he followed in her wake, out of the church, down the steps into the courtyard, blinking in the harsh July sunlight. A mole emerging from its hole. His mind spun a million miles an hour.

She belonged to him. Of that he was certain.

However, this would require careful planning, preparation. He wasn't sure exactly how he was going to pull it off, but he did know one thing.

He was her destiny.

One

Three months later

"So, which one will it be?" Eve asked, peering at Ethelwyn through the glass case.

The woman's hands were shoved in the front pockets of her saggy faded jeans, her worn plaid work shirt loose and untucked. She was staring intently at the various pies. Her lips made little smacking sounds, as if she were actually tasting the various options. "I don't know," she moaned. "The cherry looks good, but I really love Maggie's strawberry-rhubarb. It has just the right amount of tart and sweet."

Behind Ethelwyn, someone cleared his throat. Eve glanced at the fiftysomething man sporting an expensive haircut and wearing a fawn-colored cashmere sweater over a button-down white shirt. His sleeves were rolled back. There was a gold Cartier watch on his wrist and a burnished gold wedding ring on his finger.

He seemed a trifle irritated by Ethelwyn's indecision.

Eve smothered a grin. *Too bad,* she thought. *This is the Solace Island way. Doesn't matter what your bank balance is. Everyone's equal.*

Besides, Ethelwyn was one of the Intrepid Café's most loyal customers. She and her life partner, Lavina, purchased copious amounts of baked goods. Whereas Mr. Fancy-Pants had only started coming by recently and usually ordered a coffee. Black. How could anyone see the tempting treats and smell the wonderful fragrances caused by her sister's delicious creations and then just order a black coffee?

"Take your time, Ethelwyn," Eve said cheerily. "It's an important decision. I'll start boxing up the rest of your order." She slid the glass door of the display cabinet shut with her hip as she rose. Then she turned to the back counter, where her sister, Maggie, was transferring pecan-puff jam-dot cookies from the cooling racks to a display platter.

"Hey, hey, hey," Maggie murmured, a conspiratorial grin lighting up her face.

"What?" Eve said, placing a dozen chocolate cookies with caramel centers and a sprinkling of flaked sea salt on the top into a white bakery box.

"He likes you," Maggie whispered. She wiggled her eyebrows, which meant the guy she was talking about was super hot.

Eve peeked over her shoulder, took a quick glance around the café to see who had arrived. No one had. She looked at Maggie. *Who? Where is he?* she mouthed, shifting casually closer to her sister, because clearly Maggie had a better hunk-viewing vantage point.

Behind Ethelwyn, Maggie mouthed. *You should see the way he's looking at you. All hungry-like.*

The tendrils of hope and excitement deflated with a *thump.* "Eww," Eve said. "First of all, he's married."

"He is?" Maggie looked disappointed.

"Yup. Ring on the finger. And second, even if he weren't" — Eve wrapped the red-and-white string around the bakery box and secured it — "he's not my type."

Maggie started to open her mouth.

"At all," Eve said firmly.

Maggie sighed. She looked so wistful.

"I know." Eve reached over and wiped a smear of flour off her sister's cheek. "You're so happy and in love with Luke, and you want that for me."

"Yeah," Maggie said with a rueful smile.

"That about sums it up. Speaking of . . . Falling Ashes has a gig in Seattle next week. If you'd like to check the show out, it's on one of your days off —"

"Not going to happen," Eve said, cutting her off at the pass.

"But you and Levi were such a cute couple. That guy was so into you. What happened? Why'd you break up? We all loved him, Mom and Dad included."

"They were okay with him. Mom thought he was wild, and Dad wanted to keep an eye on him. 'The devil you know' and all that. It's the only reason they hired him."

"Once they got to know him, they liked him."

"Dad thought he was a slacker."

"You're being harsh. Sure, it would take Levi a while to get focused, but once he did, he pulled his weight on the construction site. The guy was *crazy* about you — still is, I bet. He's single."

Eve gave her sister a look.

"What? It's not like I've been keeping tabs on him. He sent me a friend request last week on Facebook. I was curious, so I glanced through his profile —"

"I'm going to be adventurous and take the cherry!" Eve heard Ethelwyn's raspy voice declare from behind her.

"Sounds like a plan, Ethelwyn," Eve said, turning around with a smile. "I'll box it up." She removed the homemade cherry pie with the latticework crust and fluted edges from the case.

"He still looks smokin' hot," she heard Maggie say from behind her. "Had a tour schedule posted, so he is managing to book gigs. Maybe the timing for the two of you wasn't right before."

"It wasn't timing that broke us up," Eve said, aware of a slight acerbic edge creeping into her voice. She sighed. It wasn't fair to be grouchy at Maggie. Her sister didn't have all the information. Why would she? Her family had been so fond of Levi, and he'd loved them. Even though the breakup had been brutal and he'd behaved very badly, that person wasn't who he truly was. Drugs and alcohol had sunk their claws into him. It had broken her heart to see the man she loved disappear into a shell of his former self. She'd stayed in the relationship longer than she should have, trying to save him. One day, after he'd surfaced from a three-day bender, she'd realized the only person she could save was herself.

He'd been gutted when she'd left. No need to wound Levi further by tarnishing her family's view of him, crushing the memories of happier times.

"You guys were both so young. Maybe things would be different now. Seriously, Eve, what would it hurt to go say hello? If you left right after work, you could hop on the ferry and totally make it to the concert with time to spare. You'd have to stay overnight, of course . . ."

"Maggie, honey," Eve said, squeezing past her sister to snag a pastry box. "He's a great guy and all, but —"

"But you aren't attracted to him anymore." Maggie huffed out a disappointed sigh. "I get it," she said, gathering up the cooling racks.

Attraction, Eve thought, *was never an issue.* Hell, if she'd felt any more sparks around Levi her hair would've caught fire. It was the day-to-day connection that had been the problem — or the lack thereof.

"Mmm," she murmured, even though a reply wasn't necessary. Maggie had already disappeared through the swinging doors that led to the kitchen.

Eve placed the pie on the counter and started to assemble the pastry box.

Levi. She still missed him. Correction. She missed the Levi she used to know, the bright-eyed boy-man who was overflowing with big dreams and passion, not the Levi he'd turned into. They'd met her first week at the university. Within a month he'd convinced her to move out of her dorm and in with him. He was exciting, older than her, in the graduating class. His philosophy was that one should live in the present, seize life with both fists, burn hard and bright. It was what had attracted her to him in the first place.

Their first year together had passed like a dream. Memories of music and making love, sunshine and laughter, friends and members of the band tumbling in and out of their apartment. Making sangria in the enormous pasta pot that the previous tenant had left behind. Going to the band's weekend gigs, standing in the front, starting the dancing, other people joining in. Aware of his eyes on her while he made love to his guitar, to the mic. The gigs became a protracted foreplay to what they would be doing after the set, his music and voice thrumming through her sweat-slicked body like a caress. She'd felt unleashed from the girl she used to be. The one who'd spent her high school years working weekends and summers in the family construction business alongside her sister, mother, and dad. Weeks would sometimes pass before she'd remember to drag herself out of their warm bed, put on her sensible clothes instead of her wild-child ones. She'd walk across campus to the Presbyterian Church on Whitney Avenue. But it wasn't her church, with her family, familiar faces and friends. She would sit there surrounded by strangers, a lump in her throat, imagining her family back in Eugene, Oregon. Sitting in their regular pew, freshly scrubbed and innocent of the wild university goings-on, their bellies full of homemade pancakes and cheesy scrambled eggs. Missing them had loneliness rising like a volcano, threatening to tear her apart until finally she stopped going to church altogether.

Eve placed the cherry pie in the assembled box and unspooled some string.

Looking back, it was hard to pinpoint when the shift happened and he became the other Levi, the one she didn't know. It had been an imperceptible slide. He'd graduated so certain that fame was going to reach out its golden finger and tap him on the shoulder. Over that next year, bit by bit he lost his way. He would come home worn-out, anger flaring unexpectedly, a crack of lightning exploding out of a clear blue sky. He was on the road more often than not, with a plethora of women, drugs, and booze at his fingertips. Their relationship changed, became brittle, full of recriminations, and the very quality she'd adored became the thing that tore them apart.

Eve secured the pie box with a bow, a wave of melancholy sweeping through her. *Someday, somewhere, I'm going to meet someone who's right for me,* she vowed, pushing the sadness aside. *And he's going to be a steady Eddie. A nine-to-fiver. Someone I can count on.*

She turned toward the bustling café, plastered a smile on her face, stepped to the cash register, and rang in Ethelwyn's purchases.

Two

"Aaaand that's a wrap for Rhys Thomas, folks," the first AD called. The weary film crew burst into cheers and applause. Which was very sweet, considering it was raining, they were on a night shoot, and it'd be a good three hours before any of them would see a bed.

"Thanks," Rhys said. "It's been a pleasure working with you." The crew was still cheering. "Thank you. Really." He gently thumped his fist to his heart, nodded, smiled, ignoring the excruciating headache that'd been wreaking havoc on him for the last two days.

The sound of their hands clapping was like a million ice picks driving into his skull. Rhys took a few more steps back, gave a wave, then headed for his trailer.

There was the usual crowd of fans by his Winnebago. During the day they set up barricades. Tonight, however, they were shooting bits and pieces. Needed to move fast and light, hopping from location to location, so the barricades were left behind.

He scrawled a few autographs on scraps of paper, photos of him, current and past. How people found out where he was shooting and showed up still sorta freaked him out after all these years. That they would stand outside his trailer in the pouring rain at four in the morning was mind-boggling.

"Rhys," a buxom blonde purred. "Want company?"

"Not tonight, thanks, love," he replied, polite but firm.

There had been a time, in his early twenties, when he would have taken her up on her offer. When he'd first hit it big, he'd been like a kid let loose in a candy shop where everything was free. Now, at thirty-two, screwing her would just make him sad — for her, for him.

Once the PA was able to squeeze him past the crowd and unlock his trailer, Rhys stepped inside and locked the door behind him. He'd learned early on the necessity.

He stripped out of his soaking-wet outfit. The heat was on in the trailer, but still, he was freezing his ass off, standing naked holding the dripping clothes in his arms. No sense putting them on hangers — they were filthy. Not just with sweat from the physical scene they'd filmed, but movie dirt, too, and fake blood.

He wrinkled his nose. There had been something seriously rancid in that alley they were shooting in. He was tempted to leave his briefs behind, because who the hell wanted to stuff soaking-wet underwear into their script bag? But if he left them behind, some enterprising soul would sell them to the highest bidder.

Rhys shook his head. *The world's gone crazy for sure,* he thought as he peeled his underwear from the pile of clothes and dumped the rest in the sink.

Wardrobe would launder the clothes and store them for a few months, just in case re-shoots were needed.

They'd be wise to disinfect them, he thought with a puff of laughter that jarred his head. *Acting sure is glamorous.* He strode over to his satchel, caught sight of himself in the mirror, his junk shriveled up like a scared turtle from the cold. *Yeah, I'm one sexy beast,* he thought, another puff of laughter escaping. He was glad the shoot was over. Was dog-tired. Needed to rest, to tuck away somewhere quiet for a few weeks, far from the crowds and paparazzi.

"Where's the damn . . . ?" He rummaged

around his bag until his numb fingers closed around the bottle of aspirin. "Thank God," he muttered, flipping the lid off. He shook out two pills and swallowed them with a glug of coffee left over from meal break.

Yuck.

Then Rhys turned on the shower. An anemic trickling of water emerged. At least it was hot. Wouldn't take long to wash off the grime and makeup. The shampoo his makeup artist, Pete, had given him smelled of green apples. An odd choice, since Pete was rarely seen without full biker gear on. Either it was a way for the dude to wind Rhys up, or the shampoo had been on sale.

Oh well, Rhys thought, massaging the shampoo into his scalp, tipping his head back to capture the stingy stream of water. *It's better than smelling of dumpster garbage, old beer, and piss.*

THREE

Eve leaned against the staff bathroom door at the café, her eyes squeezed shut. The manila envelope containing the disc with images of her art, her CV, and artist's statement was clutched to her chest.

After several months of persistent follow-through, Jocelyn Smith of the South End Gallery had finally agreed to take a look at her portfolio.

"Please . . . please . . . please . . ." Eve murmured, even though she knew it was stupid to pray about something that was already predetermined. Inside would either be a rejection letter or an acceptance.

She exhaled, emotionally braced herself, then opened the envelope and took the letter out.

Dear Eve Harris,

Thank you for your submission. We at the South End Gallery are fortunate to have a plethora of talented artists residing on Solace Island. We have chosen the works for our next exhibition, and yours was not among them.

Your work shows considerable talent. We hope that you will consider submitting again to us in the future.

Best,
Jocelyn Smith, owner

She felt her face flush. "Damn." She shoved the letter back into the envelope. It was stupid to feel defective every time a rejection landed in her in-box or arrived in the mail. Getting an art career up and running was difficult, and the sheer number of wannabe artists was mind-boggling.

A laugh escaped her compressed lips. "Who are you kidding?" she muttered. "You *are* one of those frikkin' wannabe artists." Never mind that she'd attended Yale University School of Art and graduated in the top five percent of her class.

"Dammit. I was *sure* . . ." she started to say, but her voice trailed off. She *hadn't* been sure. She'd *hoped.* Big difference.

"Fine." She tucked the manila envelope behind the hot water heater to retrieve later. "Nothing wrong with hoping. Onward and upward, as Grandmother would say." She straightened, shook off her disappointment, and exited the bathroom. Eve smoothed her apron, then slipped through the swinging doors to rejoin her sister dealing with customers in the front of the café.

Maggie glanced at her hopefully, eyebrows raised.

Eve gave a barely discernible shake of her head, keeping a lighthearted smile on her face. Worse than the rejections was her sister's disappointment.

"I'm so sorry," Maggie murmured, placing six brownies in a box and securing it with string.

The small bell on the front door jingled as three more customers stepped inside and headed toward a table.

Eve shrugged. "It is what it is." She turned away, making it clear that if she wasn't bothered, Maggie shouldn't be either. Eve handed Dorothy three menus and tipped her head in the direction of the newcomers.

"It's eight minutes to three and the place is still hopping. Do you think we should stay open a little longer?" Maggie asked Eve as she passed her carrying the last two brownies on a plate.

They smelled delicious.

"Nope," Eve said. "You've got places to go, people to see."

Her stomach growled hungrily. She was in need of a little comfort, and those brownies would hit the spot. "Wait!" Eve snagged the brownie plate from her sister's hand before Maggie lowered the glass display dome over them. "I'm going to take these puppies home."

"Eve," Maggie said, laughing. "You made me promise not to let you gorge when we're here."

"Exactly," Eve said, dodging her sister's outstretched hand and pushing the swinging doors open with her shoulder. "That's why I'm taking the brownies home. I want to enjoy them at my leisure rather than stuffing my face here."

Eve had learned the hard way that if she was craving something, she needed to hide it in the kitchen. Otherwise a customer might see it and she'd be forced to relinquish her claim.

Once in the kitchen she wrote *Eve's! Don't touch. Thanks!* on a Post-it and attached it to the plate. Larry, the new dishwasher, had a habit of surreptitious snacking on the job. He wasn't supposed to, but Eve couldn't blame him. It was impossible to resist the siren song of Maggie's baking. Larry was an odd duck. He didn't talk much. He had a shambling quality about him. A huge beard, shoulder-length bushy hair, abundant on the sides and back but sparse at the crown of his head. Eve made a point of keeping her gaze firmly fixed on his eyes when he spoke because he had really bad teeth and she didn't want to embarrass him.

All in all, Larry was a pretty good find. Eve did have to give him a gentle reminder to use deodorant last week, but she only had to tell him once and after that it wasn't a problem. He was punctual, fast, and hardworking, and best of all, he washed dishes like a dream!

"Mine," she called out, pointing to the brownies as an extra precaution.

Larry was hunched over the sink, up to his elbows in soapy water. His head rotated slightly, and he grunted.

"Thanks," she said, then slipped through the swinging doors and returned to the hustle and bustle of the café.

There were several people lined up at the bakery counter. Maggie was looking a little tired. Dorothy Whidbee, however, who was well into her sixties, was going strong.

"Where does she get her energy?" Eve murmured to Maggie. They paused for a moment, watching Dorothy, their rotund part-time waitress and full-time love child weaving her way among the tables with the coffeepot, topping people up. She was incorporating some kind of belly-dance move into her walk and undulating along like an overstuffed snake with legs.

"Don't ask," Maggie warned, a bemused smile flitting across her face. "I made that mistake and got an hour-long dissertation on the joys and benefits of tantric sex. Oh dear." Dorothy was now attempting to demonstrate to Big Hank — a loyal and steady customer — that she could do a shimmying backbend and top up his coffee cup at the same time.

"Dorothy," Eve called.

Dorothy straightened, looking like a kid who got caught with her hand in the cookie jar. "Uh-huh?"

Eve shook her head. "No belly dancing on the job."

"Aww," Big Hank protested. "Party pooper."

"Wouldn't be much of a party with a lapful of scalding coffee," Eve replied.

There'd been a line waiting outside the front door when they opened that morning, and the flow of people hadn't let up all day. Everyone wanted to store up on goodies before Maggie and Luke went away on their vacation.

"It's really not fair," the next woman in

line chided Maggie. "You get us addicted and then you abandon us?"

A young hippie couple complete with earth-toned fabrics, backpacks, and fresh-scrubbed faces vacated their table.

"Maggie's not abandoning us," Eve said, snagging a dishrag. She rounded the counter, gathered the two empty mugs, a crumpled napkin, and the dessert plate that had been licked clean, then wiped down the table. "She is taking a well-deserved break."

Maggie and Luke had gone on an abbreviated three-day honeymoon with the understanding that they'd make up for it with a longer vacation once the Intrepid Café was better established.

Well, the time had arrived. Eve was more than a little apprehensive about the next two weeks, but it'd be a cold day in hell before she'd let her sister know. "When Maggie comes back from her glorious holiday, she will be refreshed and rested and full of ideas for new recipes and tasty treats."

"Ooh," the soft-faced woman in the lavender dress murmured.

"And I," Eve continued as she headed toward the entrance, making sure to project her voice so everyone in the café could hear, "will be here at the Intrepid Café, keeping the home fires burning. Granted it will be a shortened week, but on Tuesdays, Wednesdays, and Thursdays, we will be open as usual. Eight a.m. to three p.m."

"Who will be doing the baking?" called someone from the round corner table of rowdy construction workers.

"I will," Eve called back with more confidence than she felt.

"But you can't cook," Big Hank said from his spot by the door.

"You don't know that," Eve replied jauntily, but she could feel her face turning red and giving her away.

"Yeah, I do," Big Hank insisted, his voice building in strength and volume. "Remember when Maggie went away for that long weekend — on her honeymoon, she was. I ordered my usual oatmeal cookie to go with my coffee, and it tasted *ter*rible."

Grizzled Big Hank was a gruff old sweetie, but at the present moment Eve would quite happily stuff her wet dishrag in his mouth.

"Well, that was an unfortunate accident," Eve said crisply. "We buy everything in bulk, and I wasn't used to the layout of the cupboards. I did, however, learn from that, and now when I bake . . ." Eve didn't bake. She was a klutz in the kitchen. The last time she attempted was three months ago, when her sister had taken her mini honeymoon. It had been an unmitigated disaster. Eve *had* planned to practice cooking, to prepare for the next time Maggie wasn't able to man the ovens. But there were only so many hours in the day. When Eve found spare time on her hands, it was much more pleasurable to be out in a field painting.

"Yes?" Big Hank said, raising a bushy eyebrow. "Now when you bake . . . ?"

"I test," Eve said, jutting her chin out. "That's right. I dip my finger in and taste, to make sure the sugar *is* actually sugar and not salt."

"Well, thank heavens to Betsy, because that cookie" — Big Hank paused for dramatic effect — "was *horrible,*" he said with relish. "Worst thing I ever tasted in my life!" Big Hank slapped his thigh, his booming laugh filling the café. "I paid good money for that cookie. My mouth was all ready . . . I took the first bite and . . . BLAH!"

Big Hank leapt from his chair, grabbed his napkin, and rubbed it wildly on his tongue. As if he were still being tortured by the flavor of the cookie Eve fed him three months ago.

Clearly, he was enjoying the rapt audience of the entire café.

Hilarious, Eve thought a trifle bitterly. *Must have participated in Ham-o-lah Community*

Theater Productions in his youth. "Well, wait and see," she said, keeping the confident smile affixed to her face. She flipped the sign on the door to closed and threw the dead bolt, so no new customers could slip in when she wasn't looking.

Just in time, too, because she could see a cluster of hungry-looking tourists heading their way. "I happen to be a crackerjack cook now. My sister has taught me all her secrets."

There was no reason to inform all and sundry that said "secrets" consisted of Maggie working day and night for the last week. She'd made huge containers of dough for the various cookies. Premade pies were waiting in the fridge and the freezer, ready to be slipped into the oven. She'd even premixed ingredients for the muffins and cupcakes, keeping the wet ingredients separate from the dry. Detailed instructions were written in a blue binder.

All Eve needed to do was mix the right amounts together and pop them in the oven. Easy-peasy. What could possibly go wrong?

FOUR

The protective gloves made him feel a little fat fingered, but they were a necessary evil when working with toxic substances. What he didn't like was how sweaty his face was getting. He longed to rip the mouth mask, safety shield, and safety glasses off and climb out of the protective coveralls, but the sodium peroxide would cause severe chemical burns. It could literally melt flesh away.

He smiled.

That was, after all, why he was using it.

He glanced at the battery-operated schoolroom clock that he had secured to the concrete wall of his underground bunker and watched the long black second hand finish its jerky sweep around the face and land on the twelve. That should do it.

He pushed away from the wall, walking past the small shrine in the corner, which was shrouded in a clear plastic tarp. It was not ideal, but special circumstances had arisen and compromises had needed to be made.

Tomorrow, once the place was dry, he'd be able to remove the tarp and bury his face in her cherry-red scarf once again. The scarf he'd stolen from the coatrack in the back room at the Intrepid. Would be able to feel the caress of silk slide across his face, breathe in the lingering notes of her scent.

Then he'd move on. Trail his finger over the grainy picture he'd taken outside a few months ago. The quality of the photo wasn't good. He'd captured it surreptitiously through the windshield of his car. He'd been too far away. Too many people had been crowding around, and she'd been moving quickly. The focus had been bad, and perhaps his hand had been shaking from the pressure and excitement. It didn't matter. He would get a better one soon.

But right now he had work to do.

He turned on the hose and started spraying down the section of the bunker where the bondage bed had been, cleansing the far wall and the floor with fresh, cool water. *Ashes to ashes, dust to dust.* Everything was dispensable.

Chhhsss . . . chhhsss . . . chhhsss . . . The water splattered against the gray concrete surfaces, streaked down the wall, then lapped its way across the floor, congregating at the stainless-steel floor drain in the center of the room. A tiny whirlpool spun around and around before disappearing down the drain. A repeat performance of what the blood had done a few days prior.

Chhhsss . . . chhhsss . . . chhhsss . . .

So fucking erotic, the tears, the blood, her helpless screams, and then the silence. Absolute, total silence.

Jesus! He was hard as a rock now. Didn't have time for this foolishness. There was work to be done. A timetable to stick to. He would have to take care of his unruly dick a little later.

He switched off the water, looped the hose and hung it.

Removed the stiff scrub brush from the cupboard and carefully, systematically, went over the area with vinegar, neutralizing any remaining sodium peroxide.

This was important for two reasons. The first: to alleviate any lingering traces of blood from the test run. *Which was* — he could feel his dick twitch just thinking about it — *very successful.*

But second, and most important: it cleansed and purified the place for *her.* Eve

Harris. His love. His light. His reason for being.

A few more days and he would be ready.

Her life was about to change. She just didn't know it yet.

FIVE

Eve locked the door of her apartment, which was situated above their café, and started lugging her gigantic suitcase down the back stairs. It was her third and final hurrah, for which she was grateful. She was sweating pretty hard by the time she got to the bottom. She stopped for a moment, shook her aching arms out, then headed toward her car, taking full advantage of the suitcase's built-in wheels.

It had taken Eve longer than she'd anticipated to pack. Yes, she was only going to be staying at Luke and Maggie's, which was a minuscule nine-minute drive away. And yes, her only company was going to be a large, shaggy wolfhound who wouldn't care what she was wearing.

But for Eve, well, she didn't have the resources to go to some tropical isle. House-sitting for Luke and Maggie *was* her vacation, and she wanted to make the most of it. She wanted to snuggle in and be cozy. One thing led to another, and before she knew it she had amassed a huge pile of stuff in the middle of her living room. She needed painting clothes, but also comfy lounging-around-the-house clothes, hiking boots and socks, a hat in case of sun — since she tended to burn — underwear, bras. And a vacation wasn't a vacation without her favorite flannel pajamas from high school. The fabric had worn through in several places. There was a gaping hole under the right arm, and the left elbow was only a few fraying strands of fabric. The fabric at the shoulder was also quite threadbare; a tiny zigzag tear was threatening further action. The pajama top was missing a couple of buttons. Yes, her favorite pajamas were really ratty-looking. Normally, she wouldn't be caught dead in them, but since it was just ol' Samson-the-dawg for company, the pajamas were coming. She also needed a couple of sweaters, a raincoat, and so her to-bring stash grew and grew.

Those were the clothes. Then came the necessities. She managed to whittle the stack of eighteen books down to a more reasonable armload of five, but it had been hard since she really wanted to read all of them. She'd dragged her easel out of her painting room, and it was now waiting in her trunk, along with a large cardboard box jammed full of stuff: her palette; a couple of cleaning jars in case of absentminded breakage; her paint box with copious tubes of paint, both full and half-used; rags. She'd also packed a can of turpentine, as well as OMS, linseed oil, charcoal pencils, and a couple of sketchbooks. There was absolutely no possible minimizing there. When she was painting she didn't want to have to stop the flow because she'd been stingy with the supplies she'd brought.

Her suitcase wasn't rolling smoothly. She scowled down at it. One wheel was stuck. *Great,* she thought. *Just what I need, another expenditure.* Money was pretty tight right now. If she could just find a way to sell a few of her paintings, it might take the pressure off. She'd taken out a huge loan to pay for her share of the building and the start-up costs for the Intrepid Café. The food side was doing well. Their customer base was growing by leaps and bounds, but people didn't seem to realize that the art adorning the walls was there to be purchased, too. Not a single painting had sold, even with her dropping the prices twice.

Sometimes, while lying in bed at night, Eve felt the weight of her debt like a large concrete slab on her chest, threatening to crush her.

It was different for Maggie.

Her sister had been Great-Aunt Clare's sole beneficiary. It raised eyebrows that she'd left her money to only one of her nieces, but Eve knew why. Great-Aunt Clare had been trapped in a heartbreaking situation of her own making. Gifting her worldly goods to Maggie was her way to try to make amends.

Her sister had used the inheritance to start her first business, Comfort Homes, with Brett, her two-timing weasel of a fiancé.

Eve knew she should feel terrible that he'd been murdered last spring by his crazy stalker girlfriend, but whenever she thought about how badly Brett had treated her little sister, the danger he'd put her in, and how he'd screwed around on Maggie and dumped her on the eve of their wedding, how he'd inadvertently played a part in Great-Aunt Clare's death, the vengeful part of Eve was glad he was dead.

Maybe that made her a bad person.

Whatever.

Thankfully, those dark times were behind them. They were living on Solace Island now. Maggie had sold Comfort Homes to fund her portion of the Intrepid expenses, and Eve secured a loan and a mortgage.

The payments were stressing Eve big-time. Gobbling every spare cent she managed to scrape together. But she'd never let Maggie know. Maggie was her little sister. She'd always looked up to Eve as if she had the answers to everything. Those were their roles in life. Eve was the ideas person, the go-getter, the passionate, creative artist. Maggie was the follower, the shy homebody. Eve had spent a good portion of her life trying to protect her sister and help her fulfill her dreams. She wasn't about to burst her little sister's bubble and let her know how panicked she sometimes felt about the fiscal burden she'd taken on.

"Yoo-hoo," a voice trilled.

Eve jerked her gaze from her suitcase wheel with a start. How long had she been standing there daydreaming?

One of their customers was making her way across the small parking area behind their building. Her diamond and gold tennis bracelets jangled as she double-waved both hands in the air. *Oh shoot. What is her name?* Eve rummaged around her blank brain. *This is not good. She comes in almost daily.*

The woman was moving surprisingly fast given her petite size and heft, huffing slightly, her chest leading the way like the prow of a ship.

"Eve," the woman said, coming to a stop beside her, her cheeks flushed. "Thank goodness. I am so glad I caught you! I had ordered one of Maggie's chocolate cakes with the broiled pecan topping and my silly husband forgot to pick it up yesterday when he dropped by. It must have slipped his mind. Poor man. I guess he's becoming forgetful in his dotage." The woman attempted a smile, but Eve could see strain and a lingering sorrow behind it. *She is quite pretty,* Eve thought. *Interesting that I've never noticed before. Always been too busy, racing from one customer to the next. How old is she? Hard to tell. Late fifties, perhaps. Lovely skin, good bone structure, delicate hands. Must have been stunning when she was younger.*

"We have a houseload of company arriving on the four o'clock ferry," the woman continued. "I know you are closed today, but I was hoping to catch you before you headed out. I'm praying that you haven't sold the cake to someone else."

Suddenly the woman's name dropped into Eve's brain like a ripe plum falling off a tree. *Irene. Irene Dawson.*

"Well, Mrs. Dawson," Eve said, making a

point to use the woman's name to try to cement it into her consciousness.

"Irene," Mrs. Dawson said, leaning in and giving Eve's arm a little pat, as if she were conferring a great secret. "You can call me Irene, dear."

"Irene," Eve acknowledged with a nod of her head. "You might be in luck. We stored your cake in the back kitchen fridge, so unless Maggie decided to sell it at the close, your cake should still be there. Just give me a second to load this up and . . ." Eve opened the door of the ancient blue Prius her mom had sold to her cheap. She wrestled her suitcase onto the backseat while Irene circled around, a friendly little fat-chested pigeon sending helping gestures and noises into the air.

Once the suitcase was safely stowed, Eve unlocked the back door of the café. She didn't bother with the light switch. There was enough daylight coming through the frosted window by the sink. A faint smell of burned oatmeal cookies still lingered. Eve had done a trial run with some of the cookie dough, figuring she could bring the cookies with her to nosh on. Unfortunately, she had misread the temperature for the oven. The cookies were beyond salvaging. Black burned blobs that were raw in the middle.

It did not bode well for the upcoming week.

Eve sighed. "I'll be right back," she said, heading into the kitchen.

"Oooh," Irene Dawson cooed, tripping after her. "How fascinating to get a chance to see behind the scenes, where the magic takes place." She seemed so pleased to be back there that Eve didn't bother pointing out that she hadn't actually invited the woman to come inside. Had said quite clearly, *I'll be right back. Ah well,* Eve thought with a shrug. *At least the place is presentable.* Unlike her apartment upstairs. After Eve's packing spree was finished, the place was in a bit of disarray. But Eve wouldn't think about that. She would deal with her messy apartment *after* her vacation was over.

"My goodness, look at that fridge," Irene said. "It's enormous. I didn't know they made refrigerators with three doors! That would be so handy to have at Christmastime. I could store all the leftovers and still have room to spare."

"Yes, well . . ." Eve murmured politely, reaching for the handle closest to the swinging doors. She was pretty sure she had seen the cake on the top shelf.

"Oh!" Mrs. Dawson exclaimed, slapping a

hand on the refrigerator door and the other hand to her chest. "I almost forgot. Did you hear the news?" Her eyes went wide.

"No. What?" Eve asked, because really, she couldn't do much else. Mrs. Dawson had now turned to face her, and the woman's backside was resting firmly against the fridge door.

Mrs. Dawson's lips pursed, her gaze darting around the darkened room as if perhaps someone might be lurking in the shadows. Then she leaned in. "There's been a . . . murder," she said, her breathy whisper seeming loud, almost harsh in Eve's ears.

"Are you sure?" Eve asked, inexplicably shaken.

Mrs. Dawson nodded vehemently. "They found human remains in Spraggs Creek, caught on one of the pilings of the walking bridge."

"Oh," Eve said, suddenly wishing she had taken the time to turn on the light. "Well, maybe it was an accident. Someone was drunk, slipped and fell, hit their head."

"I'm afraid not. We are close friends with the chief of police, Henry Lorne. He was over for dinner last night. Apparently, it was one hundred percent foul play. The body was charred beyond recognition. They were able to remove a good portion of the jaw intact and are sending it to the city in the hopes that a forensic dentist will be able to identify the victim."

"Well," Eve said, feeling rather nauseous. "That's good. I hope they are able to unravel the mystery. Now, if you could excuse me, I'll just . . ." Eve closed her hand around the refrigerator handle and gave it a gentle tug.

"Oh goodness," Mrs. Dawson said, stepping away from the fridge door. "I'm sorry. I was standing right in your way."

"No worries," Eve said, grateful to have a little breathing space. The woman had dosed herself rather liberally with Yves Saint Laurent's Opium perfume, an odd choice for someone who dressed in pastel flower tones.

Eve swung the fridge door open, the refreshing cool air from the interior momentarily soothing her. "Ah. Here it is." She slid the cake off the top rack. "You're in luck."

She boxed up the dessert, made change for Mrs. Dawson, and then ushered her out the door. She watched the woman cross the small parking lot, step out onto the sidewalk, and disappear around the side of the building, feeling grateful Mrs. Dawson had gone. Grateful for the sunshine and the light breeze and the normalness of the sounds of lives being lived all around her.

Six

After Rhys slept for a solid twenty-four hours, the headache had finally lifted. The dailies had come back clear, so Rhys was free to go. Unfortunately, the address of his beloved 1920s Spanish hacienda off Stone Canyon Road had gotten out the day before he'd left for location. The damn place had been swarming with paparazzi and overzealous fans. He was having a wall built around the perimeter of the property, but until it was completed it would be madness to return home.

"The offer of your guest room still open?" Rhys asked, his cell phone on speaker so he could multitask — pack and talk.

"Sure." Just hearing his friend's voice made him feel more relaxed. "When were you thinking?"

"Well" — he yanked the hand towel off the bedside clock and checked the time — "it'll be another half hour to pack and check out of the hotel. I'm thinking I'll be up in the air in an hour fifteen, hour and a half."

"So you're thinking sooner rather than later?" Rhys could hear the dry humor in Luke's voice.

"Yeah," he replied rather sheepishly, even though this was their relationship. They'd show up on each other's doorstep all the time.

He'd first met Luke Benson five years ago while doing research for his Blake Trenton role in the movie *Stung.* The film had catapulted him from star to superstar and had spun off a very lucrative franchise for both him and the studio. To prepare for the part, he'd trailed Luke on the job for the month prior to shooting. Trained with him, ate with him, even joined him a few times undercover as a security operative. The studio would have shit a brick if they had found out, not to mention the insurance company. A bond between the two men had been formed, and they'd become fast friends. "If it's not a bother," he said, dumping the contents of a dresser drawer into his open suitcase. "I'd arrive tomorrow morning, if it's convenient. Construction's going on at my house, so I am looking for a quiet, secluded place to crash 'til it's done." He replaced the empty drawer and removed the next one down, tipped that upside down over his suitcase. A dime rolled across the carpet.

Luke laughed. "Solace Island has that in spades. You're welcome to the house. I won't be here when you arrive."

"Not a problem at all. The solitude will do me good — what are you laughing at?"

"Nothing," Luke said, still chuckling. "Have an odd sense of humor is all. Still got your key? The security code?"

"Yep. Both are in the floor safe at home. I'll touch down in LA, pick the key and code up. Swing by Malibu to say hi to my mom. Grab dinner with my agent and head out."

"You know the drill. Help yourself to any of the foodstuffs in the house. My wife's an amazing cook. She keeps the freezer stocked, so you won't have to go out if you don't want to."

"That's right. You got married. Congratulations. Sorry the studio wouldn't let me fly out for the wedding. If you'd given me a little notice, I could have worked it into my contract —"

"No worries, Rhys. You were here in spirit. By the way, Maggs and I love the sculpture you sent."

"Look forward to meeting her in person.

Must be something special to have nailed you down." He emptied the last drawer into the suitcase. "And thanks, Luke. Really appreciate it."

"My pleasure."

"Hey, Luke, if you could not mention to anyone that I'll be there?"

"Absolutely, buddy. Not a word shall pass my lips."

He disconnected the call, but not before Rhys heard another snort of laughter. *Must be happy,* he thought with a faint flash of envy. *The guy laughed more in that one call than the entire time I've known him.*

Seven

On the drive over Eve made the executive decision not to mention the burned cookies or the local murder to Maggie and Luke. They'd just worry. Might cancel their trip. Besides, they were both probably one-offs. A single burned batch of cookies did not a disaster make, and the murderer had probably already put thousands of miles between himself and the scene of the crime. Or the murder could have been a domestic dispute gone wrong. Who knew? The one thing Eve was certain of, Maggie would not enjoy her holiday if she was worried.

"Now, you are sure you're going to be okay?" Maggie asked, fluttering around her.

"Absolutely," Eve said. "I'll feed the dog, let him out at regular intervals, take him for a long walk once a day —"

"Oh, I almost forgot to tell you. I've arranged for Ethelwyn and Lavina to swing by on Tuesdays, Wednesdays, and Thursdays and take Samson with them on their daily hike."

"That's fantastic! I was a little concerned about leaving Dorothy to helm the Intrepid while I raced back to pee him."

Maggie laughed. "You might come back to the café and find she'd attached a disco ball to the ceiling fan and set up a DJ in the corner."

"Don't even," Eve said with a grin. "You send the thought out into the universe, chances are she'll pluck it out of the air and do just that."

"You know how to set and disengage the alarm system?"

"Yes," Eve replied. "You showed me a million times. Not that I'm going to need it here on Solace Island." Her thoughts suddenly flashed to the image of a jaw being removed from a charred corpse, but she stuffed it down and continued as if the image had never occurred. "When I lived in Brooklyn, an alarm system would have been nice, but here?"

Maggie opened her mouth to argue, but Eve cut her off.

"Yes, I know you had that 'incident' this spring," Eve said, her smile feeling slightly unnatural, "but that was an anomaly, not the norm.

"However, I will make sure to set the security system so you won't worry. I'll keep the Intrepid up and running and do my best not to scare off all the customers before you return to set things right. I want you to rest and relax and enjoy all that the luxuriously romantic Laucala Island has to offer."

"You're the best," Maggie said, a little teary-eyed.

"Hey now," Eve said, giving her sister a hug. "Going away with your gorgeous husband is a happy thing."

"I know. I'm just feeling emotional. I don't want to leave you here alone. Which doesn't make sense at all."

"Hey," Eve said, dropping a kiss on her sister's head. "I'm a grown-ass woman."

Maggie nodded. "I know," she said. "Ridiculous, huh?"

"And it's not going to be all hardship and Intrepid angst. I'm planning on painting up a storm on my days off. Gonna have the time of my life!"

Little Nathan — Maggie and Luke's adopted five-year-old son — tore into the room pulling a huge navy blue suitcase that was almost as tall as he was. "I'm all ready!" he exclaimed as he charged through the living room.

"That suitcase is awfully big, honey,"

Maggie said, snagging him for a hug. "Why didn't you use the red one I left on the bed beside your clothes?"

"Nah, this one's better," Nathan said, his little chest puffed up with importance.

"You don't want to bring too much stuff, Nathan. It's more practical to pack light. Your belongings will still be here when you return," Maggie said, trying to gently commandeer the suitcase handle.

"It's mostly empty," Nathan said, tightening his already tenacious grip. "Daddy and I Skyped with Uncle Jake, and he said I need a *big* one to carry all my booty home!"

"Oh," said Maggie. "I see." She let go of the suitcase, and Nathan sprinted out the door before she could change her mind, the suitcase careening in his wake.

Luke tromped into the living room, Maggie's suitcase in hand. "This is all you're bringing?"

Maggie nodded. "Swimsuits, sandals, and sundresses don't take up much room. Who were you on the phone with?"

"An old friend."

"You'll be going out for dinner, Maggs," Eve said.

Maggie flung an arm around her shoulder. "Don't worry." An impish grin on her face. "I raided your closet yesterday, during my lunch break. I'm all set."

"You brat," Eve said affectionately as she pulled her sister in for a tight hug. "I'm gonna miss you."

"Gonna miss you, too," Maggie replied, patting her sister on the back. "It doesn't feel right leaving you behind. You're my best friend in the whole world."

"Maggie." Eve laughed. "Romance 101. You don't drag your sister along on your romantic holiday. Have a wonderful, *wonderful* time. Okay? You've been working so hard —"

"I just —"

"Seriously. Don't worry about a thing. I've got it covered. Now, off you go." Eve disengaged from her sister's grip and nudged her toward the door.

"Thanks, Eve," Luke said, tucking Maggie under his arm. "See you in two weeks. And," he added, eyes twinkling, "behave yourself."

Which was a weird thing to say. But whatever. He made Maggie happy.

Eve followed them to the door, one hand on Samson's collar, keeping a smile firmly on her face.

Luke tossed Maggie's suitcase in the back next to his, then "helped" Nathan load his suitcase into the truck as well. "Let's swing by the pharmacy and pick up some chewable motion sickness pills," Eve heard Luke say.

They felt so far away, as if she were watching a TV show. Stuck in her boring life, while everyone around her had adventures.

Luke glanced at his watch as he opened the passenger door. "The store opens in five. I figure I can zip in and still make the nine fifty ferry. Nathan will probably be fine on the plane, but —"

"Sometimes he throws up when he gets excited," Maggie and Luke said in unison, Maggie's mouth quirking like she thought it was funny.

Eww. Eve liked her new nephew, but there was *nothing* cute about vomit.

"I don't throw up," Nathan said, clambering into the truck.

"You kinda do," Maggie replied, ruffling Nathan's hair as she scooted in beside him.

"Not that we blame you," Luke said. "I'd be excited, too." He shut the door behind them and rounded the front of the truck. "Two weeks with your uncle Jake, one of those weeks at Disneyland? That's a big deal, dude. I'd be tempted to barf myself."

He hopped in the truck. Samson leaned forward, straining slightly against his collar, a low whine escaping. "It's okay, boy," Eve murmured, her voice soothing, even though she was tempted to whine herself.

The truck engine roared to life.

"Bye! Love you. Bye!" Maggie called through the open window, waving happily.

"Bye! Safe travels," Eve called back. She waved until the truck disappeared from sight and the electronic wooden gates closed with a *thump.*

Samson turned his shaggy head and gazed at her, a slightly accusatory look in his mournful eyes, as if it were her fault that they had left.

Eight

He had been sussing the place for some time now. The café downstairs had been easier to penetrate, both front-of-house and the back kitchen. Child's play how simple it had been. The apartment upstairs, more difficult, but with a little ingenuity . . .

He smiled.

The previous night he'd disabled the porch light above the door. She must not have noticed because it was still out. However, a sliver of moon created a faint illumination. So, even though he'd chosen clothes that would minimize detection and sound, it was vital he stick to the shadows created by the overhang of the roof.

His plan worked well. He blended seamlessly with the dark.

He jimmied the credit card between the door and the frame. It was proving to be more challenging than the practice runs he'd done on his own door in the past few weeks. Perhaps it was nerves, or the slick of sweat inside his gloves. Whatever the cause, this door was different, more difficult.

He jammed the card in a bit deeper and jiggled it. "Come on," he whispered. "Open for me." The dirty talk worked. He felt his dick start to swell as the lock gave way to his probing and the latch slid back.

He turned the doorknob, keeping upward pressure on it to avoid unwanted squeaks until the bolt was completely withdrawn. By the time the task was completed, his member was fully erect.

Slowly, slowly he applied pressure to the door, keeping the knob fully rotated as he passed over the threshold like a wraith. Then he carefully closed the door behind him, pushing it gently, firmly against the frame. Only then did he release the knob, slowlysliding the latch silently back into its metal slot in the doorframe. Adrenaline roared through him. His heart thundered in his chest.

He was in.

He touched the soft satchel slung across his shoulders. His handy kit. Everything he would need was there: the plastic cable ties, a roll of duct tape, a syringe of midazolam, the vibrator, the nipple clamps, and the lube, of course. After all, he wasn't an animal.

The apartment was quiet. Not even the faintest rustle or sigh. She was sleeping . . . unsuspecting . . .

Satisfaction coursed through his veins.

It was going to be one hell of a night.

Nine

Eve was pulled from the dream world by the sound of a beep or a chirp. *A bird maybe,* she thought lazily, so happy it was Sunday. She didn't have to do anything but lie there and relish the feeling of the warm sunlight streaming across her face. *Must have forgotten to shut the curtains,* she thought with a yawn. She lay there for a moment, then decided more sleep was called for. Sunshine was nice, but it would have to wait. She reached for the duvet and tried to pull it over her head.

It wouldn't tug upward. She yanked with more force and was rewarded with the sound of fabric ripping. Could feel the waft of cool air as the previously small tear in the shoulder of her beloved flannel pajamas morphed into a large one. "Dang," she mumbled, giving the covers another yank, the worn-out fabric of her pj's tearing a little more. “I should have fixed that last night.”

A low complaining groan rumbled from the base of the bed. Something large and warm was lying across it, pinning the covers down.

She opened her eyes, squinting in the bright light.

Oh yeah, Samson.

The dog lifted his head an inch or two, looked at her blearily from under his shaggy eyebrows, then flopped his head down. He stretched his incredibly long legs, claiming even more of the bed.

“My own fault,” Eve muttered, shifting to lie sideways in the large bed so her legs didn’t have to be cricked to the side. Without a large hunk of fresh meat at hand, there was no way she was going to win dominance over the dog. He was at least 170 pounds. “You’re worse than a man, you bed hog,” she said affectionately, reaching down to scratch him behind his ears. He leaned his head into the scratch. “But I don’t mind. You’re a good boy, and I appreciate you changing your sleeping arrangements to accommodate me.”

Last night Eve had felt restless, unable to settle. She’d switched on her laptop. Checked her e-mails. Nothing. No text messages either.

A wave of loneliness had swept over her. *Where did all my friends go?* Granted, she and Maggie had been so busy getting the Intrepid Café up and running, she hadn't had much free time. Every spare moment she had scraped together she'd used for painting or for the business of trying to get her foot — hell, her big toe — in through the door of the art world.

She sighed. Maintaining friendships required work. Moving from New York to reside on a small island in the Pacific Northwest was incomprehensible to the majority of the people she knew. The first few e-mails exchanged were normal, but gradually, one after another, her friends back East had drifted away. Eve hadn't noticed until this very moment how much Maggie, her husband, Luke, and little Nathan had become the nucleus around which she revolved.

Alone.

She felt so alone.

As if she were a minuscule speck of muck that had fallen off somebody's shoe.

Enough, she told herself firmly. *You are not going to walk down that path. Since you're awake, do a little work; it's a much better use of your time.*

She researched a few more art galleries. Found one in Seattle that was open to e-mail submissions by new artists. She scoured their website. The artwork they represented seemed like a match, so she personalized her query letter and e-mailed it to them, along with her CV.

She shut down her laptop and placed it on the bedside table, the room dark without the glow of the screen.

She did a relaxation exercise, visualized that her feet were filled with sand slowly trickling out. Then she moved her focus to her calves, her knees. She worked her way up her body bit by bit until the exercise was completed, but still, sleep eluded her.

She had an anxious feeling, as if she had left the stove on or had discovered the gas tank in her car was below empty and her vehicle was running on fumes.

Breathe, she told herself. *There is nothing to be scared of. You are sleeping in an unfamiliar place is all.*

But the pep talk didn't soothe her. The home suddenly felt too big, the shadows too dark, and the most inconsequential noises startled her. She levitated a good four inches when the furnace shifted on, even though she'd set the alarms for the house and the perimeter of the property.

At 11:38 p.m. Eve decided enough was enough. She roused Samson from his bed by the fireplace and made him check the house from top to bottom with her. They looked under the beds, behind doors, patted down drapery. They checked the closets, the pantry, the furnace room, and the window latches. All throughout the search Eve's heart was banging way too loudly in her chest, her mouth dry as chalk.

After she was absolutely one hundred percent positive that she and Samson were the only breathing beings in the mansion, Eve still felt jittery. So she dragged Samson's enormous dog bed down the hall and placed it by her bed. Which he had stayed in last night . . . for all of five minutes?

A muffled woof rumbled in Samson's throat, pulling Eve back to the present. She glanced over at him affectionately. "Silly old dog," she said.

Samson shifted onto his back, his stilt-like legs splayed out in the air, clearly hoping the ear rub would morph into a chest and belly scratch.

It did.

"It wasn't your fault, was it, buddy?" she crooned. "You thought the invitation extended to my bed." She'd need to wash the beautiful Frette linen duvet, as it was no longer the pristine white it once had been. She now understood why Luke had chosen charcoal-gray corduroy for Samson's dog bed. It didn't show the dog hair, slobber, and dirt.

Maybe I'll wait to wash it, though, she thought. *Samson might be homesick for Luke and need to sleep up here again tonight.*

It had been a comfort having him in her room. His solid furry presence and gentle snoring had soothed her, and she had finally fallen asleep.

Eve's stomach gave a loud rumble. *Bathroom first,* she thought, getting out of bed and stretching. *Then food.*

TEN

Rhys had traveled around the world, seen amazing sights, but whenever he stepped into Luke's home on Solace Island, it never failed to impress him. The exposed-wood beams lent an earthy quality to the high, soaring ceiling. Large windows showcased the rock cliffs, the ocean stretching outward to embrace the majestic Olympic Peninsula mountains beyond. The sky was so expansive from this vantage point, and for the first time in God knew how long, Rhys felt at peace. Had a sense of coming home.

A gargantuan prehistoric-looking bird swooped past the window, startling him for a second, then disappeared from view.

"What the hell was that?" he murmured. "Some kind of bird, clearly."

Maybe I should take up birdwatching, he thought, then grinned. *Wouldn't that be something? Rhys Thomas, voted* People *magazine's Sexiest Man of the Year, and everyone's wondering, "Where did he disappear to? Where has he gone?" And I'm bushwhacking through the woods, chasing after a pileated woodpecker, brambles in my hair, binoculars hanging from my neck . . .*

A yawn overtook Rhys. *But first things first. Birdwatching will have to wait.* He slipped his duffel bag from his shoulder and dropped it to the ground beside his suitcase.

First coffee. He ambled toward the kitchen. *Then a leisurely nap, after which I can start my new ornithology career.*

Eleven

After relieving herself, she washed her hands with the French-milled soap, the hot water releasing the clean fresh scent of cucumber and sandalwood. "So luxurious," she murmured.

Eve made the mild misstep of glancing in the mirror. Clearly, she had seen better days. The restless night had done her no favors. There were violet-smudged shadows under her eyes, exacerbated by the smears of mascara that were always present first thing in the morning, no matter how vigorously she washed her face before going to bed.

Her hair was flying every which way, and it was apparent the Frette duvet wasn't the only thing covered in dog hair.

Eve toyed briefly with the idea of using one of the fluffy fresh washcloths to clean her face. Maybe run a brush through her hair. "Nah. I'm on vacation," she declared, grinning at her scraggly reflection in the mirror. The gaping hole in her ripped pajama top was exposing the upper swell of her breast and her shoulder. She shrugged. "I'm in charge. And I say I look *fine* just the way I am." Instead of straightening her hair, she shoved both hands in it and messed it up even more. "I'm gonna be a retro punk rocker for the day!" she crowed. She struck a pose and made a fierce take-no-prisoners sneer in the mirror, then exited the bathroom feeling quite pleased with herself.

Halfway across the bedroom floor she had to stop and savor the fact that this stunning bedroom was, for all intents and purposes, hers for the next two weeks.

Life is good. She sighed contentedly.

She'd coveted this room the moment she'd set eyes on it. Seven months had passed since then, but the bedroom hadn't lost any of that extra-special fairy dust it was sprinkled with.

Tons of natural light streamed in through the floor-to-ceiling windows that overlooked the cliffs and the sparkling blue bay beyond. The view had literally stolen the breath from her chest. And when she'd turned, there was another bank of windows with an entirely different but equally gorgeous view. A spectacular outgrowth of slate-gray rock with lush emerald-green moss covering the majority of its surface. One side of the window framed the tan-and-rust trunk and undulating limbs of an arbutus tree that curved upward and disappeared from view.

Eve had wanted to stay in that room with an unholy lust. The quality of the light that afternoon had filled the space. Everywhere it touched was made warm and magical. The floor, the bed, the dresser almost seemed like living, breathing beings in the caress of that amber-golden light. And the sheer beauty of it made Eve feel weak at the knees.

Of course, she'd insisted her sister take the room. Convinced Maggie the bedroom down the hall was the one she wanted. She'd hoped with Maggie and Luke being in such close proximity, the sparks that were flying between them would turn into flames. *And,* Eve thought happily as an image of her sister's glowing face on her wedding day flashed before her, *I was correct.*

"Come on, boy," Eve said, looking at Samson and slapping her hand against her thigh as she headed for the door. "Time to do your business." The big dog huffed as he hoisted himself lazily off the bed. Suddenly, his head snapped up, eyes intent, nose twitching. He gave a short sharp *woof* and tore out of the room, his nails clattering on the hardwood floor as he galloped down the hall.

"Guess he really has to go," Eve said as the dog skidded around the corner and disappeared from view.

She broke into a jog. She didn't want to start her holiday with a lake-sized doggy accident awaiting her janitorial skills.

Twelve

Eve padded toward the kitchen, trailing her hand along the top of one of the deep gray sofas, enjoying the feel of the magnificent antique Persian Kashan rug under her feet.

Grrrrrrssh . . .

She froze.

There was only one thing that made that sound. That was the whir of Luke's posh coffee machine grinding beans. Oh shit! Someone was in the house. Hopefully, Luke and Maggie had a housekeeper they'd forgotten to tell her about. Because Samson was a smart dog, but working the coffee machine was beyond his rudimentary —

"Hey there. How you doing, boy?"

Jesus! Unlikely that warmed-honey drawl belonged to their housekeeper.

The initial wave of fear that had engulfed her had abated, and anger had taken up residence. *This asshole is going to rue the day he decided to break into my sister's beautiful home.*

Eve scanned the living room for a weapon, grateful for her mom's insistence that both her daughters be well versed in self-defense. Maggie had attended the required year of classes, going through the motions reluctantly, but Eve had flourished and had continued taking classes long after the year was up. She loved the feeling of satisfaction that came from knowing how to defend herself. Knowing how to disarm an assailant, fight standing or from the ground, made her feel powerful, like she had secret superpowers.

There. That poker will do. Stepping carefully, silently, she made her way past the thick wood coffee table to the stone fireplace where the black iron poker was waiting. She wrapped her fingers around the handle and lifted it, taking care not to let it bang against the other implements in the fireplace tool set.

She approached the kitchen door on silent catlike feet, the poker gripped in both hands and hoisted like a batter ready to hit a home run. *Isn't Samson supposed to be some kind of trained killer watchdog?* she thought, her heart thumping hard in her chest. *And how'd this guy get past the high-tech alarm system?*

She was scared, but it didn't matter. Luke

and Maggie had asked her to look after their home, and look after it she would.

She took a deep breath, then made her move.

THIRTEEN

The door of the kitchen slammed open, crashing against the wall. "What the he —" Rhys choked on the words, his mug slipping out of his fingers and shattering on the floor.

"NAAAAARRRRGGHHH!" An inhuman shriek assaulted his ears as a wild woman leapt into the doorway, the door shivering on its hinges. Her clothes were partially torn off her body, long ebony hair swirling around her like a luxurious cloak. She wielded a black iron poker, a feral snarl on her lips, clearly thirsting for blood.

For a split second Rhys was ten years old again, fists cocked, standing in front of his mom, who was cowering on the floor. "Come one step closer and you'll regret it," he'd told Howie, his mom's asshole boyfriend. It hadn't helped. Howie had thrown Rhys out the door of their beaten-up trailer. By the time he'd scrambled to his feet, the asshole had locked the door. He couldn't get in, no matter how hard he'd pounded. His mom's cries ricocheted through him like buckshot as Howie systematically beat the crap out of her. Three fractured ribs, a dislocated jaw, two teeth knocked out. After they released her from the hospital, she went back to him. She always went back.

Rhys wasn't that scared ten-year-old kid anymore. This wasn't Howie. This was a luscious green-eyed beauty. Yes, she was unhinged, but he could deal with that. Christ, half the actresses he worked with fell into the unhinged category.

"Nice entrance," he said, dryly, letting his voice negate the adrenaline coursing through him. "Quite the dramatic —"

"Shut up," she growled, shaking the poker at him. "Leave now, or live to regret it."

"Ma'am," he said, taking a slow, calm step toward the poker-wielding woman, his hands open, posture unthreatening. "I mean you no harm. If you would just put down the —"

"GET OUT OF THIS HOUSE!" the crazed she-devil roared, settling into her stance, her body coiled and ready to strike.

Rhys contemplated — for a split second — trying to disarm her, but if he miscalculated, the pick end of that poker would do serious damage to his face. His agent would never forgive him. Neither would the fans.

"All right," he said, backing toward the kitchen door. "Take it easy." If only he'd looked where he was stepping.

He hadn't.

One moment his feet were solidly on the ground, and then they weren't.

He hadn't noticed the damned dog, Samson, stretched out behind him. Rhys went sprawling ass over teakettle across the kitchen floor.

Her body was a blur as she lunged, landed on him. The poker clattered to the floor. Before he had time to process what was happening, she had him hog-tied with the toaster cord.

So much for all the skills he'd learned hanging out with Luke. "Jesus Christ," he muttered. "This is not the peaceful morning I envisioned."

"That'll teach you not to break into people's houses," she growled in his ear.

She smells good. He was aware that it was an odd thought to be having while hog-tied and at the total mercy of what was probably a deranged fan. How had she gotten past Luke's security? Must be some kind of techie. A deranged techie fan with delectable breasts pressed against his shoulder, causing his cock to make its presence known. The chorus from "I'm Only Human After All" danced through his brain. He pushed it away, forced himself into his analytical mind. *The interesting thing is her tactic: pretending I'm the intruder. First time one of them has used that trick. Reverse psychology.* And if he were being totally truthful with himself, it was kind of working.

"I didn't break in," he said, his face plastered to the floor. "I'm a friend of the owner."

"Nice try, buddy." She got off him, scooped up the poker. "I wasn't born yesterday." She moved toward the house phone. "Don't even think about moving or I'll bash your brains in." She picked up the phone.

"What are you doing?" Rhys, for the first time in this extraordinary encounter, felt a slight tendril of fear.

"What does it look like I'm doing? I'm calling the cops —"

"Don't. Please. It would be a serious mistake!" He could just see the headlines. The press would have a field day, and this quiet oasis would be ruined, not just for him but for Luke and his wife as well. "I'm Rhys Thomas." Just mentioning his name usually did the trick.

She started to dial.

Okay, the famous actor card wasn't going to cut it; she clearly had no idea who he was. "Luke Benson's a very good friend," he added hastily. "I'm here on his invitation."

"He's out of town," she said, looking at him like he'd just defecated on the floor and was telling her it was cake.

"I know. He's taking a belated honeymoon to Laucala Island. I'm the one who recommended the place."

She paused.

"My wallet is in my pocket — phone, too. You can check my ID. Luke's in my contacts. Give him a call."

Fourteen

"Okay, Maggs. Thanks. Sorry for disturbing your holiday."

Rhys watched her chat on the phone from his position on the floor. If his hands were untied he would have applauded. Her voice was light and breezy, happy even. Her face told another story. "No worries," she was saying. "We'll sort it out." A slight pause. "Why is Luke laughing?"

Ah! There it was, in that last sentence. Truth. The slight bite of irritation lurking underneath the happy-happy.

"I see." She was trying to maintain the smile, but it was more of a grimace. "Well, tell him thank you for thinking of me, but I can manage perfectly well on my own. I don't need or want his help."

She darted a glance at him. Hm . . . that was interesting. He wished he were privy to the other half of the conversation.

"All right, love you. Bye-bye." She hung

up and glared at him.

"What?" he asked.

"Just so we're clear," she said, enunciating clearly, "I'm not. Interested."

"All righty, then. Now that we've got that out of the way, would you mind untying me?"

"And I don't care who the hell you are. I am *not* giving up the corner bedroom."

"Duly noted. Although, I have to say, you have an unfair negotiating advantage, what with me being trussed up like a Christmas pig ready to be roasted."

She untied him, eyes averted. "Sorry about the unconventional welcome," she mumbled, color rising up her neck, flooding her cheeks. "I wasn't expecting you."

"Ditto," he said, getting to his feet, massaging his wrists to get the circulation going. "Kudos to you, though. You were fast. Caught me off guard." He wondered if the rest of her body flushed when she was embarrassed, and suddenly he had an image of her naked body beneath his. He cleared his throat, tried to focus, to act normal, but her pajama top was torn and hanging off her shoulder. The creamy top half of her breast was exposed. She looked pretty damned hot, in a fucked-up psychopathic way.

Samson gave a short bark by the door. "Have you eaten breakfast?" she asked, her hand gliding over the dog's head to settle behind the ears for a nice scratch. Samson leaned into her, clearly relishing the attention.

"No," Rhys said. "I'm starving."

She sighed, opened the back door and let the dog out, then turned. "I'm not much of a cook, but I am willing to attempt it." She shrugged self-consciously, still not looking at him. "To make amends."

"I'm happy to do the honors if you like," he said.

Her gaze snapped up to his. "Really?"

She had gorgeous eyes. Deep green almond-shaped eyes that had a slight tilt upward at the corners, framed by gloriously thick lashes. *Elfin eyes,* he thought. He cleared his throat. "Yeah. I enjoy cooking. Find it relaxing."

"Relaxing," she said, shaking her head as if he'd said he enjoyed a bout at the dentist, too. "Okay." A slow-blooming smile lit up her face, causing something to constrict in his chest, in his throat. "Far be it from me to battle you for kitchen supremacy." She gestured grandly to the kitchen as if presenting him to the queen. "Have at it."

■ ■ ■ ■

Eve stepped into her bedroom feeling pretty jaunty, all things considered. She had defended the house from an intruder. Granted, it hadn't been necessary, but it might have been. It was good to know that if she needed to take action, she could, that those self-defense classes hadn't been for naught.

She'd been looking forward to having the house to herself. However, given the restless night she'd had, it might be nice to have another human bumping around.

She crossed to the bathroom.

Best of all, I get to keep the corner bedroom, and the guy likes to —

She caught sight of herself in the mirror. "Ahhh!" she squawked, recoiling in dismay. "Perfect." She snorted in disgust. "I meet a gorgeous stranger, and what am I wearing?" She pulled off her ancient pajamas. "These!" She threw them against the wall, but it wasn't very satisfying. The pajamas didn't have the form or weight to make much of an impact, just plopped against the wall and slid down to the floor in a pathetic pile of fabric. "Not that I'm interested in him. I'm not. But still, a woman's got her pride."

There was a knock at her bedroom door.

"Go away," she called, staring at her reflection. Her hair looked like a chicken had been roosting in it and her slept-in mascara had given her serious raccoon eyes.

"Uh . . . how do you like your eggs?" His warm baritone slipped through the keyhole and under the door and wrapped itself around her. The man had a damned sexy voice, brandy and smoke with a touch of gravel to make it interesting. *Musicians, actors, big egos, big trouble. And you are* not *a woman who needs to drink from the same poisoned well twice,* she told herself sternly. But being strict wasn't working. There was something about the tone and tenor of his voice that called up images of hot sex on silk sheets. *Pure trouble.* She felt as if she'd downed a hot buttered rum in one gulp, restless heat pooling low in her abdomen.

Buck up! Apparently the guy is some kind of professionally trained actor. Of course he's going to have a sexy voice. No one would hire him if —

"Hello?" It sounded like he was leaning against the door. *All he'd have to do is turn the knob and . . .*

A tidal wave of sensuous heat was threatening to engulf her. Clearly it had been way too long since she'd had sex.

"I'm easy," she yelled, then slapped a horrified hand over her mouth. *What the hell?* "About breakfast!" she amended. "Don't care how you serve it, just as long as it's hot —" *Oh Jesus. Just shut up. Stop. Talking. Now.* "The food. I meant the food! As long as the food is hot —" She shook her head in disgust. What the hell was happening to her? "I'm in the shower," she said, marching over and stepping inside. "Can't hear you. Sorry. Bye."

Bye? she mouthed. *Oh brother.* She turned the water on full blast.

Cold.

Freezing cold.

She stuffed her fist in her mouth to stifle the shriek. Stayed put beneath the icy water beating down on her shivering body as she waited for it to warm up. It felt like rightful punishment. "Let this be a reminder," she told herself through chattering teeth. "I need to moderate my moods and actions. I'm too passionate, too impetuous, always leaping into situations without thinking things through. Like hog-tying what's-his-name on the kitchen floor or talking Maggie into the Intrepid Café and taking on all that debt. Let this ice-cold shower be a simile for your life. You need to smarten up."

Fifteen

Eve applied a light sheen of gloss over her lips, Maggie's words on the phone dancing through her head. *Luke says Rhys is* perfect *for you. Quirky sense of humor. He's an artist, too. Not a painter, of course, but an actor, a good one, so he understands the creative process.*

"I don't want an actor," Eve murmured to herself as she took a step back and studied her reflection in the mirror. Her cheeks were slightly flushed, her eyes bright. *I'm looking for someone steady, with a nine-to-five job. Not some lothario who's always on the road. Been there, done that,* she thought, smoothing the flowing fabric of her skirt. She loved how blurred the edges and details were of the large flowers scattered across the fabric. An impressionistic profusion of whitewashed aqua, lilac, and dusky rose with some green thrown in to represent stems and leaves. One knew they were supposed to be flowers, but their specificity was a mystery.

I am one hundred percent not interested, she told her body, which was thrumming with giddy first-date nerves. She went into the bedroom and got her ballet flats out of the closet and slipped them on. She was tempted to grab her beloved strappy velvet shoes with the square heel and the vintage glass button. The dusky rose matched her dress perfectly, but she resisted. Given the incident this morning, it would look like she was trying too hard. *Keep it casual,* she told herself as she shrugged on a faded cropped jean jacket.

She rummaged through her suitcase, found her velvet jewelry bag, removed the two antique brooches her grandmother had given her, and pinned them on her shoulder.

The first brooch Eve had received when she was twelve. Her grandmother had rented a beach house that summer so they could escape the sweltering heat wave that had blanketed Eugene. Within an hour of getting Grandmother's phone call, Mom had their bags packed, the car loaded, and they were out on the open road. Eve felt sorry for their dad. He'd stayed behind. The long-awaited fixtures for the Emerson brownstone collection had finally arrived and needed to be installed pronto.

When they'd pulled up to the beach house, Eve's mom had given a gay toot on the horn. Grandmother and her sister, Great-Aunt Clare, had tumbled out of the house with big smiles on their faces. Hugs were given all around. The welcome, cool caress of the salty ocean air made Eve feel almost giddy. She could hear the noise of the surf crashing on the packed sand behind the cottage, calling her to play.

It had been a glorious summer until that night two days before they were supposed to return home, when everything had changed.

Eve had gone to bed early with a slight fever and headache. She'd woken discombobulated. She could barely make out the profile of her little sister sleeping beside her, one arm tossed over her head. It was pitch-dark outside the window. No stars. No moon. And there were voices arguing, low and intense. Her mom and Great-Aunt Clare were fighting. Most of the words indistinguishable, but a few still managed to drift up the stairs and suck all the air out of the room around her. Maggie. They were fighting about Maggie.

Eve got out of bed quietly, intending to

shut the door. She didn't want her little sister to wake up and hear. But when she reached the door, Great-Aunt Clare started sobbing. "But Maggie's mine. She's *my* daughter, not *yours*! And I am sick and tired of pretending otherwise."

"You gave her up," her mom said. Eve had never heard her mom sound like that before. Her voice, an impenetrable ice wall. "You didn't want her. Remember? She was 'an inconvenience.' You were unmarried, 'too old.' You wanted your fancy life, the ability to travel unhindered and your high-flying career. I don't blame you. There have been times when I was so sleep-deprived and tired that I would've given anything to run out the door and never come back. But the difference is. I. Didn't."

"We should ask Bill. He might feel differently, raising a child that is not his —"

"I know one hundred percent that my husband would agree with me on this. You will not swan in after all these years and break up our family."

"Why don't we tell Maggie? Let her choose —"

"No!" Her mother's voice was harsh with emotion. "You made us *promise* not to tell anyone. I didn't want to keep it secret. Remember? You *insisted.* Said if we didn't agree to your terms, you would put her up for adoption."

"I never —"

"Don't lie. It doesn't become you."

There was a momentary silence.

Her mom started talking again, gentler but firm. "And as difficult as it was to lie by omission, we kept our promise to you. How do you think the girls would feel to find out the family has been lying to them all this time?"

"I'm sorry. It was a mistake. Listen . . . Please listen, Peggy. Don't turn away. I've sold my portion of the company."

Eve stood rooted in the doorway, unable to move. Trying to make sense of what she was hearing.

"I'm retired now. I've traveled the world. I don't feel the need to anymore. I can stay home and give her a good life —"

"She *has* a good life," Eve's mom cut in. "Clare, I understand that you are lonely and you want someone to take care of you now that your health is failing. Yes. I know all about that, and I'm sorry. Truly I am, but the solution is *not* my Maggie. You have plenty of money. Hire a nurse."

A door opened down the hall. "Eve, honey," Eve heard her grandmother say softly. "You should be in bed."

Eve turned her head. Her grandmother was standing in a pool of light spilling out of her bedroom. "Oh, sweetheart," her grandmother had said, moving swiftly down the hall and wrapping Eve in her arms. "Don't cry. It's going to be okay. I promise."

Eve had slept in her grandmother's room that night. They'd talked for a long time. Like grown-ups. About grown-up things. Her grandmother answered Eve's questions, calmed her worries, acknowledged her fears. Then her grandmother had fallen asleep, and while Eve had listened to the rise and fall of her grandmother's breath, she'd made a decision. Maggie *was* her sister. The sister of her heart. And if Maggie didn't know the truth about her birth, it wasn't Eve's place to tell her.

When they'd woken up in the morning Great-Aunt Clare was gone. "She's been called away," Eve's mom said, pouring half-and-half into her coffee. "She said she was sorry she wasn't able to say good-bye personally and to give you both her love."

Maggie had popped a bite of syrup-drenched French toast in her mouth, her legs swinging happily under the table, her feet not yet able to reach the floor. "I'm going to make a big sandcastle today," she'd declared. “The biggest one in the whole wide world, and I’m going to decorate it with clamshells and sand dollars. Wanna help?”

“I’d love to,” Eve had said, even though she was much too big for childish things like sandcastles.

The next day, when they were loading the car for the long drive home, Grandmother pressed a blue velvet pouch into Eve’s palm and closed her fingers around it. “I want you to have this,” she’d murmured. Eve had looked up at her in surprise, and her grandmother had tapped a finger to her lips. *Our secret,* she’d mouthed, her eyes twinkling as she motioned for Eve to tuck the pouch into the front pocket of her jean shorts.

It had burned a hole in Eve’s pocket while she’d sat in the front seat next to her mom, Maggie in the back. Resisting the urge to take the pouch out and see what was inside was one of the hardest things she had ever done in her short life. But she knew how to keep a secret. Two secrets she now had: Maggie’s real mom and the mystery present in her pocket. Five and a half hours on the road. Another hour while they greeted their dad, unloaded the car, and had a quick snack. She and Maggie kissed their parents good night, brushed their teeth, and went to bed. Minutes ticked slowly by as she waited for the house to settle. She could hear the low murmur of her parents in their bedroom behind closed doors. Then they, too, got quiet.

Finally.

Eve took the pouch and a mini flashlight out from under her pillow. She loosened the drawstring and turned the soft velvet pouch upside down. A beautiful bejeweled dragonfly brooch fell out into her hand. *Magic,* she thought, having to close her eyes for a moment, overwhelmed by its delicate beauty and the magnitude of the gift.

After that summer they didn't see much of Great-Aunt Clare.

Once Eve thought she saw her standing against the back wall by the door during their school's winter concert. But Great-Aunt Clare must have slipped out the moment the concert was finished, since she wasn't by the refreshment tables with everyone, eating holiday cookies and drinking juice.

The second brooch had arrived in a bubble-wrapped pouch addressed to Eve from the offices of Jenkins, Bunting, and Co. It was the end of January. The world was blanketed in dirty, stale snow, sludge, and ice, and fifteen-year-old Eve was beside herself with grief. Her grandmother had been battling a cough through the Christmas holidays. "It's just a little cold," her grandmother had said. But by December 28 she was gone, and Eve missed her desperately.

The second brooch was also in a small blue velvet pouch, and when Eve opened it, a beautiful deep blue flower brooch dropped into her hands.

"Oh my goodness," her mom had breathed. "Her forget-me-not brooch."

Eve started to pin the brooch onto her shirt above her heart.

"Oh no, sweetie," her mom said. "That's not to wear. These leaves and the stem are made from high-quality diamonds. And here" — her mother slid her finger over the flower's petals — "these are large sapphires. Do you see how strong and vivid the color saturation is? This brooch is very valuable and needs to be kept in Daddy's safe."

"No," Eve said, anger rising in her belly, even as tears blurred her vision. "Grandmother gave it to me to remember her by. I am not putting it in the safe. I'm going to wear it whenever I want so I can feel her close to me."

It was the first time she had gone directly against one of her mother's decrees. In hindsight, her mother had probably been right. A fifteen-year-old probably shouldn't have been running around wearing an expensive diamond and sapphire brooch, but it had given her great comfort and had helped ease the grief.

If anyone glanced at her brooch for longer than a second or two, she would say, "Costume jewelry made out of paste." Eve helped the assumption along by frequenting vintage shops and purchasing a couple of rhinestone brooches, which she wore as well. Gradually, over the years, the dragonfly brooch with its ruby head and emerald eyes joined the forget-me-not adorning her shoulder. After she graduated from Yale, the rhinestone companions fell by the wayside, and it was just the two brooches from her grandmother keeping Eve company.

And today, Eve thought, *after my grand torn-pajamas-wild-hair-poker-wielding entrance, I need the feeling of my grandmother's support and wisdom with me.*

Eve's hand rose to rest on the sparkling dragonfly and blue forget-me-not, and she let the memory of her grandmother surround her. She could almost smell the gentle scent of her lilac perfume. Feel the coolness of her fingers as she had pressed that first pouch into Eve's hand. Could almost see the translucent, papery quality of her grandmother's skin with the network of blue veins that had gotten more and more pronounced as the years slipped by.

"It's time to beard the lion," Eve said, straightening her spine, setting her shoulders back, and then, as calmly and regally as she could, she exited the safety of the bedroom.

Sixteen

Eve took another sip of her coffee, drawing comfort from the full-bodied creamy flavor and lingering caramel aftertaste. Her hands cradled the mug, enjoying the heat emanating from it.

"Here you go." Rhys placed a plate laden with piping-hot scrambled eggs, thick slices of perfectly cooked bacon, and buttered toast on the table in front of her.

Eve's stomach rumbled loudly. It was a massive amount of food, and boy did it smell good. The only thing she had eaten since the peanut butter sandwich she'd slapped together for yesterday's lunch was the handful of jelly beans she'd found rolling around the bottom of her purse. She could've heated up something from Maggie's fridge, but she'd have had to clean the pan. Seemed like a lot of effort for one person.

Her mouth was watering. "Thank you."

"My pleasure." He rounded the table, plopped his plate down, and sat. "Dig in," he said.

And so she did.

The scrambled eggs were cooked to perfection, not too wet, not too dry, lightly seasoned. The bacon had just the right amount of chew and crispness, and the buttered toast was sourdough, Eve's personal favorite. "Wow," she said, trying not to gobble the entire plate of food down in five seconds flat. "You're a good cook."

He shrugged, but she could tell he was pleased. "I enjoy it, which is lucky. It's less work to eat in. More convenient."

"Less work?" Eve laughed. "Are you kidding me? First you have to decide what you're going to make. Then you have to shop —"

"Not necessarily. It is quite easy to go online and purchase groceries to be delivered."

"Whether you go to an actual store," she said, "or do your shopping on the World Wide Web, it's still shopping. Once the groceries arrive, you have to cook and do a mountain of cleanup. Convenient-con*shme*nient. I'm telling you right now, if money were no object, I'd never cook again."

"Wait a minute," he said, shaking a finger

at her. "You're pulling my leg, aren't you? Because I'm pretty sure Luke mentioned something about a café you and your sister opened that has *amazing* food —"

"Amazing food? Yes. That is correct. Do I cook it?" Eve shook her head. "Nope." She popped a piece of toast in her mouth. "I hate cooking, and I refuse to feel less than about it." This had been a bone of contention between her and Levi. "Why is there this expectation that the only way a woman can keep a man is if she's a whiz in the kitchen?"

"I can only speak from personal experience, but a woman being good in the kitchen isn't a requirement of mine." Rhys tilted his head, regarding her with that dark-eyed gaze of his. "Although," he continued, "I certainly have no complaints if a woman wants to . . ."

He paused.

"What?" she asked, because even though his face hadn't changed, she had the feeling that he was enjoying a private joke.

He shrugged, the internal smile she'd suspected blooming into a real one on his face. "If a woman I'm dating wants to be *bad* in the kitchen, I'll make every effort to accommodate her."

And just like that, she felt her body shift

from combative to fuck-me-now. *Don't even!* she told herself sternly. *This guy is one hundred percent trouble, and you, my dear, are not going to touch him with a ten-foot pole.*

"Why are you glaring at me?" he asked, voice bland, eyes twinkling.

"I'm not," she snapped.

She was.

She pushed away from the table. Crossed the kitchen to the fancy coffee machine and added a shot of espresso to her coffee to top it up. Her mug hadn't needed topping. She'd used it as an excuse to put some distance between her and Mr. Hunk-on-a-Stick, or she would likely jump him and screw him senseless.

The shot of espresso brought the contents up to the brim of her mug. She bent over and sipped some off the top so she could return to the table without it spilling. She took another sip, glancing out the window. The wolfhound was lifting his leg on various stones and bushes. "I wonder how long Samson's going to need out there?" she said, her voice more breathless than she would like. Her body was thrumming. She could feel his gaze on her like a heat-seeking missile, like he knew what she was thinking.

"So, you opened a café but you hate to cook?" He looked amused, which made her want to kick him in the shins.

"My sister, Maggie, is a brilliant cook," she said, taking another nonchalant sip of her coffee. "So she cooks, and I handle the rest."

"The rest?"

"Decor, the bills, the orders, serving customers, dealing with the staff . . ."

"You have staff?"

"Are you being condescending? Because if you are —"

"Not at all," he said. "Why so prickly?"

She felt a flush start to travel up her neck to her face. She wasn't being fair. Just because he had a drop-dead-gorgeous hard body and a killer smile didn't mean that he was a carbon copy of her ex. The actor dude hadn't freaked out when she'd tackled and hog-tied him, not that she would have blamed him if he had. But it was kind of refreshing that he wasn't a drama queen. Levi would have been supremely pissed off. Then, not only did this guy volunteer to make breakfast, but he'd turned out to be a damned good cook to boot.

"I'm sorry," she said. "My bad. Woke up on the wrong side of bed."

He nodded. "Been there," he said. "You're welcome to come back to the table and finish your breakfast. I won't bite. Promise."

There was that smile again, the one that was slightly naughty and almost a dare, as if to say, *Unless you want me to.*

She shut her eyes briefly, trying to erase the flash she'd had of hot sex, entwined bodies, sinking her teeth into his shoulder. She could almost taste the salt of his sweat.

She exhaled, opened her eyes. "We have a dishwasher," she said tartly. "A part-time waitress. On weekends and holidays we hire a couple of students from the local high school." Samson gave a short *woof* at the kitchen door. She was glad for an excuse to look away. "Hey, boy." She opened the door, gave the dog a scratch behind the ears as he leaned into her.

"Wasn't intending to grill you. Was curious is all. Always had this fantasy if the acting work dried up, I'd open a restaurant."

Eve laughed. "Well," she said. "It's a lot harder than it looks." And then she got an idea. A gloriously inspired idea. "But if you'd like," she said, ambling casually over to the table and sitting down, "I'd be willing to let you ride shotgun at the café for a few days." She speared some eggs onto her fork, sneaking a glance at him through the curtain of her hair, which had fallen forward. "You know, as a test run, to see if it's even a viable alternative for when gravity wreaks havoc on" — she gestured toward him as if presenting a plate of fish — "all of that."

"You'd let me?" The poor sucker actually looked excited.

"Sure," she said. "Don't see why not. Maggie's out of town. You're a good cook. You can commandeer the kitchen. You might love it." She could see him thinking it over. Reminded her of fly-fishing with her dad. Landing the fly just so, seeing the trout through the crystal-clear water, circling, contemplating. *Come on,* she thought. *Take a nibble.*

He shook his head, pushed his chair back from the table. "Nah," he said. "Sounds fun, but it's not practical." He gazed out the window. Seemed wistful. "I'm kinda famous, and fans can be weird sometimes."

"Fans? What fans?" Eve shrugged with her palms upward as if checking for rain. "No fans back there, just me and a morose, monosyllabic dishwasher. Our part-time waitress, Dorothy, mostly stays in the front of the house, but even if she strayed into the kitchen, she's a sixtysomething love child. If *I* didn't know who you were, I am *certain* those two wouldn't. You could cook with impunity. Totally safe from fans."

He was looking seriously tempted now.

"I'm not a professional cook."

"But maybe you could be," she said encouragingly. "You'll never know 'til you try."

He rubbed his palms on his jeans-clad thighs. "It's a new business. I don't want to mess you guys up."

"Let me worry about that. Unless" — she paused, dabbed her lips with her napkin — "you're too scared."

"Wha—"

"No judgment. Totally understandable," she said, giving a delicate shrug.

"I'm not scared. I just —"

"Perfect!" She catapulted from her seat and captured his hand in hers. Gave it a firm shake. "Welcome aboard. So glad you've decided to join the Intrepid team while you're here. Can only pay you minimum wage, but luckily you aren't doing it for the money." She was talking fast so he couldn't get a word in edgewise. "We are operating on a shortened schedule while Maggie's gone, so that will make it easier as well. We're open Tuesdays, Wednesdays, and Thursdays, eight a.m. to three p.m. Of course, we'll need to arrive a little earlier to prep, but no need to get into all those pesky details now. This is *fantastic*! Thank you *so* much for volunteering to be the Intrepid's cook for the next two weeks. I can see why

Luke likes you so much." She leapt to her feet. "All right, I'm off," she said, dashing across the kitchen. "The muse is calling. You know how it is. Ta-ta!"

She ran through the kitchen, down the hall, into her bedroom, slamming the door shut behind her, and just in time because laughter had her collapsing on the floor.

The expression on his face when I railroaded him into cooking for the café? She hugged herself. *Priceless.*

Humming happily, she shucked out of her clothes and into her grubby painting ones, then gathered up her supplies. She stuffed her car key in her pocket — she'd need to get a canvas from the trunk — and headed for the door.

She paused. No sense wandering past Rhys. *Don't want to give him a chance to correct the "misunderstanding."*

She scanned the room. Floor-to-ceiling windows were beautiful, but not so good if one wanted an emergency exit.

She sussed out the bathroom. Aha! There was a latched window of frosted glass over the sink. It might be a little tight in the hips department, but she was pretty sure she'd be able to manage. *Better this way,* she thought as she opened the window, folded up her easel, and chucked it out. *If Rhys has to sit with my heartfelt gratitude all day, it might make him too embarrassed to back out. I'm a frikkin' genius!* She chuckled happily and maneuvered her paint box out of the window. It was a tight squeeze, but turning it diagonally worked. She flinched as the box hit the ground, the metal clasp popped, and tubes of paint scattered. Luckily, the box itself didn't break. "All right. My turn now." She pulled herself onto the counter and began the arduous process of wedging herself through the small window.

Seventeen

"And to think," Rhys said to Samson, who was waiting beside him expectantly, "that I was worried I might get bored here on little old Solace Island. Ha! Not with that eccentric warrior woman residing down the hall." He tossed another slice of bacon and watched the dog leap up and snap it out of the air, his jaws closing over the fatty strip of pork like a steel trap. The wolfhound made like an anaconda and swallowed it in one gulp. "Note to self," he said, "keep dog well fed and appendages away from his mouth."

He leaned back in his chair, took another slurp of coffee, contemplating the morning's unusual events. It had been a refreshing change interacting with her. He'd watched her carefully, waiting for that moment when she realized just who he was, but it never came. There was no fluttering about and clutching her heart. Her eyes didn't get that dazed, stunned look while she hyperventilated herself into a stupor.

Granted, there was a sensual awareness on both sides, but the sparks appeared to stem from her awareness of him as a man, not him as a movie star.

"Jesus," he said, taking another sip of coffee. "Wouldn't that be something? To stand or fall on my worth as a man, as a human being, without having my movie-star status tattooed on my forehead. I wonder what her name is. Luke must have mentioned it."

"Oh crap!" a voice shouted from down the hall, jolting him upright. "Helloooo! I need some help here!"

It was the woman. She was in distress!

Rhys leapt to his feet, tore through the living room and down the hall, Samson hot on his heels.

"Helloooo! Good God, is the man frikkin' deaf?"

He burst into her bedroom. She wasn't there.

"RHHHHYYYS!"

She's in the bathroom.

Samson bounded in, no problem. Gave a *woof.* Poked his shaggy head back out the bathroom door and looked at Rhys as if to say, *Come on, dude.* Rhys was unsure of what he would find, but hey, a guy's gotta do what a guy's gotta do, so he followed Samson in.

She was clothed. At least the lower half of her body was, which was all that was visible from his vantage point. She was wiggling quite vigorously. Her faded jeans clung lovingly to her luscious ass, which was prominently displayed and level with his face.

He was filled with an irresistible urge to step between her flailing legs. Remove her beat-up tan construction boots with the laces untied and dangling, and peel off her jeans. Once he had her lower half stripped bare, he'd touch her, taste her, he'd spread her petals, and look at her as intimately and as long as he liked. He could have his way with her. Make her moan and undulate with need, totally at his mercy as he licked, lapped, buried his tongue and fingers deep inside her, until she was boneless and satisfied.

Nevertheless, he resisted. There was a big difference between indulging in a harmless two-second fantasy and acting like a misogynistic dickhead.

"Hey there," he said, his voice raspy, as if he'd been wandering in the desert without water for days.

"Whaaa!" was her startled reply.

"It's me. Rhys." He cleared his throat.

"You seem to be stuck."

She muttered something under her breath. He couldn't make out the words, but he could read the intention loud and clear.

He knew he was a terrible man, but good God it was enjoyable to find her in this predicament. "What was that?" He grinned.

"Would you help me, please?" It sounded like she was speaking through clenched teeth.

"Sure," he said, putting on a cheerful air that he knew would bug the hell out of her. Since there was no way scenario one was going to happen, he might as well get some sort of satisfaction out of this interlude. "You coming or going? Kinda hard to tell. By the way, how'd you get stuck up there?"

She gave an angry kick with her legs. Muttered something else.

"Pardon?" he said politely. "I'm afraid I couldn't make that out."

"Something . . . fell." She was pissed, trying to sound calm, but he could tell. She was enunciating way too precisely. "Out. The window. I was *trying* to get it."

"Ahhh . . . I see. Well, do you want to continue your outward journey? Or would you rather I pull you back in?"

There was a short pause while she seemingly sorted through the pros and cons presented by the two options.

"Continue out," she said.

"All right. I'm going to have to —" He blew out a breath. He didn't feel jokey anymore. How was he going to manage this? What was he supposed to push on? He could leverage his shoulder against her ass, but after where his mind had gone, that would make him feel like a letch. Maybe he could wrap his arms around her thighs and push that way. It was either that or shoving on the bottoms of her feet, which would be too precarious and unlikely to work.

"Hello?" she said, her butt shifting up and to the side as if she had twisted her body around and was trying to glare a hole through the wall at him.

"Yup. Just . . ." Taking a hold of her ass and giving it a good firm shove was the most straightforward solution. However, she was not a dude. Proprieties had to be observed. "Hang on." He stepped to her side, crouched down, and wrapped his arms around her warm thighs. The moment his skin made contact with her, heat coursed through him like an electrical charge. *Thank God she chose to go* through *the window,* he thought as he hoisted her legs up onto his shoulder. *It would be pretty damned embarrassing if she had decided to come in this way.*

There would be no way she'd miss the enormous woody he was suddenly sporting. *You are carrying a rolled-up rug, nothing more,* he told himself as he tried to help navigate her hips through the window. But he was lying. She was the most delectable bundle of woman he'd come across in a very long time, and his cock was not fooled. He tried to shut down his senses, but it was impossible to do. Her ass was near his face, and when he breathed in, he was surrounded by citrus, verbena, a touch of cucumber, and woven throughout was a scent that was all her.

She smelled right. Like she was the missing piece he hadn't known he was searching for.

Almost there. Her palms were now flat on the ground. She walked them forward a couple of steps to make room for her body to land. "Okay," she called over her shoulder. "You can let go."

"You sure?"

"Mm-hmm. I've got it. Thanks." She felt Rhys release his grip on her ankles. She kicked off with her feet, tucked her abdomen.

"Oomph!" She heard him grunt.

Damn. Must have clipped him with her

foot. "Sor—" She hit the ground with a *thump.* Not the most graceful of descents. Oh well. *It's done and I'm in one piece.*

She got up, brushed herself off. "You okay?" There was a red mark riding high on his cheekbone. It hadn't been there at breakfast. "Didn't mean to . . ." She gestured toward his face.

"No worries." He seemed deep in thought.

"Well. Thanks for the . . . ah . . ." *What does one call it? For helping stuff my fat ass out the bathroom window? And by the way, Miss Evelyn Harris, what possessed you to try to force your way through that minuscule window like an overstuffed sausage when there are plenty of operating doors available to walk through —*

"Hey, I was thinking about your whole be-a-chef-for-a-day scheme and —"

She puffed out a breath. "Look," she said. "I understand. It's a lot to ask. The thing is . . ." She shook her head, squatted down, and started gathering the scattered tubes of paint, wiping the dirt off on her shirt and replacing them in the paint box. "I don't just hate cooking. I'm a terrible cook to boot. I love my sister to bits, and I'm *really* glad that she and Luke are having a vacation, but I'm terrified, too."

"Terrified?"

"That my horrible cooking will scare off our regulars and I'll personally be responsible for bankrupting the café. That I'll somehow manage to burn the place down. Yes. I *am* that bad of a cook. I'm worried, because even when both Maggie and I are working full-tilt, we're running our feet to the bone. How the hell am I going to juggle both the kitchen and the front of the house? Of course you don't want to be a chef for a day. I get that. You're some kind of goddamned movie star — if my sister's to be believed. Why the hell would you want to spend your vacation slaving over a hot oven?" She slammed her paint box shut, latched it, and stood to face him. "I understand. Truly. I do."

He blinked once. Twice. And she was momentarily mesmerized by what a gorgeous color his eyes were. Blue. With a deeper hue, almost a midnight-blue, encircling the pupil and the outer rim of his iris. And then, if that weren't beautiful enough, he had a starburst of steel gray scattering outward from the center.

"I'd like to do it," she heard him say. She transferred her gaze from his eyes to his mouth. *Strong, firm, full lower lip, slightly chapped, totally kissable.*

"Do what?" she said. *Maybe he'll let me*

paint him. She didn't usually do portraits. Landscapes were what called to her. However, for him she'd make an exception.

"Help out at — what was that you called it?"

His face was its own sort of landscape. Beauty and symmetrical perfection, hiding shadows and secrets. "Called what?"

"Your café?"

"What about it?" Maybe she'd paint his face as a landscape —

"What is the name of your café? As a matter of fact, why don't you give me your name as well? You already know mine from riffling through my wallet, but I never got the privilege of learning yours."

She was vaguely aware of the fact that she was being rude and forced herself to pull away from her creative mind and back to the present. She blew out a breath, her mind clearing. "Sorry," she said. "Daydreaming. We named our café the Intrepid. I'm Evelyn Harris, but most everyone calls me Eve."

"Well, Eve, I'll help out."

"You will?" She wasn't sure if she'd heard him correctly. "Seriously?"

He nodded. "Whether I'm an unmitigated disaster or not remains to be seen, but I am happy to do what I can. Can't promise I'll last the two weeks. After the first day, we might agree that having me as your chef was a colossal miscalculation."

"Seriously, Rhys, *anybody* would be better than me!" She laughed, relief flooding through her. "I have to admit, that was the *last* thing I expected to come out of your mouth," she said, a huge smile on her face. "Thank you. Thank you so much!"

"Also, if I *do* last out the week, I have a previous engagement Thursday night, but since you close at three p.m., that shouldn't be an issue."

"Absolutely. No problem."

"I can't promise you miracles. I will need to get acquainted with the kitchen beforehand. See if what you're asking is doable. If I'm going to attempt this, I want to give it my best shot."

EIGHTEEN

"We'll go in through the back door," Eve said, leading the way. "If people see activity in the front of the house, they'll think we're open and we'll be mobbed." She inserted a key into the lock, first the dead bolt and then the door handle. The door swung open and they stepped inside. "Here we are," Eve said, switching on the light.

Rhys flipped his sunglasses to the top of his head and looked around the kitchen, a low whistle escaping from his lips. "Nice setup," he said, a feeling of anticipation and nerves tingling through him. There was a stainless-steel beast with glass doors lurking against the wall. He tipped his chin in its direction. "I take it that's the oven?"

"Yeah." Her brow screwed up slightly. "What the hell's it called? Ah . . . a double deck bakery oven." She paused, obviously trying to recall her sister's commentary. "Convection."

"Electric or gas?"

"Gas. With a preheat time of . . . What was it? Oh yeah, fifteen minutes."

"Nice." He ambled over to take a closer look. "Looks like each of the four ovens has their own individual temperature controls."

"Yeah, that's so you can cook pies at the same time as cookies, cakes, and so forth."

"Jesus." He shook his head ruefully. "What have I gotten myself into?"

"Not to worry. Maggie premade the pies; they just need cooking. Ditto with the cookie dough, muffin mixes, et cetera. We should have enough to get us through the —"

There was a muffled *thump* overhead.

Eve clutched his arm, eyes wide. "Wait —"

"You okay?" he asked.

There was a *creak,* then a few more soft *thuds* across the ceiling.

"Shhh," she whispered, listening hard. "Did you hear that?"

What? he mouthed. She seemed freaked out. "The footsteps," he whispered. "Is that what you're talking about?"

She nodded, face tense.

"It looked like there was an apartment over the café."

"There is," she hissed back. "Mine."

"You don't have a roommate?"

"No." She shook her head. "It's just me."

"Stay here. I'll check it out." He headed out the door.

"Like hell I will," she retorted. "I've seen you in action. You'll probably get yourself killed."

He shook his head. He would have argued, but there wasn't time. He took the metal open-rung stairs up to her apartment two at a time, Eve hot on his heels.

Eve grabbed the back of his shirt. "The door," she whispered, her stomach in knots. "I locked it."

Her front door was not only unlocked, but it was slightly ajar. Over Rhys's shoulder she could see a hairline sliver of her living room.

Slowly, quietly, he pushed the door open.

Shhtt . . .

They froze.

The intruder was definitely in there. She could hear someone moving around her apartment.

Rhys charged inside.

"Hold on!" she called. "It could be dangerous." But it was too late. He'd already disappeared.

"Hells bells," she muttered, racing in after

him, her heart pounding. "Now I gotta go save him."

She could hear yells coming from her bedroom, the *thump* of bodies hitting each other, crashing into walls, things breaking.

By the time she got to the bedroom Rhys had already immobilized the heavyset man. *Who knew the pretty boy could move so fast?*

The intruder was quite hairy. She couldn't see his face as his head was turned away from her and smashed against the floor. Rhys had the intruder's beefy tattooed arm wrenched up high behind his back. It looked painful.

"Call nine-one-one," Rhys barked.

"Right." Eve reached into her purse, her mind spinning in overdrive. *I've seen a forked-tongued dragon tattoo on someone's biceps recently, but whose?* "Damn, having difficulty with the zipper." The inside pocket zipper's teeth had caught a piece of the purse lining and wasn't budging.

There was a scuffle, a *thump,* followed by a low pain-filled moan.

"Don't try that again," she heard Rhys say. He didn't raise his voice, but the deadly warning was clear. His voice sounded so different from the amused drawl she associated with him.

Eve gave another hard yank, and the zipper gave way. "Okay." She jammed her hand in the purse, her fingers closing around the phone. "Got it."

"Eve?" the intruder grunted. "Eve, is that you?"

"You know this man?" Rhys asked, his head swiveling to look at her, his eyes fierce, intent.

The intruder's voice sounded familiar. Eve moved so she could see the man's face. The guy had a hell of a lot of hair splayed across his —

"Larry?" she said cautiously. "Larry Shumilak?"

"Yeah, it's me. Um . . . Can I get up now? This is very uncomfortable."

Yes. It was definitely Larry. "I know him," Eve told Rhys as she slowly straightened, her mind reeling.

An impenetrable mask slid over Rhys's face. "He your boyfriend?" he asked, his voice cool, detached.

He thinks I'm dating this guy?

"No," Eve said, determined to keep her face as expressionless and detached as Rhys's. "Of course not. He works at the Intrepid, and I'm sure he has a reasonable explanation for what he is doing here." Eve squatted by Larry's head. Never mind that she was furious. She was going to question

Larry calmly and collectedly.

"Larry," she heard herself bellow. "What the *hell* are you doing in my apartment?"

"Milk?" Eve was asking. "Sugar?" Had the world gone insane? Rhys shook his head. When she'd thought he was an intruder, she'd slammed him to the floor and hog-tied him. But this guy? Who they'd caught red-handed in her bedroom —

The thought of this asshole in her bedroom, pawing through her things, made Rhys want to punch something. But the guy had started crying, and Eve made Rhys release him. Wouldn't let him call the cops and report the intrusion. Wouldn't let Rhys throw him out on his ass.

No.

She was serving this low-life *tea.*

"B-both please," Larry answered from the little kitchen table, his head in his hands.

"There you are," Eve said, placing a delicate china teacup and saucer in front of the hulking Neanderthal of a man, who was *still* weeping. She glanced over Larry's head at Rhys. "Would you like some?" she asked.

"No," Rhys said. The thing that pissed Rhys off the most was the anger that was surging through him. He prided himself on being able to maintain his cool in the most difficult of circumstances. So why was he feeling so damned furious now?

She shrugged. "Suit yourself." She reached into the cupboard and removed a pale blue teacup with gilt around the edge and on the handle and placed it on the counter. "No need to snarl."

Rhys briefly considered the merits of arguing that point but decided against it.

"And stop pacing," she added. "You are scaring Larry and making me dizzy."

Rhys slammed to a halt, arms crossed over his chest, and glared at the intruder. "Better?"

"Now you are towering over him. Sit down." Eve reached over and patted Larry's arm. "Drink your tea, Larry."

Rhys didn't budge. It was taking all of his control not to rip Larry's arm — that she was so tenderly patting — right out of its socket. The weeping act this dude was putting on pissed him off big-time. Howie would always cry. Every single time his mom came home from the hospital, battered and bruised, the litany would begin: "So sorry — don't know what got into me — will never do it again."

Ha! Fucking asshole.

Larry took a shaky slurp of tea. "Do — do you hab some Kleenex?" he asked. "I gotta blow my dnose."

Rhys stomped into the bathroom, grabbed a roll of toilet paper, stalked back into the main living area, and slammed it down on the table, causing Larry to jump slightly. It was a good feeling.

"All right," Rhys said. "Time for answers." He turned to Eve. "Did you give him a key to your apartment?"

"No," Eve said, looking troubled.

"No." Rhys placed both hands on the little vintage Formica table and leaned in. "She didn't give you a key, and yet the door was open and you were inside. Care to tell us how that happened?"

Larry unspooled a long length of toilet paper and blew his bulbous nose loudly. There was a lot of liquid up there. He unrolled another long streamer of toilet paper, mopped up the excess snot, then dropped the soggy mess. Eve winced as it made contact with her table.

"We're waiting," Rhys said.

Larry lifted his shaggy head and looked at Eve mournfully. "I came to work, see, and —"

Rhys could see Eve's spine stiffen out of the corner of his eye. "We're closed, Larry," she said. "There's no work today."

"I know," Larry said hastily. "But my mom

was hosting her knitting club, didn't want me hanging around the house. So, I came here. I — I sometimes do on my days off, to clean up the perimeter. No time to do it properly when we're open. Too busy."

"The perimeter?" Eve asked, looking wary.

"Yeah." Larry nodded. "I sweep off the sidewalk in front of the establishment. Sometimes little weeds poke their way through, right along the base of the building, so I pull those out." His hands were miming the various activities. "Can't leave them there to proliferate. They'd weaken the foundation. And then there's the windows."

"Windows?" Eve was sitting back in her chair and seemed slightly dazed at this outpouring of words.

"They need washing!" Larry said, arms waving, head nodding, his long beard making the movement seem even bigger. "And that's why I was here. Gonna wash the outside of 'em and try to get the inside cleaned when we had a midmorning lull."

"Larry, we have a window-washing service," Eve said, shaking her head. "There's no need to come here on your day off to —"

"They don't come often enough. It's bad for business. Gotta have clean windows. The windows are the eyes to the soul!" Larry must have realized that his voice had built to a shout because he flushed deep red and snapped his mouth shut.

The kitchen was silent.

Eve blinked. "Oh," she said softly. "I see."

See what? Rhys thought. *He hasn't answered the question.* "Window washing," Rhys said, not the least bit bothered that Larry visibly cringed whenever he spoke, "is all well and good, but that doesn't explain what you were doing in Eve's bedroom."

Larry's hound-dog gaze darted from Eve's sympathetic one to Rhys's. Larry blanched. "It . . . It was open," he said, swallowing hard. "The door. It was already open."

"So why didn't you just shut it? Walk away. Why did you feel the need" — Rhys could feel white-hot anger rising as he flashed back on the image of Larry standing among Eve's private things — "to enter her apartment, walk through to her bedroom, and who the hell knows what else?"

"I heard a noise, sir," Larry whispered, his eyes welling up. "Wanted to make sure Ms. Harris was okay."

NINETEEN

"You aren't gonna fire me?" Larry asked, a quaver in his voice. And Eve thought, not for the first time, what an odd contradiction Larry was, the rough external appearance and the vulnerable sweet inside.

"No. You're my A-one worker. Couldn't manage without you."

"Really?" Larry said, his face brightening.

"Absolutely," Eve said firmly. "I'll see you Tuesday, bright and early."

"You don't want me to wash the windows?"

"No. You go on home." Eve could feel Rhys's gaze on her as she stood at the door watching Larry reluctantly start to lumber down the metal open-rung stairs.

"All right," Larry said. "Bye-bye."

"Bye, Larry," Eve said, and then stepped back into her apartment and shut the door. She remained for a moment with her back to Rhys, trying to calm her body. *These heightened waves of sexuality that are roaring through you are the residual adrenaline from the drama before,* she told herself. *Do not make an ass of yourself.*

"He lives with his mom?"

"Yeah," she said, keeping her voice soft so it wouldn't carry through the door to Larry. "He went through a rough patch, got tangled with the wrong people, but he's turned himself around. Is back on the straight and narrow."

"You hope," Rhys said. She could hear the taut frustration in his voice. "You should have let me question him."

Eve turned to face him. "I believe Larry," she said. "I must have forgotten to lock the door and the wind blew it open."

"Or (a): He was blowing smoke up your ass," Rhys said through gritted teeth, "or (b): He interrupted someone in the midst of a burglary. The place has clearly been tossed."

Eve glanced around her apartment. No tossing had happened here. It looked pretty much how she had left it. However, no need to admit to that. "Or (c):" she said. "You are a tiny bit paranoid." He glowered at her, but she paid him no mind. "Understandable," she said, giving him a reassuring pat on his shoulder, "given your dramatic inclinations . . ." The rest of her pithy comment had vanished like a mouthful of smoke. She stared at his large sun-bronzed hand, which had captured her smaller one, her knees suddenly weak. The solid warmth of his hand, the slight roughness of calluses were so unexpected. She had thought an actor would have soft, unused hands. Rhys's hands could have just as easily belonged to one of the construction workers on her dad's crew.

There was a thin white scar that ran between the first two knuckles and disappeared just past his wrist. How did he get it? A shiver went through her, and without meaning to, she leaned forward and rested her cheek on it, barely touching his skin, as if that would somehow take the wound away.

A growl rumbled from his chest, snapping her gaze to his.

He was watching her intently, the pupils of his eyes almost obliterating the deep midnight-blue irises.

"How did this happen?" she asked, her voice coming out lower, husky, as if she were recovering from a cold. Her gaze dropped again. Her finger, skimming lightly, followed the scar's trajectory, traveling across the tanned, warm skin on the back of his hand.

■ ■ ■ ■

"I don't remember," he said. He forced himself to release her hand.

He took a step back, then another. Needing distance from her, from memories of his childhood, which had roared to the forefront.

"Liar," she said, her voice soft, eyes sad. As if she could see deep inside him to the wounded, scared kid he hid from the world.

He turned. Looked out the window. Larry's hulking form was leaning against the brick wall of the building, his shoulders bowed. Why was he lurking in the parking lot? Keeping hidden by the dumpster from passersby on the sidewalk?

Rhys lifted his hand to rap on the window. Let Larry know he could see him. Was aware he hadn't left. But before his knuckles reached the glass, Larry's head snapped up, his eyes staring daggers at Rhys through the glass. Gone was the weeping, wishy-washy giant.

"Well, fuck you, too," Rhys murmured.

Larry jerked his arms outward as if taunting a gored bull, his teeth bared, then spun around and stalked off, muttering angrily to himself.

"What are you staring at?" Eve asked.

He shrugged, turned away from the window. "We need to go through your apartment." He was relieved to discover his voice and body were calm again. "Make sure nothing's missing. That the place is safe."

Twenty

Right there. Behind that copse of trees. He pulled over. His vehicle bumping, bouncing as its wheels left the asphalt. Once he was totally hidden from the road, he shifted to park, applied the emergency brake, and switched off the engine.

He was feeling light-headed, nauseous. His breath was coming too fast, too hard. The sound harsh, loud in his ears.

Shaking. Whole body shaking.

Caught. Almost caught. He dragged a sweaty hand across his face, dropped his forehead to the steering wheel. *That was close. Too close.*

He wasn't sure how long he stayed in that position, but gradually, along with the adrenaline and fear coursing through him, came glee as well.

Granted, the night hadn't gone as he'd planned. However, he'd successfully breached her defenses, broken into her apartment with relative ease.

Eve.

Last night had been amazing. He'd lain in her bed. Slept with his head on her pillow, pleasured himself in her sheets.

Which he'd removed from the premises — of course — DNA and all that.

He reached into his satchel. Yes, the sheets were still there. Had survived the drop from the second-story window. He'd worried someone would run off with his prize before he managed to retrieve it.

But no, his satchel had been there on the ground, waiting patiently.

Fortune had smiled upon him yet again.

He removed one of her sheets and wrapped it around himself, covering his head, his shoulders. He gathered huge handfuls of the fabric, lifted it to his face, and inhaled deeply. He could smell her, could smell himself. The combination of their two scents intermingled was unbelievably erotic.

He unstrapped his seat belt, unzipped his fly, lifting his hips for easier removal. Didn't want his stiff dick to snag on the small metal teeth of the zipper.

"Soon, my love. Soon," he murmured, wrapping his hand around himself, envisioning her on her knees, hands tied, being forced to bring him to satisfaction.

Twenty-One

Eve stared at her bed in disbelief. "My sheets are gone." She felt sick to her stomach. "Why would anyone do that? Such a creepy thing to steal."

"You want to call the cops?"

"I don't know." She rubbed her face, suddenly tired. "Not sure what the right thing to do is." She sank down to her bed, but it felt weird. She stood up quickly. Her bed didn't feel like a safe haven anymore.

You don't have time to be grossed out, she told herself. *You need to figure this out. Someone has been in your room, taken your sheets? That's such a personal thing to do. Must be someone I know, but who? Was Rhys right? Could Larry be the culprit?* The thought made her feel guilty. Ashamed. As if she'd kicked a puppy when no one was looking. No. He didn't have the sheets. If he had taken them, wouldn't he have been carrying them when Rhys tackled him? It didn't make sense.

"You okay?" Rhys asked. He put an arm around her shoulders. "You look pale. You need some water."

"No. I just . . ." She was feeling lightheaded. "I wanna get outta here."

"Okay," he said. "Let me lock up." He gave her shoulders a quick squeeze, then rounded the bed to the window, started to slide the window frame down when something on the floor caught his eyes.

He crouched down.

"Oh shit." His voice sounded deadly serious. He blew out a breath, long and slow, then looked at her. "Eve, do you use plastic cable ties for anything?"

"No," she said, stepping toward him. "Why?"

He straightened, his face like granite. "That's it. We're calling the cops."

"They didn't seem too concerned," Eve said, easing her car onto Rainbow Road. "Guess stolen sheets don't rank high on the crimes list." She was trying to act nonchalant. Unfazed, even though her insides felt as though she'd drunk battery acid.

She glanced over at Rhys, who hadn't spoken since they'd left the apartment. "They weren't that interested in the cable ties either."

"That's because they're idiots," Rhys bit out, his face grim.

Well, at least he was finally talking. She couldn't take much more of this stone-cold silence. "Why were you so freaked out when you found them?"

"You don't want to know," he said, as if that was the end of the conversation.

"Actually," she said, her voice coming out sharper than she intended. "I do. That's why I asked."

Silence.

She drummed her fingers on the steering wheel. "Well?"

"Look." He turned to face her. "I hope I'm wrong. As you said, I'm an actor. I have an active imagination. It's just . . ." He huffed out a breath. "I did a movie where I played a corporate raider who got kidnapped. He was held for ransom. It was based on a true story. The kidnappers used plastic cable ties to secure him, then wrapped him from head to toe in duct tape, only leaving air holes to breathe through. That movie fucked me up. Even now, three years later, every time I hear someone ripping off a piece of duct tape — which happens a *lot* on movie sets — the sound makes my skin crawl. Hated that bloody movie. If I'd known what it would take out of me, I never would have agreed to do it."

He turned away, stared through the windshield with unseeing eyes. "So yes, finding plastic cable ties on your bedroom floor is worrisome. The upside of all this is, you've got yourself a cook until Luke and Maggie return. No way in hell I'm letting you go to the café alone."

When they got back to the house, Rhys reset the property's perimeter alarms. Reached to activate the interior ones as well.

"No," Eve said. "Don't. It's pointless. We would be hostages of the house. Not able to let the dog out to go pee or open a window to get a little fresh air without having to disengage the damned alarm."

"What if you have a stalker?"

Eve snorted, acting nonchalant even though she was feeling anything but. "Puuleaze. Who's gonna stalk me?"

"Any number of people."

"I'm not the movie star."

"Doesn't matter. You're a heart-stopper," he said, which was really quite sweet of him.

She forced a laugh out. "Look, it was probably an isolated incident. Some homeless person saw the lights were off, car was gone, and decided to spend a night on a comfy bed."

"And the sheets? How do you explain that?"

"Maybe he accidentally peed the bed and didn't want to leave the mess for me to find?" But even as the words came out of her mouth, she knew it was a stretch. Her body knew, too, because that jangly nervous feeling was starting up again in her belly. "I just . . ." She shrugged, unable to find the right words. "I . . ." She shoved her hands in her jeans pockets.

"You just what?" he prompted. The compassion in his eyes loosened something inside her, made her want to explain.

"This was supposed to be *my* vacation," she said. "I can't really afford to take a trip. I wanted to have these few days to live a carefree existence, with no debts to pay, no clock to punch. To be able to come and go freely, with endless hours to paint my heart out." She squeezed her eyes shut, but it didn't help. A tear escaped and then another. She turned her head away, hoping he wouldn't notice. "If I . . . have to be turning the house alarm on and off every time I want a breath of fresh air . . . every time I need to run inside to refresh my water or get a different paintbrush that I didn't know

I would need, it would disturb the muse. Block the process, and I . . ."

"I get it," he said, his voice gentle, and then she heard him move. Felt the heat of his body stepping in front of hers, the warm pads of his thumbs slide across the crests of her cheeks.

She blew out a shaky breath and opened her eyes. The sight of him, his totally *there* presence made her feel as if she'd just slammed into a brick wall. *So goddamn beautiful,* she thought. Momentarily lost. Drowning in the dark pool of his eyes, his soul. He understood. Didn't think she was weird. Totally got what she was saying. Got *her.*

She wanted to lean forward, taste his mouth, twine her fingers through his sun-kissed hair. Wanted it more than she wanted her next breath, but she didn't move. He had women throwing themselves at him all the time. She would not take advantage of his kindness that way.

"We won't turn the house alarm on during the daylight hours," he said, his thumbs making another pass across her cheeks. "Unless circumstances heat up. Then we will reassess. We'll leave the perimeter alarm on as a safeguard. This way no one can breach the perimeter of the property without triggering the alarms. This will give us plenty of advance warning to get inside and secure the house, et cetera. Sound good?"

She nodded, unable to trust her voice. She felt humbled by his kindness.

"There . . . there. Don't cry." He slid his hands to gently frame her face. "Come on, now, sweetheart." He dropped a gentle kiss on her forehead, his lips warm, tender. "Things aren't so bad." Another kiss placed near the corner of her eyes, capturing a tear. "We'll work it out. Promise."

She raised her hands, meaning to stop him, his kindness, before it undid her completely. It was her intention to be good, to give him space, not give in to her baser impulses, but the minute her hands covered his, all her noble ideas flew out of the window. Resisting was as futile as trying to put out a forest fire with a child's plastic bucket. She plunged her fingers through his hair, grabbing fistfuls of it, forcing his head down so his mouth fused with hers. Lips parting, teeth bumping, the stroke of his tongue, rough and silky velvet all at the same time. The taste of him roared through her like a thunderbolt. His arms, his scent surrounding her, engulfing her senses, sending shivers coursing through her, both hot and cold.

"Oh my God, oh my God." Along with

the heat, panic rose, too. *What have I done?* She forced herself to wrench away from him, from his beautiful seductive mouth. "Oh my God," she murmured, her fingers rising to her swollen, hungry lips. "What the hell?"

"I know, *right*?" he said.

That his eyes were mirroring the rampaging hunger she felt was exhilarating. It also frightened the hell out of her. "I just . . . I don't want . . ." she said. "I *can't* — fall for someone like you."

Twenty-Two

What the hell did that mean? Can't fall for someone like me? Rhys paced the confines of his bedroom. *I'm a damn good catch!* She'd given him a taste of her — and a boner the size of Montana — then had torn out of the living room as if the devil himself were on her heels.

He glanced out the window. Yep. She was still there, out in the far field. Painting. It was clear, even from this distance, that for her painting was a full-body, all-encompassing experience. Her lithe form moved as if she were being buffeted by a windstorm, creativity and passion spiraling outward from her like the advancing wave front of a sonic boom.

His phone chimed. He strode to the dresser and glanced at the screen.

A text from his agent, Jon: UPPED OFFER. 14 MIL. 11% OF GROSS. GREAT OFFER! RECOMMEND WE ACCEPT.

Rhys shook his head. He'd had this conversation with his agent numerous times in the last week. The script was shit. Didn't matter how much money they tried to throw at him; he was *not* going to agree to star in *Busted.* To do so would be career suicide. He switched his phone to vibrate and returned his attention to the conundrum that was Eve Harris.

Why is she so averse to starting a relationship with me? Not that I'm looking for a relationship. God, no. But still. One kiss made her run from the room?

He cupped his hand around his nose and mouth, exhaled, and took a whiff in through his nostrils. *Breath's fine, doesn't stink.*

He glanced in the mirror as he passed. *Mug's still the same. Body's toned. I can string two sentences together, three if need be. I'm well off. Hell, Rhys, call a spade a spade — you've got a shitload of money. No debt. Clean bill of health. All your teeth.* He attempted a laugh, but it came out hollow. *So why the hell did she run like I was a card-carrying member of the zombie apocalypse?*

He turned and stared out the window.

He couldn't make out her features. She was too far away, but he could feel her energy tugging at him like an invisible silken cord gently spooling him closer and closer.

■ ■ ■ ■

At first she had difficulty finding her way in. Circled her easel, the blank canvas staring back at her. Mocking her. *You aren't an artist,* it said. *You are a time-wasting untalented fraud. There is a reason no one has purchased your paintings.*

"No, I've sold a few —"

Sales to family and friends don't count. Snide. So snide, her inner critic.

"Enough!" she shouted, causing a flock of white-crowned sparrows to spiral upward until one took charge and chose a direction. The rest followed in a dark flurry of wings. Eve's gaze flew with them over the treetops until they disappeared from view.

"Right," she said. "No more of this foolish discourse."

She dug into her backpack and pulled out her noise-canceling headphones. Even though the offensive noise was in her head, she was hoping they would help. She plopped them on, synced her playlist to Adele's "Rolling in the Deep," and cranked the volume loud.

Good move, she thought as the music stormed through her. There was absolutely no way she could listen to that song and be stuck in her head.

As a matter of fact . . .

She put "Rolling in the Deep" on a continuous loop. Pushed up her sleeves and got to work, the power and fury of the song booming through her veins, inspiring her to roar as well.

Possible stalkers, mind-altering kisses, a movie star so handsome her eyes ached to look upon him? Gone. Vanished into the ether like a mouthful of smoke. She was an artist now, and she was damn well going to paint!

Finally. Took forever. Rhys clicked off the Dropbox site, having finished the kills on the stills from the *Rider* movie. The set photographer had been the overzealous, click-happy type, took *way* more stills than was necessary.

He shut his laptop and stood, rolling the tension out of his shoulders. Glanced out the window. She was still in that field painting, but she'd have to stop soon, as the sun was setting.

He went into the kitchen. Got a cup of coffee, then returned to his bedroom and shifted the armchair so it faced the window. Sat down, drank his coffee, and enjoyed the view.

■ ■ ■ ■

He'd watched the sun disappear behind the mountain range, the sky start to shift to gray. The wind picked up, whipping off the ocean, cold and brisk, causing the trees to sway and rattle their branches.

By the time he reached the far end of the field, she didn't appear to be painting anymore. Had pushed off her headphones and stepped back from the canvas, a slight frown on her face, arms crossed over her chest. She didn't seem displeased, just focused.

"How'd it go?" he asked. She seemed surprised. Must have been so deep in the work that she hadn't registered him and Samson approaching. He recognized her dazed look, a combination of fatigue and exhilaration. He'd experienced it often enough when he was deep into a character, the feeling of straddling two worlds, the real world and the creative, imaginary one.

"Hi," she said, dragging her eyes away from her canvas. He could sense the moment he slowly came into focus for her. It was almost as if he were watching her wake from a dream.

The sky was shifting to dusk, but there was still enough light to see the flush sweeping up her face. She must be remembering the kiss.

He smiled, a little wolfish perhaps, but who could blame him? The kiss was on his mind as well.

She turned back to her canvas.

The temptation to make his way around to the front of the easel was enormous. He was curious to see what she'd spent the day working on, but more than that, he wanted to stand beside her and breathe her in.

However, he didn't like it when he had to share a character that wasn't yet completely formed. He found sharing something he had been working on too soon could stunt the process. So he stayed where he was.

She yawned, stretched out her arms, her shoulders, reminding him of a sleek cat stirring from a favorite perch.

Her shoulders must be cramped from painting for so many hours without stopping. Maybe she'd like a massage? But the minute that thought arose, he vetoed it. *When I know her better,* he thought. *I don't want to spook her. Whoa! I'm thinking about a possible future with her?* He shoved his hands deep into his pockets and took a large step back.

She yawned again, stretched some more, her high, small breasts thrusting upward.

What would it be like to wake next to her? Her shimmering ebony hair spread over the pillow. Her eyes at half-mast, sleep-filled and lusty, her body lit by moonlight coming in through the —

She placed her paintbrush in a jar with the others and stirred it, the sharp smell of turpentine adding a bite to the air. "What time is it?" she asked, rotating her wrist.

"A little after seven."

"Wow. I had no idea it was so late."

He nodded. "Sometimes it's like that when you get in the flow. Means it was a good day. Jacket?" Rhys asked, holding out the spare he'd grabbed along with a flashlight as he exited the house.

"Oh. Yeah. Thanks." She put it on and rubbed her palms briskly up and down her arms. "Didn't realize I was cold." She smiled at him like she was grateful, and the expression on her face caused an unexpected warmth to bloom outward from his chest.

Rhys's foresight in bringing a flashlight proved to be fortuitous. Her favorite filbert brush slipped out of her hand while she was packing her supplies. With the sun's light now long gone, it would've been extremely difficult to find.

They walked back to the house in comfortable silence, Samson loping beside them. Eve was carefully carrying her partially finished painting out from her body, so as not to smear paint on the jacket Rhys had loaned her. The jacket smelled of him, a fresh, clean scent with a touch of wood smoke. She liked wearing his jacket, as it made her feel warm and protected.

"You happy with the day's work?" he asked.

"Mm-hmm," she said. "For now. Who knows what I'll think when I look at it tomorrow?"

The pool of light caused by Rhys's flashlight bobbled. She glanced over. "You sure you're okay? I can handle my equipment. I brought it out here on my own."

"I'm fine," he said. "Just shifting hands." He'd insisted on lugging her easel and paint box back up to the house.

"All right, then."

When he'd picked up her stuff, she'd felt all elbows and knees. Shy. Hopeful. Which was a totally weird sensation. She was thirty-one years old, with way more experience under her belt than she ever wanted to cop to. Yet something about walking back to the house with him made her feel young. Like how she'd thought her teenage years would be. A boy she liked carrying her books home from school.

They deposited her painting and equipment in the gardening shed. On the way to the house they saw a great snowy white owl flying overhead, magical in the moonlight, making Eve's breath catch in her throat. A rush of wings and then it was gone, only a faint *hoo . . . hoo . . .* in the distance as a reminder of its existence.

"Wow," Rhys said, more breath than voice.

"Yeah," she said. The two of them stood staring up at the night sky.

Samson broke the spell, nudging her with his head as if to say, *Come along now. I'm ready for dinner.*

Once in the house, Eve fed the dog, then got out a frying pan and heated up some lasagna Maggie had left in the fridge, while Rhys opened a bottle of Chianti.

He handed a glass of wine to her. "Cheers," she said, and took a sip. He did, too, watching her over the rim of his glass with those sexy, soulful eyes of his. Damn him. She did not want to be feeling this way.

"Listen," she said, turning back to the lasagna and giving it a poke. "I think we should set some boundaries. Do I want to jump your bones? Yes. I do. Who wouldn't? You're hot as hell." He started to open his mouth, but she held up the goopy spatula as if she were wielding a red stop sign. "However, that doesn't mean I'm going to act on my baser instincts. I've been down this road before. I know where it leads. Being in the kind of relationship you could offer is something I have no interest in exploring."

He crossed his arms and leaned back against the counter. "And what kind of relationship would that be, pray tell?" he asked, his voice deceptively smooth. She could see the tension that had settled around his eyes.

Who the hell says "pray tell"? she thought irritably. "Short-term. A fling. A vacation fuck buddy." She turned the lasagna a little too vigorously, and a splatter of red sauce spackled across the toe of his clearly expensive, well-made boot. "*Not* interested."

"Okay. First." He held up one long tan finger. The man had nice hands. She'd give him that. "We had one kiss. *One* kiss does *not* a relationship make. Two." Up came another finger and with it an image of what he could do with those fingers.

Eve blew out a breath and swallowed as she struggled to compose herself. *Stay focused. This is important. You can't just fall on your back because you like his hands.*

"I've had," he continued, "short-term

flings and vacation fuck buddies up the wazoo. And I can tell you right now, I'm not interested —"

"Don't bullshit me," Eve spat, feeling a surge of anger. "I know I'm not feeling this heat all on my own."

It was his turn to hold up a hand. "Let me finish."

She snapped her lips together, gave a short nod.

"What I'm *not* interested in is starting a relationship with a timer ticking. Yes, I'm attracted to you. No, we don't know how things will turn out. Might be, we get to know each other and realize we don't particularly suit.

"However, for the record, I'm tired of short-term. Am looking for something more. Whether that 'something more' is you?" He shrugged. "Who knows? But I'm not so chickenshit that I'm going to tuck tail and run without exploring if there's a possibility for something more."

He reached around her and turned off the burner.

Eve could feel her face flush. She'd thought he was reaching for her. Had wanted him to.

"Starting to get crispy," he said.

"What?"

"The lasagna," he said, tipping his head toward the pan. "You were drying it out." He went to the cupboard and removed two plates. "Mind if I ask whatcha got against actors?"

"You're on the road a lot."

"And?"

He was right. He deserved an explanation. "My ex was a musician. He was on the road all the time and . . ."

"Fooled around."

She nodded.

"Okay, so I get where your prejudice comes from. You've been burned. But in the defense of actors and musicians worldwide, perhaps it's not fair to paint us all with the same brush. That would be like me avoiding you because Vincent Van Gogh cut his ear off. Yes, some actors and musician types are hound dogs, but some" — he gestured to himself — "aren't."

He was looking at her with those gorgeous eyes, a slight furrow on his brow, as if he were a surgeon waiting to see if the sutures were going to hold.

"Point taken," she said. It was embarrassing to concede that he was probably right, she wasn't being fair, but there was a feeling of lightness, too. A sense of relief, as if she were finally releasing a fist that she had kept clenched for far too long.

She plated the food and they brought it to the table.

Rhys was right. She'd dried the lasagna out some, but it was still edible and they were hungry, so they made fast work of it.

"I hope you don't mind," Rhys said, scraping the side of his fork along his plate to capture the last scraps of food. "I made an appointment for a locksmith to meet us at your apartment tomorrow."

His lips closed around his fork. *Such a great mouth,* she thought, calling on her stores of self-control not to lean over the table and devour him. *It's a sin that a man like him is allowed to roam the streets looking like sex on a stick.*

"I figure we can get two birds with one stone." He was still talking. "I need to spend some time acclimating myself to the Intrepid kitchen so I can hit the ground running for Tuesday's opening. While I'm doing that, the locksmith can be changing out the locks."

Locksmith? Changing the locks? Sheesh, you were just zoning out there, basking in a sea of lust. "Rhys," she said, clearing her throat. "I really appreciate the idea, but —" Yes, now that she was thinking with her mind rather than her nether regions, better locks made sense. It was sweet of him to think of it. However, there was no way she could afford the kind of outlay that specialized locks would require. Not now. Maybe in six months, if the business kept growing the way it was.

"My treat," he said. "And save your breath, because there is no way I'm going to back down on this."

"But —"

"Yes, the break-in might have been a one-time thing. But just in case it wasn't, let me do this. Please. I would not be able to look your brother-in-law in the eye if I didn't take some kind of preventative action."

Twenty-Three

"Holy Mary Mother of God," Rhys groaned. He rolled over to grab his cell phone from the bedside table and switched the alarm off. "Four a.m. I volunteered for this?"

He forced himself out of bed, showered, dressed, and staggered out of his room. Eve was waiting by the front door, bleary-eyed and holding two travel mugs. He could hear Samson's dog tags jingling in the mudroom as he wolfed down his breakfast.

"Coffee," Eve said, handing him one of the mugs with an apologetic smile. "Early, huh?"

"You're not kidding."

"I really appreciate you helping me out like this."

"Better save your thanks 'til we see how I do." He took a long slug of the hot liquid. "Thanks for the coffee." He followed her out the door as he took another long slug, feeling the caffeine starting to make an inroad through the fog. "Let's get this party started."

He ladled tomato soup into a bowl, glanced at the soup page in the blue binder.

> Drizzle a little spiral of cream on tomato soup.

Right. He drizzled, then plopped the heavy cream in the fridge. Sprinted to the stove, flipped the grilled cheese onto the chopping board, and cut it at a diagonal.

The buzzer on the third oven went off.

Too much to do. Too little time.

He arranged the bowl of soup and the sandwich on a plate, added a sprig of parsley, and hit the bell.

Eve dashed in, grabbed the soup and sandwich combo, then dashed out again. No way in hell she would've been able to handle this on her own. Even with the help of her possible-convict dishwasher and her kooky senior-citizen waitress. He shoved his hands in the blue-and-white-striped potholders, removed the sheets of fresh-baked chocolate cookies from the hot oven, and placed them on the counter. Yanked the mitts off, then flipped to the page for salted chocolate caramel cookies.

"Okay, next . . ." He glanced at the hand-written instructions in the binder. "*Melt caramel.* Caramel? Where would that be?"

"Hey, you," Larry barked.

Rhys turned. Larry was glaring at him, hands on his hips. "Can't leave 'em like that," Larry growled. It was the first full sentence the man had uttered to him since arriving at work four hours ago.

"Like what?"

Larry stomped over to a cupboard, yanked it open, pulled out several wire racks, and slammed them on the counter by the baked sheets of cookies. "Gotta cool 'em on these, like Maggie does." He slapped a spatula on the counter as well.

"Thanks, Larry. Appreciate the help."

"Ain't helping you. It's for the girls. Don't want you scaring off their customers with your soggy-assed cookies. Tested one of those oatmeal cookies you made this morning. They sucked."

"Now, come on . . ."

"No crisp around the edges. Shoulda used the cooling racks. Don't mess up again," Larry snarled. "I got my eye on you."

"Well, that makes two of us," Rhys said. He thought he'd kept his tone pleasant, but the guy flinched as though he'd gotten a flash of what Rhys was really feeling behind the smile. Then, pale-faced but defiant, Larry hoisted his middle finger in the air, his jaw thrust outward like he was begging for Rhys to break it.

Rhys was tempted, but he'd promised Eve he wouldn't do anything to upset Larry, and a broken jaw might fall into that category.

"You are allowed to have your suspicions," Eve had told him on the drive over that morning. "But unless you come up with concrete proof that Larry was lying, I want you to be civil to him. When Luke gets back from vacation, he can run a check on him, make sure no red flags pop up — knowing Luke, he probably already has. He's so damn protective of Maggie. But even if he hasn't, I can't afford to lose Larry. He's hardworking, *never* late, and a fabulous dishwasher to boot."

"Who might just happen to —"

Eve didn't let Rhys finish. "Let me make this absolutely clear: if you run him off, you're the one who will be staying here until midnight up to your elbows in dirty dishwater. Not me."

Rhys picked up the spatula and started transferring the cookies to the cooling racks. *The woman is tough,* he thought with a grin. *No doubt about it. She'd never let some assh-*

ole use her as his private punching bag. Then the sorrow hit. As it always did when he thought about his mom.

Eve came through the swinging doors, a stack of plates in her hands. "It's finally calming down out there. Thank goodness. What a madhouse it's been. Everyone talking about that poor person whose body was found under the bridge."

Rhys was standing motionless by the cookies cooling on the rack, spatula in hand.

"You okay?" she asked, because he had a funny look on his face, sort of lost and forlorn.

"Yeah," he said. He headed toward the fridge, then paused. "You mind if I take five?"

"Anytime," she said. "I'm so grateful you're here. I would have been well and truly screwed without you."

He smiled, his mood lightening. "I'd have preferred that sentence with the 'out' removed."

" 'Screwed: a difficult or hopeless situation; ruined or broken,' " she said with mock severity. "Not generally considered a positive thing."

"Depends who's doing the screwing," he said, a slight smile quirking the corners of his lips. Then he stepped outside into the parking lot and the door swung shut behind him.

"He didn't finish the cookies," Larry said. He'd been acting sullen ever since he'd arrived and seen that Rhys was installed in the kitchen.

"He will," Eve said, scraping the dishes.

"Hi, Sue Lynn." She heard Rhys's voice drifting in through the cracked-open window. "It's me." Eve glanced out. She wasn't spying, just human curiosity was all.

Rhys had parked himself on the stairs leading up to her apartment. He was sitting against the brick wall, his head tipped back, cell phone to his ear. His eyes were shut as though he were savoring the burst of midday sun that was beating down. There was a vulnerability about him.

She felt a flare of something. If she didn't know better she'd think it was jealousy. Which would be ridiculous. She'd started to share a kiss with the man, then shut it down. What was there to be jealous about? She didn't give a rat's ass if he was talking to some stupid girlfriend named Sue Lynn. It just reinforced the absolute correctness of her decision not to let her hormones drive the bus.

"Things are fine." The familiarity in his

voice as he spoke wrapped around Eve's chest like a boa constrictor. "It's very beautiful here." There was a pause as he listened, the corner of his mouth quirking up. "Well, 'peaceful' isn't exactly the word that springs to mind."

"Have they figured out how the person died?" Larry said, his gravelly voice drowning Rhys out. "Or who did it?"

"No." Eve dumped the scraped dishes at Larry's station. "No clue. They've sent the jaw into the lab to check dental records."

"Ah." Larry grunted. He said something else, but she didn't hear what. She'd already slipped through the swinging doors to deal with her hungry customers.

"How's she doing?" Rhys asked. He felt weary, as if the air around him was pressing in, weighing him down.

"Oh, you know," Sue Lynn said with her seemingly ever-present good cheer. "She has her good days and her bad ones. She was mighty glad to see you. We all were, if you want to know the truth. You're a ray of sunshine."

"Yeah, that's me," he said, a wave of self-loathing washing through him. If he was such a ray of sunshine, he wouldn't have hopped on that Greyhound bus headed for

LA the day after he graduated from high school. Couldn't have fled that hellhole fast enough. If he had stayed, maybe things would have been different.

"You should've seen us, Rhys. Last night" — Sue Lynn was still talking — "the entire day staff went to see your movie *Laws of Attraction.* Mr. Abrams, the activity director, let us use the Sunnyvale bus. Actually, he came with us — his wife and daughter, too. We *pre*bought tickets to make sure we all got in. We filled up that theater like nobody's business."

Rhys jumped in. Sue Lynn could talk the leg off a cat. "Well, thank you all for going. That was awful sweet of you. I'm on a bit of a time crunch, but I was hoping I could talk to her for a moment."

"Oh, certainly. Let me put her on."

Rhys could hear the rustle of fabric, then footsteps as Sue Lynn made her way to his mom. "Lorelai? Lorelai, it's your boy, honey."

"Who?" he could hear his mom say.

"Rhys. Your boy, Rhys, the movie star. He's on the phone. Wants to say hello."

"Who?"

"No, that's all right, Lorelai. I'll hold the phone. Okay, Rhys, she can hear you now."

"Hi, Mom."

"Hello. Who's this?"

"It's Rhys, Mom." It was one of those days. She had them. He always thought he was prepared, but it still caused a pang of sorrow on the occasions when she didn't remember who he was.

"Rhys . . . I have a son named Rhys."

"Yes, Mom. That's me. I was just thinking about you and wanted to call and tell you that I love you."

"Come for a visit?"

"Yes. I'll be there Thursday evening."

"Thursday?"

"That's the day after tomorrow."

"Bring candy?"

"Uh-huh. I always bring candy, Mom."

"Oh good. Fudge. I like fudge."

"I know. I'll bring some."

"Good."

"Is there anything else you'd like me to —"

"Who is this?"

Rhys made himself concentrate on the feel of the warm brick wall behind his back, the sunshine on his face, the slight breeze. "Rhys. It's Rhys, Mom."

Twenty-Four

"I can't believe we have to do that all over again tomorrow," Rhys said, rolling his shoulders and rotating his spine while Eve locked up. He felt like he'd been run over by a Mack truck. "The restaurant business is hard-core. I'm knackered." He fished his car keys out of his pocket. "Need anything from upstairs before we head out?"

"I'm good," she said, removing the restaurant key from the lock and dumping it in her purse as she walked past him toward his SUV rental.

"I checked upstairs during my lunch break," he said. "No sign of entry."

"Great." There was a tinge of sarcasm in her voice.

"I didn't go in," Rhys said. "Wouldn't violate your privacy like that. Just checked the tell I left in the doorjamb. It hadn't been disturbed. I walked around the building —

your upstairs-window tells were in place as well."

She gave a short nod. Didn't answer. No *Thank you for thinking to do that. What a relief. So glad the break-in appears to be an arbitrary incident, not someone with a personal vendetta against me. And by the way, I am so grateful you had the presence of mind to install high-security locks on my front door and windows yesterday. I'll sleep much better knowing they're there.*

Nope. Nothing.

Rhys didn't consider himself to be on the short list for Mr. Intuitive-Man-of-the-Year. However, it didn't take a genius to ascertain that she was pissed off about something. He watched her climb into the vehicle, her back stiff.

He got in, started the engine. "Wanna tell me what's going on? Or are we gonna play the guessing game?"

She didn't say anything, just strapped herself in, acting as though his voice were background static on a radio station.

He strapped in, backed up, shifted into drive, and pulled onto Rainbow Road. "Okay, guessing game it is. This is fun. You're never gonna believe this, but in my experience, it's usually the woman in the relationship who wants to talk things out.

You know, get all touchy-feely with the emotions, analyze the minutiae." He shook his head. "If my buddies could see me now, they'd laugh their heads off."

Silence. She didn't even crack a smile.

He sighed. "Eve," he said. "Talk to me." Her lips were compressed into a flat line.

"I heard you on the phone," she finally said, as if that would explain everything.

"And . . . ?" He waited.

She opened her mouth to speak. Shut it again. Glared out the window.

"Spit it out. You'll feel better."

She turned the full force of her glare on him. "Who's Sue Lynn?"

He couldn't help it. He had to laugh, unexpected warmth bubbling through him. "She's one of my mom's caregivers, early sixties, generously proportioned, married to her childhood sweetheart . . ."

"Oh," Eve said. Her voice was so soft he almost didn't hear it.

She looked at him, eyes dark with compassion.

"Brain damage," he said, answering her unspoken question.

"Has your mom always been that way?"

He shook his head.

"I'm sorry," she said. "Must be difficult."

He managed a shrug, throat suddenly

constricted. "Could've been worse." Keeping his eyes focused on the road. "The neighbors called the cops before Howie — her dipshit boyfriend — could finish her off. Even so, the damage was pretty extensive. Didn't know if she was going to pull through." He paused, tangled in the past for a moment, and forced himself to exhale. "She seems pretty happy most days. She's still my mom, just more childlike is all."

She nodded. Neither one of them felt the need to disturb the gentle silence that had filled the car.

A white-haired couple in their late seventies stepped into the crosswalk. Rhys slowed his vehicle to a stop. The woman was speaking, the man leaning toward her slightly to catch her words. Her thoughts, what she had to say, still important to him after all those years.

Rhys felt something click into place, as if this were a sign. He glanced at Eve. She was watching their slow progress across the road, a wistful smile on her face. "They remind me of my mom and dad," she said, tilting her chin in their direction. "In another twenty years or so."

"Could be us" — his words surprised even himself, and yet out they came — "in forty or fifty."

He heard her breath catch. "Don't play me," she said, her mouth more shaping the words than speaking them aloud.

"I'm not," he said. "I won't," he added. Like a vow. His gaze locked on hers. He could feel his pulse pounding slow and steady in his throat.

She watched him, eyes wary. She extended her hand, pinkie outstretched. "Pact?" Almost like a dare.

"Pact," he said, interlocking his finger with hers.

Someone honked behind them. Rhys took his foot off the brake, pulled forward with a mix of exhilaration, peace, and a sense of rightness thrumming through him. Her pinkie still clasped in his on the console between them.

Twenty-Five

He'd trailed his ladylove all the way from the café parking lot until the high-end glossy SUV she was riding in turned off Morningside Road onto a long driveway. He couldn't slam on the brakes. It would've drawn attention to him. Instead, he rounded the bend, pulled to the side of the road, threw open the car door, and sprinted back just in time to see the solid wooden gates closing securely behind them.

He started to move closer but noticed a security camera perched in a tree at the head of the drive.

Shit!

He needed to think fast. He bent over, hands on knees, pretending he'd been running for a while and needed to catch his breath, peeking under the shelter of his arm to get the lay of the land.

He spotted more security cameras on the gateposts and along the six-foot wall. *What the hell?* he thought, anger surging. *This is fucking Solace Island! Who the hell needs a security setup like that? She must be two-timing me with that asshole!* Rage filled his mouth with bile. *Not so fucking pure, is she? Little slut.*

He couldn't stay bent over forever, pretending to suck in air, so he straightened. Rolled his head, stretched out his calves, and started running again.

Now what? he thought as every footfall took him farther from his car, farther from her, his preordained destiny.

He was not wearing appropriate footwear. Could feel a blister forming on his left heel.

Another thing she was going to have to be punished for.

Twenty-Six

They'd decided to forgo a hot dinner. *It's a pleasure,* Eve thought as she perused the contents of the refrigerator, *to forage in my sister's fridge. It's so clean and shiny and bursting with tasty food.*

Her own fridge was usually quite barren, boasting a couple of Tupperware containers with ancient leftovers from dinner at Maggie's. A few withered carrots lurked in the produce drawer. On the shelves were several food products that had morphed into science projects.

"Ah, what do we have here?" she exclaimed, her mouth watering. She removed a couple of crisp Granny Smith apples, a local garlic and chive goat cheese, a wedge of four-year cheddar, and a triple-cream French Brie from the fridge. Next she sliced the apples, plopped them on the chopping board along with the cheese, a jar of wine jelly, and a baguette.

As she passed through the living room, Samson lifted his shaggy head from his dog bed, his nose twitching. She broke a small chunk of cheddar off the wedge and tossed it to him. Could hear his lips smacking as she exited through the doors and onto the deck.

She stepped past Rhys and placed the cheese board on the small table that was nestled between the two chaise longue chairs.

"Mm . . . Perfect," he said, looking at what she'd brought and then up at her, his smile warm and uncomplicated. His hair was still damp from the shower he'd had after taking Samson for a run.

Rhys swung his long legs off the lounge chair, setting his feet on the wooden deck so they straddled an uncorked bottle of red wine and two elegant crystal wineglasses. He picked up a glass and tipped it toward her. "Wine?"

"Absolutely," Eve said, feeling shy and hopeful all at once. Which was discombobulating, because she hadn't felt like this since the early Levi days. Like the world was freshly washed and full of possibilities.

She watched him pour, the wine splashing into the wineglasses, the ruby-red color growing deeper and darker as more wine was added.

"Cheers." He handed a glass to her, the slight brush of their fingertips causing electrical tingles to *zing* through her.

"Thanks." Awareness vibrated in the air around them. She took a sip. It was an excellent bottle of cabernet sauvignon. Balanced. Complex. She could taste undertones of dark, savory fruit. "So good." She waited for a second, enjoying the lingering rich finish, then took another sip. "Wow."

"Glad you like it," Rhys said. "It's one of my favorite wines. A little mom-and-pop vineyard I discovered when I was shooting a film in Napa. It's totally off the beaten track. No signage." He took a sip of wine, head tipped back.

She watched him swallow, wanting to trace a parallel path of the wine's journey.

And so she did.

She placed her wineglass on the side table and stepped in, her fingertips skimming the corded columns of his throat with the lightest of touches. The tanned skin beneath her fingers was warm. She could feel the slight prickle of stubble on the underside of his jaw, the upper portion of his neck. His gaze collided with hers, a multitude of emotions swirling — there was a hunger and wildness waiting to be released.

"Eve," he murmured, her name on his lips sounding almost like a prayer.

She continued her exploration downward, until the tips of two of her fingers rested gently in the hollow of his throat.

She took another step closer, only inches separating them now. She could feel the heat of his body calling her. To resist would be as futile as iron filings thinking they could escape the lure of a neodymium magnet. She couldn't help herself; she leaned forward and replaced her fingers with her mouth, her tongue continuing the caress her fingers had started.

His skin tasted of salt and wild midnight dancing under a full moon. He tasted of whiskey madness, sin, and sex, but innocence, too. He tasted like a man she wanted more desperately than she'd ever wanted anything in her life.

"Eve." Her name on his lips again. A groan. A plea. A benediction.

He was the one who closed the final distance. Must've put his wineglass down because she felt the controlled strength of his hand slide around her waist, arching her upward. His other hand was looping silky strands of her hair around his fist, tugging her head back. Forcing her gaze to meet his, the heat and intent in his eyes unmistakable.

"You're in trouble," he murmured with a hint of a smile. Then he bent his head and laid claim to her mouth.

She could taste the wine on his lips, his tongue rough and silky, causing liquid lightning to course through her, to the very ends of her extremities. Her knees gave way, buckling under the onslaught, but before the ground could rise to greet her, he'd scooped her up.

As he moved, with her cradled against his chest, a slant of warm, yellow light shining through the kitchen window fell across his face, illuminating it against the night sky. And the expression on his face, the tender beauty of him made her want to weep.

Another step and his face was in shadow again, but the prior image was seared into her brain. She pressed her face against his chest, could feel hard muscle beneath the soft fabric of his charcoal-gray T-shirt, the thump of his heart against her cheek, his chiseled, hard body. She inhaled deeply. He smelled wonderful, like the forest after a hard rain.

His muscles contracted as he shifted his weight, using his foot to release the back of the chaise, and she heard the *clunk* as the teak wooden frame fell to a flattened position.

Then the night sky tilted again and she was laid out on the cushioned surface like a feast. He stood above her, sexy as hell.

"Come here," she said, her voice a lower register than usual. Huskier. Full of need.

"Dammit." He groaned, squeezing his eyes shut, his hands fisting at his sides. "Woman, I want you more than I want anything on God's green earth. But if I join you there, I won't want to stop."

"Good," she said, sitting up. She reached out and latched her forefingers in the front belt loops of his faded jeans, tugging him toward her. She wrapped her arms around his narrow waist, hugging him tight, as if in this way she could fuse her body to his. It wasn't enough. More. She needed more. Skin against skin.

"You're so damned beautiful," she murmured. "It's not fair." Her fingers, like heat-seeking missiles, flicked open the metal buttons of his jeans, one by one, their progress torturously slow.

A groan escaped his lips.

She peeled back his jeans, and he watched as her hands disappeared beneath the elastic waistband of his briefs. He sucked in a breath, wrestling for control, not wanting to spend himself the second her long artist's fingers wrapped around his tool.

"Ahhh . . ." Her voice was barely more than a dandelion puff floating into the summer sky. He held his ass and his abdomen taut, everything clenched tight, trying not to embarrass himself as if he were a milk-on-the-cheeks virgin.

"Wait," he ground out. "I don't . . ." He grabbed her hands, stilled their sensuous progress.

"Don't want me?" she said, her gaze rising from his crotch to his eyes, a knowing siren's smile on her face.

"I don't . . ." Shit. Her little finger had escaped his grip. She was tracing small swirls on the upper curve of his balls. His balls that were sucked up tight against his rock-hard cock, her beautiful hands wrapped around the shaft, making coherent thought impossible. "Have a condom." His voice — like the rest of him — was strained.

She paused. "Damn."

"Do you?" he asked, hoping against hope.

"Nope." She shook her head and sighed, reluctantly releasing him, removing her hands from his briefs. "I gave my last batch to my sister. Haven't replaced them. No need." He could see the glisten of a smear of precome on the soft curve of flesh between her thumb and forefinger. Made himself drag his gaze away and look up into the night sky. "And what's your excuse?" he heard her say, her voice light, teasing. "Aren't you supposed to be a famous lothario? I would have expected you to be more prepared." He could feel her buttoning up his fly. No small task given how engorged he was.

"I, too, wasn't planning on any seduction. Was expecting to come to a deserted house for some quality alone time — what the hell are you doing?" She'd buttoned his fly and had just given his stiff cock a little pat. "It is not a fluffy white kitten you have tucked in for a nap," he said sternly.

She laughed. "You men and your penises," she said. "You take them so damn seriously."

"Well, yeah. You would, too —"

That just made her laugh more. "Yes, okay, you have a mighty staff. But put the ego aside for a minute. Let's look at it logically. The penis —"

"The *penis* —" He was playing it up now, because her belly laugh was the most beautiful thing he had ever heard. "Great — yes, *very* sexy. Please, ma'am, I'd very much like to place my pe*nis* inside your genitalia." She was laughing big-time now. "Good thing we don't have a box of condoms, *extra*-large, naturally, or you'd be in big trouble. I'd have you every which way to Sunday."

"With your" — she was having to wipe her eyes — "massively big pe*nis*?"

"Yup." He shoved his thumbs in his belt loops, settled back on his heels. "That's right, ma'am," he said, leaning on the Texas drawl he had worked so hard as an actor to erase. "We Texans pride ourselves on leaving our women with a smile."

"Typical man," she said, grinning at him. "You're already planning the exit route. Actually, we don't have to wait until your massive penis is clad. There are plenty of ways for us to —"

"So damned tempting, but I'm going to try to wait, so there will be no limits," Rhys said as he ambled across the deck, his body a symphony of confidence and controlled strength. She enjoyed watching him walk. Would actually be willing to pay good money for the privilege.

"I could jerk you off," she drawled, loving that her offer caused his step to hitch slightly, with a sharp intake of breath. "I'm *super* good at it."

"I'm sure you are." His voice came out a

husky growl.

"Then why are you over there instead of here?"

"You'll see." He was in profile now, and she could see that for all of his casual languor, he was still highly aroused. He inserted his smartphone into the sound-system port, made his selection, and suddenly she was surrounded by music. Aching notes that held within them both sorrow and joy. A piano. The composition so patient and tender, a gentle unfolding that filled the night air with glorious music.

And just like that, the mood changed. Swooping from sensuous laughter to heart-searing longing.

Rhys returned to her, his blue eyes turned almost black and filled with some indefinable emotion. Eve's breath caught in her chest at the beauty of the night, of him.

Ah . . . she thought, her eyes suddenly hot with tears. Romance. *How long has it been since someone took the time to romance me? Has anyone ever?*

It felt almost as if the music were emanating from him, spilling out of his pores, his soul. As if he *were* the music.

He extended his hands, palms-up. No words now. She placed her hands in his, and almost as if she were sleepwalking, she let him pull her to her feet and into his arms.

They danced, body against body, languid and slow, contained heat wrapping them together. One arm around his neck, fingers tangling in his hair, her other hand surrounded by his, nestled between their chests, in a way that made her feel protected. Cherished.

With the heat of his palm at the small of her back, her body thrummed, longing for him to explore her, to claim her more thoroughly.

They danced. Breathed each other in, at times barely moving, their bodies drifting through the slanted warm light that spilled from the kitchen window, then back into the quiet, cool embrace of the night's darkness again.

Twenty-Seven

"Ha!" he shouted, scooping up his vodka on the rocks as he pushed back from his desk, the glowing computer screen lighting the darkened bunker like a beacon of hope. The wheels on his chair whirred as they spun along the concrete floor.

"It's her brother-in-law's house," he sang, taking a deep slug of his drink and embracing the icy cold as the liquor burned its way down his throat. "Of course. I should have guessed. And they are away on holiday. She's house-sitting!" He tipped his head back, drained the glass of liquid, then crushed the remaining ice between his molars.

"The guy shadowing her is probably a relative, a brother or a cousin. Or maybe one of Luke's bodyguard security friends that he's stuck her with until Luke returns home with his wife. No sweat. Adds another challenge to this fascinating board game."

It felt good to know where she was, to have sorted out what was going on. He spun his chair in a happy twirl, then got up, went to the makeshift bar, and made himself another drink.

My fourth? He used the silver tongs to drop a second ice cube in his tumbler. *Or maybe it's my fifth alcoholic beverage of the evening?* He shrugged. The sort of nonchalant shrug a man about the town would do. *Who's counting?*

He laughed out loud.

No one. That was the beauty of this place. There was no old nag with sagging tits shuffling around, peering over his shoulder, wanting "conversation," or counting his drinks.

He was his own man here. King of his castle. Could do whatever the hell he liked.

TWENTY-EIGHT

Usually, for Eve, navigating the early-morning hours took a lot of self-negotiating before she could drag herself to consciousness.

Not today. When the alarm went off, she found herself instantly awake and filled with tingling awareness of her body and her surroundings. Also present was a slight sense of vertigo, as if she were blindfolded and perched on the edge of a precipice.

She showered, got dressed, then went into the living room and roused a sleepy Samson from his bed, took him out to do his business. The dog didn't even glance at the food and water she put down. Just staggered to his bed, circled twice, then flopped down with a noisy groan. *No worries,* she thought as she headed into the kitchen to make the coffee. *He'll nosh on his food later, when we're gone.*

She felt shy, meeting Rhys at the door.

They'd only danced. Danced and talked until the wee hours of the morning. And yet here she was, a couple of hours later, feeling more vulnerable and exposed than if she'd spent the whole night fucking his brains out.

Driving into town, the sky still dark, headlights on, the whole world in bed but them. "How much sleep did we actually clock?" Rhys asked. His hands solid and firm on the steering wheel, shirtsleeves rolled back exposing tanned skin, a light dusting of sunkissed hair. She wanted to lean forward and lightly skim her cheek over it, feel the feather softness caressing her skin.

"Two and a half hours," she said.

They both laughed, soft and warm, like a secret.

He took a long drink of his morning coffee, then ran the back of his knuckle across his lush lower lip. Suddenly it felt as if she were his knuckle, reveling in the texture and taste of his lip.

Last night, while they were dancing, she'd reached up and traced his lips with her finger, then pulled his head down and followed her finger's journey with the tip of her tongue, slipping inside the welcoming warmth of his mouth.

A single moment, a few seconds where

time and space slowed until her entire world narrowed down to the feel and slide, the suck and pull of their tongues' explorations.

Throughout the day, as they worked, shoulder to shoulder, keeping the Intrepid Café running relatively smoothly, she found herself bombarded with memories of the night before.

There was a lull in the front of the house, so she lingered in the doorway and watched him cook. Granted, his presentation skills weren't up to Maggie's standards, but the food wasn't burnt or undercooked, and it tasted pretty darn good.

She loved how he knew his way around the Intrepid kitchen as if he had been working there for months. Such a turn-on, how fast he'd picked everything up.

She ambled over and plucked the BLT croissant and an asparagus and leek frittata from under the heat lamp, where he had deposited them. *Imagine how well he could learn his way around your body if you gave him the chance.* And just like that, heat shimmered through her like a promise.

He looked up from the beets he was prepping for the next day's borscht — a recipe of his mom's he wanted to make — as if she'd tapped him on the shoulder or called his name. His gaze captured hers, a slow-growing smile curving the outer edges of his lips, like he knew exactly what she'd been thinking.

Waves of longing coursed through her as she added the green side salad to the frittata plate and arranged sliced fresh fruit beside the croissant. Then out the swinging doors she went, back to the hustle and bustle of the café, cheeks flaming, clothes chafing her overly sensitized body. *This is what happens when one has gone too long without sex,* she told herself, but it was a lie. She had never felt like this.

Never.

She tried to stay in the front of the house, dealing with customers, filling orders. It was the sensible thing to do. She couldn't walk around in a sensual stupor, emitting fuck-me pheromones like a dog in heat. But knowing that he was there, just beyond the swinging doors, called to her like a lodestone.

Within twenty minutes she was back there again, watching him gently sprinkle powdered sugar on the jam-dot cookies. The tenderness and care with which he was doing it made her need to turn away to hide her smile. The man was powerful enough to take down Larry and pin him to the floor — which was no small feat; Larry was six foot four and weighed two hundred and something pounds — and yet Rhys appeared equally comfortable wearing Maggie's pink heart-patterned apron, humming to himself while knuckle deep in powdered sugar.

She walked to the freezer, taking the roundabout route that required her body to squeeze past his.

"Hey, now," he drawled under his breath as he leaned back a little to prolong the brief contact. "No harassing the help."

"You wish," she said, an answering smile on her lips as she tugged the freezer door open, removed the vanilla ice cream, and brought it to the counter beside him. She reached up, brushing against him again under the guise of getting two dessert plates, even though there were plenty still in the lower cupboard. She felt his warm breath caress the slope of her neck as she reached past him for the ice cream scooper. There was so much electricity zinging between their bodies, Eve was surprised her hair wasn't swirling around her head like in a sci-fi movie.

He placed a hand on her hip as she plated the pie, leaned in with his pelvis. She could feel through their clothes that he was fully erect. Hot and hard. She laughed low in her throat and danced away from his grasp, out through the swinging doors.

Certain her cheeks were flaming, she ducked her head down as she placed the two plates of warm plum-apricot pie à la mode on the table.

"Thanks, Eve," Dusty said.

"Looks delicious," Dusty's sister, Sandy, chimed in. The two of them were so similar in appearance. Clouds of white fluffy hair, a multitude of soft wrinkles lining their faces, and delicate print dresses that were soft and faded from years of wear.

The two sisters would arrive like clockwork every Wednesday afternoon. They would order warm pie à la mode and a pot of Afternoon Blend tea with cream and sugar.

"I had a slice of this delicious pie for lunch," Eve said. "You won't be disappoint —" Eve froze. Someone had just slid their hand between her legs and fondled her privates.

She jerked upright, the movement dislodging the hand from her body.

Had the person done it because they could tell she was horny as hell? Was it visible to bystanders that she was walking around in a dazed state of arousal?

Riding the heels of self-doubt and shame

came anger. White-hot, incinerating fury.

Eve spun around, ready to read the riot act to whoever the asshole was, but no one was looking at her or acting in the slightest bit suspicious.

A young couple was heading to the cashier. A family was pushing past, snagging a couple of spare chairs to squeeze six people around the corner table that was meant to seat four. The mild-mannered balding husband didn't look like a sleaze, but sometimes appearances could be deceiving. Hank was in the middle of telling a raucous joke to the Wilson brothers and two members of their crew, men whose names she didn't know. Mr. La-de-da-black-coffee-please was on his computer, being the big man, placing stock orders, looking at graphs. Ethelwyn and Lavina were sharing a cheddar and chive scone and an oatmeal-raisin cookie while huddled over a worn copy of the *Paris Review.* No one else had been within reaching distance.

"Did you know" — Eve could hear Dusty speaking to her, but the woman's soft-spoken voice seemed far away, as if she were in another room — "that the police have confirmed the corpse they found was the body of a young woman? When we heard this, we got worried about you."

The kitchen doors were swinging slightly. However, if Larry had dashed in and touched her inappropriately, he would've had to sprint in order to disappear before she spun around. Wouldn't she have heard footsteps, even with the chatter of voices and the clang of dishes? Besides, Larry would never do something like that. And he definitely wouldn't dare behave like that when his mother was standing in line waiting to order baked goods.

Dusty patted her arm. "Promise us you'll be careful, dear. With a murderer of young women on the loose."

Eve nodded, a polite smile on her face. Dusty and Sandy weren't the first of her customers to express these sentiments. "I'll be careful. Thank you for your concern," she said absentmindedly as she rescanned the faces at the tables surrounding her, then the faces of the family by the corner table. No one was looking lecherous or smug.

Had she imagined it?

"Everything okay, honey?" Dorothy asked as she swung past with a fresh pot of coffee for refills.

"Did you see . . . ?"

"See what?" Dorothy asked, pausing midstep, looking at her with a concerned expression.

"Anything . . ." Eve wasn't sure what to say. "Odd or out of place?"

"No. You just had a funny look on your face," Dorothy said. Then she gasped and clutched her generously endowed braless bosom. "OMG! You're *preg*nant!"

"Jesus, Dorothy." Did the woman need to bellow her wacka-doodle theories across the frikkin' restaurant? "I'm not preg—"

"Are you feeling faint?"

"No, Dorothy," Eve said firmly. "I am *not* feeling faint. And since inquiring minds want to know" — conversation in the café had screeched to a halt, and the entire place was staring avidly at her — "I'm most definitely *not* pregnant."

"All it takes is one insertion and . . ." Dorothy said helpfully.

"Well, that'd be one more insertion than I've had" — she knew from the heat in her face that it had turned beet-red — "thank you very much," Eve replied, stopping Dorothy's baby-fantasy train in its tracks. "Nothing to see here, folks." Eve gave a jaunty wave. "Nobody's pregnant. Go back to whatever it was you were previously doing." She plastered a calm, professional smile on her face as she walked behind the counter to deal with the to-go bakery customers.

Twenty-Nine

Rhys sprinted out of the pharmacy and hopped into the SUV. "Sorry it took me so long. There was a bit of a line at the cash register."

There was no need to tell Eve that the cashier had recognized him. Eve was already skittish about him being an actor. The fact that people recognized him would not help his cause.

Rhys had tried to keep the interaction with the swooning woman brief and low-key, but the young lady was "a *huge* fan" and wouldn't stop squealing. This attracted the notice of several other customers. Selfies had to be taken, scraps of papers signed, plus a T-shirt, an arm. Finally, he'd fled before a mob could form.

It was a close call. As he pulled out of the shopping center parking lot, he could see several shrieking girls chasing after the SUV in his rearview mirror. They were taking pictures of his fleeing SUV with their phones.

Shit.

He'd have to switch out his vehicle.

It didn't used to be like this on Solace. The place was usually pretty mellow, and he could get by without too much of a fuss. Just an acknowledgment of, "Yes, I am Rhys Thomas. Glad you liked the movie," and he could move on.

When he was younger the fame thing had freaked him out, made him feel hunted. The lack of privacy, the intrusion had made him want to lash out. He'd devised ways of coping.

However, it had been foolish to think he could waltz into the pharmacy — no matter how rural Solace Island was — and expect no one to notice him. Hanging out with Eve, he'd let his guard down. He'd need to be more careful. He blew out a breath, letting the frustration go. To hold on to the negative feelings would be allowing the past to control his present.

"The good news is," Rhys said, presenting the bag from the pharmacy with a flourish. "We are now fully stocked and ready to roll."

"Great." Eve smiled at him, but the joyful enthusiasm of the past twenty-four hours was missing.

"You okay?"

"Yeah," she said, but she looked subdued. "Long day."

As he drove, the interior of the vehicle was quiet, the world outside the windows irrelevant, a blur of color and sound. His mind sorting through the various connotations.

"Just because I bought condoms," he finally said, his voice gentle, "doesn't mean we have to use them."

"It's not that. I'm looking forward to being intimate with you. It's just . . ." She drew in a large breath, then exhaled. "I was thinking about work."

"What about it?"

She shrugged. "Everyone's talking about the body that was found, a young woman, apparently. And I was thinking, does her family know? Does she even have family? Or was she a drifter, one of those homeless kids that are camping in the woods behind ArtSprings? Who was she? Was she scared right before she died? I hope she didn't suffer." Her gaze flew to his, and he was struck by the bleakness in her eyes. He placed one of his hands over hers, the other firmly on the wheel.

"I know what you mean. It is one of the blessings, but also the curses of possessing an artistic sensibility. We've trained ourselves to see and experience things deeply, more viscerally than the average person. We use these insights in our art, but sometimes one feels like an exposed nerve."

"You're right." Eve nodded. "This woman, she's more than a corpse, more than titillating gossip. She was somebody's daughter. Might be someone's wife or girlfriend, sister or mother. Are they worried and looking for her? And then I thought of my sister, Maggie. We had a scare with her last year. Everything's fine now, but I can't deny how easily it could have gone the other way. If she'd been killed, the trajectory of my life would've been altered forever, Mom's and Dad's, too.

"Such maudlin thoughts, huh?" Eve shook her head with a self-deprecating half laugh. "Guess I'm missing my sister something fierce. Which is weird, because Maggie's only been gone for five days. And goodness knows, when I lived in New York, sometimes six months would go by between visits, but I've gotten used to seeing her every day."

"You're lucky to have each other," he said. "Why don't you give her a call? Bet she'd like to hear from you."

"Nah. Don't want to disturb her vacation. She'll ask me what's new, and I don't want to lie. But if I were to tell her about the break-in at my apartment, she might cut her vacation short and hightail it home. Especially if someone from the island e-mails her and mentions the body being found." Eve bit her lip. "She's a bit of a worrier."

"I can see how that would be problematic. I imagine Luke's not much better. All his years in the Special Forces and the private security business . . ." There was no need for him to finish that sentence since they both knew Luke only too well. "You could talk about the weather, how the café is doing . . . You could tell her about us." He said it jokingly, but once the words were out of his mouth, he realized he did want that. Wanted to be important enough in Eve's life that she would tell her family about him.

He removed his hand from hers and took hold of the steering wheel with a two-handed grip, shaken by the realization.

"Yeah, right." She laughed dryly. "I'll wait until there is an *us* before I mention you to my sister. And on top of all the murder talk flying around the café, this afternoon some asshole touched me inappropriately while I was serving. Pissed me off, so I guess I'm feeling a little —"

"Wait a second. Back up a minute. Somebody did what?" He was aware of anger rising, possessiveness, too.

"Touched me inappropriately."

"Point the asshole out to me next time they come in."

"That's the problem. I don't know who it was. Couldn't start yelling arbitrarily. Would be bad for business. And no —" He felt her hand alight on his thigh. "I don't want you to start putting my customers in neck holds and slamming them to the floor, as you so aptly demonstrated with Larry, thank you very much." Clearly she'd read his mind. "However, I have to admit," she continued, "I hate that there's someone in our café who thinks it's okay to treat women like pieces of meat."

As Eve spoke she felt the tight knot in her stomach unwind. She was glad her sister had found her happily-ever-after in Luke. However, she hadn't realized how much she'd missed this sort of companionable talking over the day after the work was done. Having someone to share the preparing and eating of dinner, laughter, and conversation. The silence that fell once Maggie hopped in her car and drove home to Luke and Nathan was sometimes overwhelming. Of course they'd invite her for dinner, but she couldn't go every night. It wouldn't be appropriate.

"As much as it pisses me off," Rhys said, "I agree. Me slamming the customers to the floor" — a text message lit up the screen of his phone, which was resting in the drink holder — "until we discovered the guilty party wouldn't have been good for your bottom line." Another message appeared below the first.

"You got two texts. Want me to read 'em for you?" she asked.

"Nah."

Another text appeared, followed by another and another.

"Three more. Might be important."

"Doubt it," he grumbled. "Should have turned the damned thing to airplane mode." But he handed her his cell.

She tapped messages and scrolled up. " 'Pick up the goddamned phone!' '*Busted* made another offer.' 'Too good to refuse. Call me!' 'Fifteen-point-eight mil, sixteen percent of the gross.' " Eve cleared her throat. Her voice at the tail end of that last message had emerged as a squeak. " 'They've hired Andy Mitchell to do the rewrite. You love him.' " That was better. She sounded cool and nonchalant. She had been able to keep her voice steady, as if millions and millions of dollars were no big deal. As if she weren't spending sleepless nights worrying about how she was ever going to get out from under her three-hundred-and-eighteen-thousand-dollar mortgage. Not to mention the fifty-eight-thousand-dollar line of credit for the renovations that had transformed the ground floor of their building into the Intrepid Café. " 'Offer expires ten tonight,' " she continued. " 'Stepping into a screening. Will leave my phone on vibrate.' "

Rhys huffed out a frustrated breath.

Eve studied his face. "You don't want to do it?" It was hard for her to believe that Rhys might consider turning down such a mammoth amount of money; it was even crazier that someone had offered it. *Shit.* The realization hit like a cast-iron frying pan over the head. *He must be a* real *big deal in Hollywood.*

"Didn't," he answered, his fingers absent-mindedly drumming on the steering wheel. "Andy changes the equation somewhat. He's a brilliant writer."

He must spend his days surrounded by brilliant people, beautiful women. She swallowed hard, her chest suddenly constricted. "Does it take long to shoot a movie?"

"Three months — give or take — on location." He shrugged. "Prep, of course, but you don't get paid for that. A couple of days in post. Probably four months of my time, all in."

"Rhys, that kind of money, it's nuts. You know that, right?"

He laughed, his head thrown back, eyes crinkling at the corners. He was beautiful in repose, but laughing, the man's appeal was beyond intoxicating. "Yeah, I'm a lucky son of a bitch, that's for sure."

She placed his phone back in the drink holder, moving cautiously, as if it were a poisonous snake that might strike.

"I'm going to have to work tonight," he said. "I hope you don't mind. I know it's not what we'd planned, but —"

"I totally understand."

He captured her hand in his and placed a gentle kiss on her palm, then curled her fingers closed, as if to keep the kiss safe. "Thanks," he said, glancing over briefly, the expression in his deep blue eyes warm. Then he refocused on the road. She could see the wheels turning as he sifted through his thoughts. "I'll need to call Andy, see how he thinks *Busted* can be fixed. Then I'll need to reread the script while keeping his ideas in mind."

Even though he was including her, Eve felt a little lost, as though she'd just been plunked in the middle of the Pacific Ocean without a lifeboat. His real life was so foreign, so far removed from the cozy existence they'd started to carve out on Solace Island. *We're playing house, make-believe,* she realized, a wave of wistfulness sweeping over her. *You'll have to make up your mind, Eve, a short-term affair or nothing.*

"I'll enjoy an evening to myself," she said, but the pleasant expression on her face felt like a mask. "I can do some painting." She glanced at the clock on the dashboard and sighed. In the time it would take her to set up, dusk would have fallen. No painting was going to be taking place tonight.

"Great," he replied, oblivious to the internal war she was waging. He swung the SUV into their driveway. "You're the best. Should be a couple hours max." He suddenly slowed the vehicle. "Who the hell is that?"

Thirty

Rhys scowled through the windshield. There was a long, lean male resting with his back against the trunk of an ancient red cedar tree by the gate. He was wearing faded jeans, scuffed boots, and a black T-shirt that hugged his cut, hard body. He was strumming on some small instrument. As the vehicle drew closer, it became clear it was a ukulele. Who the hell played a ukulele? Even worse, this guy looked totally cool doing it.

As they drew closer still, Rhys heard Eve's sharp intake of breath. He glanced at her, but she didn't notice. She was staring at the guy as if she were seeing a ghost.

The dude straightened as they pulled up next to him in front of the gates, the ukulele dangling loosely in one hand, the other pushing the tangle of dark curls out of his face.

Rhys opened his window. He had a bad feeling about this. "Can I help you?" he asked, voice cool, expression unwelcoming.

"Hey, yeah, I'm looking for . . ." His gaze drifted over Rhys's shoulder. "Eve, that you?"

Shit.

Rhys had to shut his eyes for a second to block out the fucking joy in this guy's smile.

"Levi?" Her voice drifted past Rhys, barely audible yet full of feeling.

Better to have my eyes wide open, Rhys thought grimly. It didn't take a genius to figure out this asshole was the ex-boyfriend. The musician who'd left Eve damaged and reluctant to trust.

"Babe, I've been looking for you," the Levi guy said as he loped around the front of the SUV to where she was sitting. "Can I?" He tipped his head toward the back.

"Sure," Eve said, reaching behind her, fumbling with the lock. "You don't mind, do you, Rhys?"

It wouldn't matter if he did. The guy had already hopped in the vehicle and made himself at home, hands on Eve's shoulders, dropping a kiss on her cheek.

Eve glanced over at him, looked slightly startled. *Damn. I must have growled out loud.* Rhys did an internal shrug and punched in the security code for the gate. *Better a growl than to leap into the back seat and rip the guy's head from his torso.*

The guy draped his arms over the back of their seats and leaned forward so his body was positioned between them. "Thanks for the ride, man. Hey, do I know you?"

Oh crap. Here we go again. Rhys huffed out an internal sigh. "No," he replied. "Never met you."

"Come on, man. I'm sure I know you. Where'd you go to school?"

"Silsbee."

"Shit, man. Gigging, I've crisscrossed this country a million times and never come across Silsbee. Where the hell is that?"

"Texas. Outside of Beaumont." Rhys pulled the SUV to a stop in front of the house.

"So we didn't go to school together." Levi snapped his fingers as if that would activate the memory in his brain. "Don't worry. We know each other." He thumped his fist against his chest. "Just gotta figure out how."

Rhys unlocked the front door and disengaged the interior alarm. Eve stepped past him and gave Samson the *friend* signal. Samson's body relaxed. His tail swished. He poked his wet nose into her hand in greeting. She gave him the requisite scratch around his ears. Then the wolfhound headed out the door. "The dog won't bother you," she told Levi, who had a cautious look on his face, arms crossed around the ukulele and his hands tucked safely in his armpits.

"Gotta protect these babies," he said, wiggling the fingers of his free hand once Samson was safely past. "That dog is a monster. Who knew they grew dogs that big?"

"Samson's a sweetheart once you get to know him."

Samson peed, started to stretch languorously, when he caught the scent of something and took off at a dead gallop, disappearing into the woods.

"Holy shit!" Levi exclaimed. "That hairy beast can move. Glad that's not me he's chasing. You think it's okay to let him run free like that?"

Eve shrugged. "Luke says it's fine. Samson knows his way around. He'll come home when he's run off some steam. Come on in." She was acting calm, as if Levi descending on her doorstep was an everyday occurrence, but her mind was spinning. *Why is he here? How did he find me?* "Would you like a drink — beer, cider, red wine?"

"I'll have mineral water with lemon if you have some," he replied.

Eve glanced at him, surprised.

"Yeah," he said, a sheepish grin on his

face. "Stopped boozing, doing drugs. I'm clean. Totally clean."

A wave of happiness swept over her. "Levi, that's wonderful. Wow." She crossed the living room and entered the kitchen, Levi following in her wake. "I'm so proud of you."

"Well," he said with a shrug, laying his ukulele on the kitchen table. "Taking it day by day. We'll see. It was hard as hell when I first gave it up. Bit easier now, but the wanting remains. Always present. The whisper in the ear."

"Still." She opened the fridge and removed a bottle of mineral water and a lemon, her mind flashing to all the times she'd found him wasted, the fights they'd had. "It's a huge deal." She took a couple of glasses from the cupboard, placed them on the counter, and started to pour.

Levi glanced around the kitchen and let out a low whistle. "This is some digs you've set yourself up in."

Eve suddenly felt protective. Levi was clean, but what if he slipped up and needed cash for a fix, and who knew what the rest of the band was doing? "This place belongs to Maggie and her husband, Luke. Great guy. Ex-Special Forces. Can handle anything you throw at him and is a total whiz with the security. The property is more secure than Fort Knox." She felt the moment Rhys entered the kitchen. Didn't need to look up. "Rhys, you want some mineral water?"

"No," he replied curtly.

What had crawled up his ass and died?

"Fine." She topped up Levi's glass, sliced a wedge of lemon, and stuck it on the rim. "Here you go," she said, handing the water to Levi.

Rhys stalked past, his body brushing against hers. It felt purposeful, as if he were staking a claim. Which was pretty damn ballsy of him, seeing as how he was planning to sally back to his fancy Hollywood life without a backward glance.

"How long you been clean?" Eve asked Levi politely. She was determined to keep a pleasant, breezy look firmly attached to her face no matter which primitive caveman behavior Rhys had decided to emulate.

"One year, four and a half months, not that I'm counting. I think me cleaning up my act is what put the final nail in the coffin in my last relationship. The reverse of what broke the two of us up." Levi laughed. "Guess I swung from one extreme to the other. Tiffany was *not* pleased. She was the quintessential party girl. If she could smoke it, ingest it, or inject it, she was a happy camper. Did you hear my song 'Candy Flippin' '?"

"Uh . . . no. I . . . uh . . ." Did he really think that after they broke up, she had nothing better to do than to sit around waiting with bated breath for his next album?

"No worries. I can e-mail you a download if you like. I wrote that song about her. She'd been on a five-day bender. Almost OD'd." He laughed. "Grist for the mill, man. Grist for the mill. She was pissed off when she heard it. Didn't mind spending the money the song brought in though," he said, tossing Rhys a jaunty you-know-how-women-are wink.

Rhys just looked at him stone-faced.

"Yeah, I've been doing real well. 'Candy Flippin' ' charted in the top one hundred for a week and a half."

Typical Levi, Eve thought wryly. All bravado and narcissism. "So, what made you come to Solace Island? It's not really your cup of tea."

Rhys yanked the fridge open, got a beer, snapped the tab, and took a long swig.

"Ahem . . ." She coughed, giving him a swift glare, but Rhys pretended not to notice, took another slug of the beer.

"I came to this rinky-dink island to see you," Levi said, extending his arm like he was an actor in a Shakespearean play. Then he picked up his ukulele and started strumming it, improvising a song. " 'Drove a hundred miles,' " Levi sang. " 'Maybe a hundred more. Weathered two ferry rides through the wind and the snow . . .' "

"There's no snow," Rhys interjected. Clearly he didn't know Levi the way Eve did. A sarcastic comment or two would have no effect once Levi was in performance mode.

" 'Ahhhh . . . drove to the caaaafé you and Maggie own.' " His hips were swiveling now, and he was going to town big-time on that little ukulele. " 'Buuuut was lo-ahhhhcked up tight. Nobody waaaahz home. Ah called your liddle sistah. Woke her up from a nap.' " He winked. " 'I explained my dilemma, and that was that!' " Levi finished his song with a grand flurry of strums. All the while stomping his boot against the floor, which created a makeshift drum.

"That answer your question?" Levi asked, giving her that wicked smile of his, the one that had never failed to make her weak at the knees.

Interesting, Eve observed. *My knees feel perfectly sturdy.*

"People pay you for that?" Rhys scoffed.

Uh-oh. Must've figured out Levi's the musician I used to date.

"Cute song, Levi," Eve said, keeping a cautious eye on Rhys. "Thank you." She turned her head so Levi couldn't see her face. "Be nice," she whispered to Rhys through gritted teeth.

"Why?" he said, not bothering to temper his volume.

"He's had a hard time."

"I'm standing right here, folks," Levi interjected. "I'm not deaf."

Rhys ignored him, kept his eyes locked on hers. "And you haven't?" he asked.

Eve shifted uneasily. That was the thing about Rhys. When he looked at her, he really looked, as if he had X-ray vision and could see well beneath the skin.

"Uh-huh." Rhys smiled. "Just as I suspected." He crushed his empty beer can in his hand, then tossed it in the recycling bin under the sink. "Anyone want nachos? I'm thinking of making some."

"Don't you have some work to do?" she asked Rhys pointedly.

"It can wait," he said, suddenly cheerful as he took a metal baking sheet from the cupboard and set it on the marble counter.

"You like the ukulele, babe?" Levi said.

Babe. That had been his pet name for her.

"Picked it up at a garage sale as we drove through Medford. Fifteen dollars, including the case. I'd forgotten I had it. This old thing was banging around on the tour bus for a couple of weeks."

Or did he call all of his women that? An easy way to make sure he didn't accidentally call out the wrong name in the throes of passion.

"Then, last Friday TJ was rummaging in the overhead storage . . ." Levi was still rambling on. "And there it was. I was bored, picked it up, never held a ukulele in my life, but started playing around and —"

"Hey, dude," Rhys interrupted. "Look, I know the ukulele is supposed to be having a resurgence and all, but" — Rhys strode to the pantry, removed a large bag of tortilla chips, ripped it open with his teeth, and dumped the chips on the baking sheet — "personally?" He smiled the way a shark does before it devours its prey. "I'm not a fan." He removed a grater from the lower cupboard, straightened, opened the fridge, and got out some cheddar cheese, salsa, and a jar of jalapeños. "But hey, I guess if you're one of those unfortunate men who got stuck with a small instrument," he said with a sympathetic whatcha-gonna-do shrug, "it's probably best for everyone involved if you learn how to use it."

Thirty-One

"Hey." Andy leaned toward the camera and waved his hand. "Something wrong, man? Did I freeze?"

"No," Rhys said, pulling his attention away from the feminine laughter he could hear drifting from the kitchen and back to the screen. "Sorry. I spaced out for a moment. You were saying?"

"Basically, the premise is good, but the script is shit. We throw it out and start over. In the right hands . . ." Andy cleared his throat modestly.

"Yours —"

"That is correct." He grinned. "With me writing, you acting . . ."

Rhys heard footsteps, then a light knock at the door.

"And if you're able to get the right director attached, we could create something quite spectacular."

Rhys held up his hand. "Someone's at the

door. Hold on a sec." He removed his earbuds, pushed back from the computer, crossed the room, and opened the door.

"Hi. We're going to —" Eve glanced into the room, saw Andy on the computer screen, and flushed. "Sorry," she whispered as she pulled on her faded jean jacket. The whimsical brooches attached caught a slanting ray of sunshine. Every breath she took, every slight movement caused tiny rainbow flecks to dance around the room. "I didn't know you were talking to someone." A lentil-sized rainbow was quivering on his forearm, as if entangled in his sun-lightened hair. "We're going to grab a bite to eat. Want to come?"

She shifted her weight so that the brooches no longer caught the light. The rainbows were gone, and he was aware of a faint sense of loss. "Nah," he said. "I had the nachos." The incident at the pharmacy proved that even in places like Solace Island, he couldn't roam free. It would create havoc. Eve would look at him differently. "If I get hungry later, I'll forage in the fridge."

"Okay. Samson's back. I've fed him and given him fresh water. I should be home by nine at the latest, but if for some reason I'm not, could you let him out to pee?"

"Sure," he said.

She looked up at him with her inquisitive eyes, her head tilted to the side. "Are you all right? Your voice sounds funny."

What could he say? *I don't want you to go out with your old boyfriend?* He wasn't the boss of her. "I'm fine. Totally fine. See you later. Have fun."

"All right, then. Hope you get everything sorted out with your work." She waved her fingers at him and disappeared down the hall.

He couldn't see Levi, but he could feel his presence in the house. "Nah. Don't feel much like pub food," he heard Levi say in his smoke-and-whiskey rasp. "Get too much of that on the road. The guy I hitched a ride with mentioned a great French bistro on the island."

A French bistro? They were going to a French bistro? That was just great. Romantic music, candlelight —

Rhys heard Eve murmur something in response, her voice too low for him to make out the words. He could hear the front door open and then swing shut. And with the *thunk* of the door closing, more doubts arrived. Maybe he'd read Eve wrong and she still was into this guy. He was making a big mistake leaving her alone with him —

Frustrated, Rhys slammed his palm

against the doorframe. "Fans be damned," he muttered. "This is an emergency." He'd better move and move fast!

Rhys ran to the computer. Didn't bother sitting. He crouched down, jammed the earbuds in his ear. "Look, Andy, sorry. Something's come up. Gotta run. Will discuss these story ideas later." He hung up, ripped out the earbuds, grabbed his wallet, and sprinted out of the room, down the hall, and out the front door.

"Hey!" he yelled, even though it was clear his efforts were futile. The driveway gates were almost closed. He ran down the steps, waving his arms. "Wait for me." But it was too late. He saw a flash of blue as Eve's car turned out of the long driveway and disappeared down the road. The gates slammed shut, and all that was left was the sound of the wind rustling through the trees.

Thirty-Two

Eve flipped the white napkin in the breadbasket open and took another slice of bread. The baguette didn't have the proper crisp and chew that a good French baguette should, she thought as she slathered it with salted butter. Either they didn't buy their bread from Luke, or they'd run out while he was on vacation and were making do with store-bought.

"How's your soup?" Levi asked, his knife slicing through his steak au poivre. Eve loved a good steak drenched in peppercorn sauce, and that side of crispy potatoes and onions cooked in duck fat looked delectable. However, given her present financial circumstances, splurging on steak au poivre was out of her price range. Alternatively, there was no way she was going to let Levi pay for her meal. Didn't want to send the wrong message. "Want a taste?" he asked, holding a forkful of food toward her. She could smell the rich cream, cognac, and shallots.

Her mouth was watering, but eating from his fork was too intimate. It would feel almost as if she were cheating on Rhys. "No thanks," she said. She picked up her spoon, forcing her eyes away from the tempting mouthful of food. "I'm very happy with what I ordered." The cheapest item on the menu at $5.99. "French onion soup, mmm, so good." She dipped her spoon back into her bowl. The logistics of this particular soup required some maneuvering. The trick was to get the melted cheese and savory broth onto her spoon without leaving some dangling cheese strand to *thwack* her in the chin. Also, she needed to time it. She didn't want to empty her bowl too fast and be left drooling over his food.

"Are you still painting?" he asked, spearing another chunk of juicy steak onto his fork and popping it into his mouth.

"Of course," she said, feeling defensive. "Painting is my passion."

Levi had never taken her painting seriously. He'd wanted her to drop out of Yale and go on the road with him, which had been a huge bone of contention between them.

"Come on, babe. We'd have a blast," he'd

said, pacing around their tiny apartment. "You know you want to."

"No. I don't."

"Why not?" he'd demanded, turning to glower at her.

"I can't just drop out of college, Levi. My parents and I worked so hard to pay for this."

"My point exactly! You'd be doing your parents a favor. Attending Yale to be an *artist* is a waste of time and money. The tuition fees are exorbitant, and in your line of work" — he'd laughed mockingly — "even if you sold a few paintings, you'd never earn back the money you'd spent on tuition, and forget about making enough money to sustain yourself."

"And you make so much money as a musician? Huh? You guys are playing for tips, barely covering your gas money."

"For now," he'd said with absolute conviction. "It's early days, babe! You gotta look at this in a practical manner. There's way more musicians running around with bling on their fingers and driving Rolls-Royces than artists. I could easily name a hundred musicians who are living the big life. Can you name even twenty current artists doing the same thing? Okay. Name ten. Five? You can't, can you? See! I'm our big shot at fame, babe. Come on the road with me, and we'll build our dream together."

"Levi, I just need to clarify. Are you asking me to marry you, to share your life for better or worse? Is that what this is? Your idea of a proposal?"

Levi recoiled. "Hell no, baby. You know I don't go for that white-bread establishment bullshit! I'm asking you to come on the road with me. Take it or leave it."

She left it. Left him.

"Are you having showings?" Eve heard Levi ask, bringing her back to the restaurant and the present. "Sold any?" He was sorting out his next bite, his attention on his plate, which was lucky because he didn't see her flinch.

Eve tilted her chin up, as if bracing for a blow. "It takes time to build a customer base," she said. She removed another slice of mediocre bread. "I paint for me."

"Whoa. Okay." Levi held up his hands. "No need to take my head off, babe. Just asking a simple question."

Eve blew out a breath. She'd buttered the hell out of her slice of bread. "I haven't sold any yet," she said. "But I have paid off my student loans, if that's what you're getting at."

He reached over and captured her hand.

Weird, she thought, feeling slightly removed from her body. *It used to be the feeling of his calloused fingers on my skin would cause tingles to course through me.* "I wasn't getting at anything," he said, looking at her now with an uncharacteristically earnest expression on his face. "I didn't mean to hurt your feelings."

It seemed really important to him to be able to tell her whatever it was he wanted to say. *Probably part of his recovery treatment,* Eve thought. *Make amends. Apologize to those you have hurt.* So, although his hand on hers made her feel a mixture of squeamishness, sadness, and a touch of regret, Eve left her hand where it was.

His grip was scrunching her hand, causing the overly buttered and now squished slice of bread to extend from her fingers like a bulbous question mark.

"I'm trying," he continued, "to show you I've changed, to show an interest in your work, so you'll know that I regret what a self-involved fool I was."

His other hand landed on the hand pile. It reminded Eve of that game she and Maggie used to play on road trips. *He sure would be surprised if I slipped my hand out from the bottom fast and slapped it on top of his.* She kept her smile secret because for some reason Levi was acting super serious.

"I've missed you so much, Eve. You have no idea. You complete me." He stood up abruptly. "I was going to wait until dessert to do this, but what the hell, since we're on the subject." He pried the slice of bread from her suddenly numb fingers and dropped it on his plate, her hand still firmly clasped in his.

"What subject?" she said nervously, a feeling of foreboding washing over her, but it was too late. He'd already rounded the table and dropped to his knees.

"Eve, you are my heart, my life, my reason for living."

He was talking so loud. Everyone in the restaurant was staring. In her peripheral vision Eve noticed the waiter rushing toward their table. He was carrying a sweating silver ice bucket with a bottle of champagne chilling inside. Two champagne flutes dangled from his fingers.

Suddenly the penny dropped, along with her stomach. *Oh shit.*

"But never let it be said," Levi brayed, "that I don't learn from my mistakes. I love you, Eve. I've always loved you. My life without you is nothing."

"Oh my goodness," she heard a woman behind her say. "So romantic . . ."

"Levi," Eve whispered through clenched teeth as she tried to tug her hand free. "Please, you have to get up."

"No way, my love," he announced, releasing one of his hands to thump it on his heart. "I am not getting up. You deserve me on my knees, after all these years of trials and tribulations! Nothing but the best for you. Speaking of . . ."

Out came a velvet ring box, which he flipped open with his thumb. A small solitaire diamond set in a black rhodium ring blinked up at her accusingly.

"Evelyn Ashley Harris," Levi said with an expectant smile on his face. "Will you marry me and make me the happiest man alive?"

THIRTY-THREE

Rhys tried to focus on the script. He'd printed the notes Andy had e-mailed earlier to cross-reference. Usually this type of work was a breeze. He was lucky that way. Could drop into business mode at the drop of a hat.

Many actors had difficulty with the business side of their work. They were amazingly talented actors but couldn't handle money to save their lives. Saying yes to the wrong movies could trash a career. Handing their finances over to a hotshot business manager or lawyer only to discover years later that the bulk of their wealth had been stolen. Those unfortunate actors usually ended up trapped in drawn-out court cases. Eventually, they would declare bankruptcy in their twilight years. It was heartbreaking.

Rhys did what he could to help, but it was never enough. Most actors were like children, too trusting and easily distracted by short-term gratification and acquiring the trappings of success.

Tonight, however, it was impossible to focus. He was on his second read-through of the script and still wasn't seeing how the fixes Andy wanted to implement would help.

Was it because he couldn't stop his mind from veering off track to obsess about Eve, wondering where she was and what she was doing?

He glanced at the time. It was 7:12 p.m.

Rhys sighed. Even if Eve and Levi ate fast and had nothing to say to each other, it was doubtful they would be home before eight. And from the peek he'd had of Levi, Rhys was pretty damned sure the guy had lots to say.

He forced himself to read through Andy's notes again.

No. It wasn't the Eve distraction. Something was not adding up.

He opened FaceTime and called Andy. It rang a couple of times, and then Andy's beaming face appeared on the screen. "Rhys, my man, wassup?" Rhys could hear the TV in the background, some cop drama from the sounds of it.

"Andy," Rhys said. "I've been reading this thing over, and it doesn't make sense."

"I know it's a bit of a stretch, but I think

if we —"

Suddenly he knew what had happened, could see it spiraling out before him as if someone had laid down a map. "Andy," Rhys interrupted. "The script is garbage, and it's not fixable because the premise stinks."

"That's a little harsh," Andy interjected.

"What I think happened," Rhys said, steamrolling over him, "is they offered you a shitload of money to put rouge on the corpse. They knew having you on board would be an incentive for me."

Andy blinked in visible surprise behind his trendy glasses. His lips formed an O shape, which made him look as if he hadn't realized someone had removed a Popsicle from between his lips.

"Look, Andy, I don't blame you if that's the case. They've offered to back up the dump truck full of cash to my house as well. That kind of payday is tempting."

Andy exhaled. Rubbed his face. "Yeah. You're not kidding," he said, looking depressed. "You've pretty much summed up the entire situation. The financing for the project I was working on fell through. Didn't get green-lighted in the final hour. I got bills to pay. Need the money."

"I understand. The movie business has

changed. Times are tough."

"Jesus, you're not kidding. And the wife spends money hand over fist. The kid wants to go to Harvey Mudd next fall. A great college, but do you know how fucking expensive it is? Sixty-nine thousand seven hundred and seventeen dollars for tuition, plus room and board! That doesn't include 'spending' money, books, or clothes. And we're talking after-tax money, so let's just add another 39.6 percent to that whopping sum and I've put her through *one* measly year of college . . . for a *liberal arts* degree! What kind of work will she ever get with a liberal arts degree? And why go to Harvey Mudd if that's what you're after? It's because her *boyfriend* wants to go there for the mathematics program. Kill me now. I swear, Rhys, never have kids. It's too damned expensive."

Rhys hated being in this position, but he'd learned over the years that the kindest thing to do was to rip the Band-Aid off fast. "I'm sorry, Andy. I can't do this film. Not even for you. It would be career suicide."

Andy's shoulders slumped even further. "Shit." He sighed wearily. "I had a feeling you were going to say that."

After Rhys hung up, he sent a text to his agent telling him to pass on the project.

Then he switched off the sound on his phone, so he wouldn't have to hear the bombardment of eleventh-hour texts and phone calls that were sure to pile in until the deadline had passed.

The smart panel on the wall chimed, causing a tiny jolt of happy adrenaline to course through him. *The front gate. Eve must have misplaced the code.* He pressed the button activating the camera.

Damn. Some middle-aged balding dude in a truck.

"Yes," he said into the speaker. "Can I help you?"

"I'm here from Prestige, to switch out the rental for Mr. Thomas."

That was fast. "I'll open the gate."

He activated the gate, told Samson to stay, and headed outside.

"You sure this is what you want?" the guy from Prestige asked, looking at the nondescript low-value truck. "I got all sorts of luxury brands on the lot — Range Rover, Ferrari, Tesla, Audi?"

"This is perfect for my needs," Rhys said, signing the new lease agreement. Now that word was out that he was on the island, people would be looking for a flashy, expensive car. Hopefully, implementing the hiding-in-plain-sight strategy would buy him a few more days of privacy.

Rhys fished the keys for the SUV from his pocket, laid them on the clipboard, and passed it back.

The guy shook his head. “Hard to believe you are trading this excellent piece of machinery for that piece of junk. Guess what they say about you Hollywood types is correct. You are all crrrrayzy.” He laughed — the guy had a lot of fillings in his teeth — then opened the SUV door and tossed the clipboard on the passenger seat.

“Mind if I get a selfie with you before I head out?” He didn’t wait for an answer. Wrapped a large sweaty arm around Rhys’s shoulders as if they were best buds. “Say ‘cheese,’ ” he ordered, holding up his phone and taking a couple of shots. “Thanks, man. My wife is going to *flip* out.”

“If you could keep this location and the type of vehicle you dropped off to yourself, it would be greatly appreciated,” Rhys said, shaking the guy’s hand with a hundred-dollar bill folded neatly in his palm. The transfer went off seamlessly. The guy didn’t look, just slipped the money in his pocket faster than bacon disappearing down Samson’s throat.

“Absolutely, Mr. Thomas,” he said, laying

a thick finger against his lips. “You can count on me.”

Thirty-Four

He almost lost them.

It had been a welcome surprise when his ladylove magically appeared in the restaurant where he was eating. Even more unexpected was when the imbecile she was dining with dropped to his knees and pulled out a ring.

Eve, however, was a woman of high standards. Refused the guy. Clearly saving herself for something better.

It was a little startling when they left the restaurant in the middle of their meal.

Made things a touch awkward for him. He had to make his excuses to his dinner companions. Dropped a handful of cash to cover his portion of the bill, then wound his way through the tables, dodging the waitstaff carrying plates of food.

The tricky part had been palming her soup spoon. He'd accomplished it with the simple matter of letting his fingers settle over the spoon in the guise of resting his hand on the table. Meanwhile, making good use of the old distraction technique, he'd thrust his unoccupied arm outward, retracting the sleeve of his shirt and exposing his watch. "Ah!" he said loudly. "So that's the time." While the other hand slyly slipped the coveted spoon into the pocket of his jacket. Then, smooth as silk, he continued his journey out the door of the faux French restaurant.

The little side excursion to collect her spoon had almost lost him the trail of his quarry. He caught the briefest glimpse of the glowing taillights of her first-generation blue Prius before it disappeared around the bend.

He took the porch steps two at a time, leapt into his vehicle. Gravel spitting from under his tires caused him to skid slightly as he tore out of the parking lot.

At first he was trying to catch up, but once he had her car firmly within his sights, impotent fury started rising like bile in his throat. *Where is she going? She's not returning to her brother-in-law's house. She's headed in the wrong direction.*

When her beat-up Prius pulled into the Harbor Motel, he couldn't pull in after her. He had to cruise on by, looking straight ahead, nothing to see here, until he was able to park a block and a half away.

He doubled back, crouching down low and keeping to the shadows.

By the time he arrived at the motel parking lot, her car was gone and the idiot with the ukulele was exiting the lobby, a key dangling from his hand.

Ah, so that's their game. He'd danced this dance himself a million times before. The guy checks in, gets the key, and unlocks the room, while the woman parks elsewhere. This way her car isn't recognized in a sleazy motel parking lot. Then she gets the text on her smartphone, ambles by the motel, and if no one's around, she makes a sharp right turn into the room.

Perfect. He rubbed his hands together in anticipation. *That's when I'll grab her.*

THIRTY-FIVE

The sound of Samson's bark yanked Rhys back to consciousness. *I must have fallen asleep,* he thought as he stretched and enjoyed an enormous yawn. Samson's tail thumped against the coffee table leg on his way across the living room to wait by the front door.

A second later Rhys heard Eve's car pull into the drive, the crunch of gravel under her tires.

That's right. The events of the past few hours came roaring to the forefront. *She went out with her ex. A hot-looking wannabe rock star who is clearly still in love with her.* Rhys glanced at the clock on the mantel of the huge stone fireplace. It was 8:23 p.m. *She didn't stay out late.* Cautious hope began to bloom. He hadn't realized how stressed he'd been that they might have chosen not to return. He stayed on the sofa, envying Samson's absolute certainty that if he greeted Eve at the door, she'd be pleased to see him.

She entered quietly, a silhouette in the darkened room. She bent over and nuzzled her face in Samson's wiry gray fur. "Hey, old boy. How are you?" She seemed tired. Subdued.

"You have a good time?" Rhys asked.

She jumped slightly, startled. "What are you doing sitting in the dark?"

"Seemed like too much bother to switch the lights on. Once my eyes adjusted, I wondered why we do it. Was so pretty without. The moon and starlight shimmering off the bay, pouring through the windows, the sound of the water lapping. Peaceful. I dozed a little."

"We didn't get a lot of sleep last night," she said, dropping her purse on the floor and joining him on the sofa. She kicked off her shoes and tucked her feet beneath her, nestling next to him. He could feel the cool night air still clinging to her clothes. She tapped his glass. "What are you drinking?"

"Whiskey. It's very smooth. Want some?"

"Sure," she said, removing the crystal tumbler from his hand, electric sparks zinging through him from the brief contact of her cool fingers sliding past his in the hand-off. She took a sip. Her eyelids drifted shut as she savored the smoky liquid fire going down. She took another sip. "Mm . . ." she murmured, her voice husky. "Tastes good." The pink tip of her tongue snuck out and gathered the lingering traces of whiskey shimmering on her luscious, bee-stung lips. And just like that, his cock was rock-hard and aching.

"Where's Levi?"

"He's gone," she said.

"I thought he was going to crash on the sofa."

"Well . . ." She stared into the tumbler of amber liquid as if the words she was looking for were floating there. "Dinner ended up being . . . um . . . rather unusual. So, I made an executive decision. Dropped him off at the Harbor Motel near the ferry."

Tension he didn't know he was carrying unfurled gently. "So it's just you and me," he said, putting his arm around her shoulders and snuggling her closer. Her hair was silky soft beneath his cheek and smelled of citrus and springtime. "Bit of a drive to the ferry," he said.

She shrugged, then burrowed her face into his chest as if needing to draw warmth, physical and emotional, from his body. So he held her, savoring the magic of the moonlight and the sense of peace that surrounded them.

She felt right. As if she and no one else belonged on that sofa beside him. His arm tightened around her, wanting to claim her for his own. But he could tell from her posture when she'd come in the front door that tonight had wearied her. So he opted for dropping a gentle kiss on her head while breathing her in and trying to disregard the gigantic boner he was sporting.

"I thought it best," she murmured, her sultry voice coursing through him. He took a healthy swallow of whiskey and tried to focus on the burn as it went down. "It will make it super easy for Levi to hop on the morning ferry back to the mainland." She yawned mightily. "So tired," she said, another yawn escaping as she wrapped her arms around his waist and squeezed him tight, snuggled in even more. Her jean jacket had fallen open. He could feel her soft breasts pressed against his chest through her cotton T-shirt, the rise and fall of her breath. "I'm so glad" — her voice was getting quieter, like a slow fade in an old-time movie — "to be home . . ." She smiled sleepily at him, her eyelids drifting to half-mast, then sliding closed as sleep overtook her and pulled her into its embrace.

Home, Rhys thought, feeling her body relax into his, growing heavier as her breath took on a gentle, even cadence. *That's how I feel when she's in my arms. As if I've arrived home.* He'd always associated the word with a physical place. Had spent most of his life longing for a home, where there was beauty, comfort, and safety like he had read about in books. He'd purchased a beautiful Spanish hacienda in Bel Air hoping to create that sort of sacred oasis. He'd hired an award-winning interior designer to decorate it and a landscaper to create gorgeous lush gardens for him to enjoy and entertain in. However, as beautiful as the place was, it felt as if he were living a lie, presenting a pretend life to the world that had nothing to do with who he really was. *I've been looking at it wrong. Home is not a physical place,* he thought, smiling up into the darkness. *It's a state of being. And right now, in this very moment, I am home.*

Thirty-Six

The wind had picked up, rattling through the tall trees. Leaves, browned needles, and small branches were plummeting to the ground all around him. A light, steady rain had started a little after nine p.m. Not a big deal at first, but now, forty-five minutes later, he was soaked to the bone. Decisions had to be made. He told himself the tremors running through him were from the cold, but they could have been caused by nerves.

He had made a miscalculation. She must have looped back to the motel when he'd dashed to the trunk of his vehicle to retrieve the tools he'd collected for this venture.

The matrix had shifted, and he must shift with it.

Then, like a sign from heaven, the final light in their motel room was extinguished.

It was time.

She wasn't coming out, so he would retrieve her.

If things had gone according to plan and he'd been able to intersect with her outside the motel, he would've used the knife to obtain her cooperation. That way, if punishments needed to be doled out for bad behavior, it could be done quickly and effectively without irreparable damage.

However, since she was in the room and there was a man in the equation needing to be neutralized, he would start off the party with his Walther P22. He returned to his vehicle, opened the trunk, and removed old Walt from its case, then screwed on the gorgeous suppressor he'd special ordered from Finland. He didn't remove his satchel, however. Best to be prepared for all eventualities.

A couple of minutes later he was standing before their motel room. A worn Do Not Disturb sign was dangling from the doorknob. He smirked. *Ah, well, needs must.*

He tapped on the door.

No answer.

He knocked a little louder. "Front desk. It's essential I speak with you, please," he called. He could hear movement inside, feet hitting the ground, a few choice curse words through the paper-thin door. The door opened a crack. The security chain was on.

"What the fuck?"

"So sorry to disturb you," he said, keeping his tone mild-mannered and unassuming. Shoulders rounded, eyes down and apologetic, making sure to keep old Walt out of the guy's sight line. "There's a problem with your credit card. Probably just a computer glitch, but the main office has requested that I run it through again. I've brought up a machine for your convenience."

"Jesus Christ." The guy fumbled with the chain, and the door swung open.

Eve wasn't in the bed. In the bathroom maybe, hiding. Perhaps feeling shy.

"I'll get my card," the guy said, flipping on the overhead light and turning away.

He shut the door silently, waited until the prey had crossed the room. No need to get blood splatters on his shoes.

The guy was reaching for his wallet on the bedside table when he pulled the trigger. Once. Twice.

The guy made an "ugnuh" noise, turned, a stunned look in his eyes. Childlike almost. Confused. "Why did you do that?" he croaked, hand rising to the newly acquired hole in his chest, crimson blooming outward.

He fired again.

Watched the bullet rip through the forehead, the head jerk back.

"You shithead," the guy managed to get out, a trickle of blood escaping the corner of his mouth. Then he crumpled to the ground as if he were a puppet whose strings had been cut.

Thirty-Seven

Eve was having a marvelous dream. She was in a warm hammock. Swaying slightly. It reminded her of something. What was it? Oh yes, that summer when she was nine, getting up while it was still dark outside to go fishing with her dad. The rock of the boat after the motor had been shut off. Bobbing on the waves. "Mm . . ." The hammock smelled good, clean and male. "Delicious," she murmured, opening her eyes at the sound of her own voice.

Hmm . . . not a dream. She was in Rhys's arms, nestled against his gorgeous mouthwatering bod as he carried her down the hall toward her bedroom. The man's muscles clearly weren't just for decoration. His chest and shoulders were rock-hard, and he didn't seem to be winded in the slightest. *Should probably let him know I'm awake and can make the journey to my bedroom on my own two feet.* But being carried by him, surrounded by his arms and his masculine scent, was just too delicious. *When does this kind of thing happen? Only in the movies. No need to truncate this once-in-a-life-time experience.*

Decision made, she quickly shut her eyes, feeling a tiny bit guilty, which added to the fun.

He grunted slightly as he shifted her weight so he could open the door to her room. *So, maybe he* is *feeling the burn a little,* she thought, biting her lip to keep her smile from taking over her face.

She could hear the door swing open, felt him move to the bed.

He paused.

She could feel him problem solving. She lifted her eyelids a fraction, so she could watch him through her lashes. His face had a wide-open sweetness that she hadn't seen before, all the harsh angles softened somehow. He was chewing the inside of his cheek, deep in thought. Then his face lightened. He bent slightly and used his knee to push the covers back. The gentle tenderness with which he carefully lowered her to the bed caused something to shift inside of her, as if a shard of glass, embedded in her heart throughout her twenties, had just dislodged and was dissolving in the bath of his kindness.

He slowly eased his arms out from underneath her, then pulled the covers up to her chin. He smoothed a strand of hair away from her face. "Sweet dreams, my love," he whispered, a barely there kiss alighting on her forehead.

His love? Surely he was just using that word. He was from Hollywood after all. It was probably an affectation, but still . . .

She could hear his body shift, turn to go.

Her eyes flew open as she captured his hand. "Stay," she said, her heart brimming to overflowing with emotion.

He turned, sleepy surprise on his face.

"I had a nap," he said, clearly wrestling with his better intentions, because she could see the ridged outline of his swollen boner pressing insistently against the fabric of his jeans. "You only got a couple hours of sleep last night. Been on your feet —"

"I don't care about sleep," she said, sitting up, her other hand joining the first and tugging him toward her. "I need you. Tonight. Naked in my bed."

His eyes darkened as the flickers of hunger flared into flames. His strong, calloused hand slid behind her neck, cradling the back of her head and tilting it so his mouth swooping down could claim hers.

Yikes! She'd just eaten a huge honking bowl of French onion soup. *What if my breath stinks?*

"Wait!" Her hand flew to his chest, stopping his descent. "I've gotta brush my teeth, take a quick shower. I'll be super fast. A couple minutes tops." She scrambled out of bed and slipped past him. "Be right back!" she said apologetically and shut the bathroom door behind her.

She brushed her teeth and stripped off her clothes in record time. Turned on the shower, bundled her long hair on top of her head and secured it with a tortoiseshell clip, then stepped inside. The water wasn't fully heated yet. Didn't matter. Liquid heat was coursing through every molecule of her body. The lukewarm water pounding down on her highly sensitized skin acted as an aphrodisiac, causing her nipples to tighten and jut out. Washing her skin, her fingertips encountered a different kind of wet as they slid between the sensitive folds nestled between her legs.

She heard a husky groan over the running water and whirled.

Rhys was standing in the bathroom, towel in hand, staring at her hand. His gaze traveled upward to lock with her eyes, a savage, almost feral expression on his face.

"I was going to dry you off," he growled.

"Better yet," she said, swinging the glass shower door ajar, "you could join me."

The towel plummeted to the white marble floor. He yanked his T-shirt over his head and dropped that as well. *The man is fucking gorgeous,* she thought, licking water droplets off her lips, her fingers itching to explore every millimeter of his beautiful body. "My God," she murmured, needing to place a hand against the shower wall. The sheer beauty of Rhys's near-naked form was making her dizzy with longing and lust.

He unfastened his jeans, removed a condom from his pocket, and held it between his two fingers like an unlit cigarette. Then he latched his thumbs under the waistband of his jeans and briefs and tugged them downward. Her breath caught in her throat as her gaze followed the slow, tantalizing descent. His swollen cock snagged on the fabric momentarily and then bobbed free, his long, lean muscles rippling as he moved.

He bent over, stepping out of his garments, giving her an excellent view of his gorgeous, muscular ass. Her knees suddenly felt as if they'd been pumped full of Jell-O.

She blew out a shaky breath. This was *ac-*

tually going to happen. She was nervous, but greedy, too. She was starved for him, for his body to meld with hers and fill all the lonely, empty spaces.

It'd been a couple of years since anyone had caught her eye. She talked a big game, but she didn't actually *do* short-term flings. Sure, there was the disastrous one-night stand she'd had last winter when an old friend from New York had arrived on her doorstep. He'd spent most of the weekend a broken wreck, weeping because his girlfriend had left him for her best friend. His self-esteem had been at rock bottom. On the final night of his visit he'd made a pass at her, and she hadn't had the heart to turn him down. It was her first — and *last* — mercy fuck.

Yes, this is short-term, Eve thought with a satisfied grin, *but it sure as hell ain't no mercy fuck.* Rhys straightened, and her gaze was drawn back to his cock, huge, thick, and proud, arching upward as if it were attempting to caress his beautifully defined washboard abs. *This is going to be totally worth it. Heartache probably lurks on the horizon, but I don't care, because this is going to be an experience I will remember until my dying day.*

Then there was no time for thoughts. He'd bridged the distance between them, dropping the condom on the soap rack, and she was in his arms. She heard the *clatter* as her clip hit the shower floor. Her hair tumbled down, Rhys grabbing fistfuls to angle her head upward.

His mouth descended on hers, demanding a response, their tongues tangling as their kisses turned wild. Ferocious. She bit down on his sinfully decadent lower lip, tugging it gently with her teeth, her tongue gliding along the captured portion in her mouth. His groan reverberated off the tiles.

The heat and the weight of his erection against her belly was driving her insane.

His hands, slick on her body, glided over her rib cage, cupped her breasts. His thumbs circled, teasing her nipples, his head bending so his hot mouth could worship them, too.

"I need . . ." She moaned, undulating against him, wet, so slippery wet and ready. She wrapped her leg around his thigh. "Oh God . . ." The texture of his legs against her smooth ones was a glorious undernote of sensation, a bass cello, giving weight and strength to the lighter string instruments. Skin against skin, the water, piping hot now, was raining down on them, steam rising and fogging the glass. "Rhys . . ." She dragged her teeth along the muscle at the base of his neck, leaving a red mark in their wake. "I . . . can't wait. I want . . . I need you."

"Eve," he said, his voice a harsh rasp as he grabbed the condom, the bottle of shampoo crashing to the shower floor. He ripped open the foil packet with his teeth, his hands shaking.

"Let me," she murmured, kissing the inside of his wrist. Then the tip of her tongue traveled upward until it reached the packet. "Thank you," she whispered as she removed the condom from his fingers and sank to her knees. She unrolled it over his stiff, jutting cock using her mouth, her lips and tongue slipping and sliding, enjoying every millimeter of the journey. Enjoying even more the desperate groans that she lured from his throat.

"Good God, woman," he groaned, pulling her to standing. His large, sure hands spanned her waist, hoisting her into the air as if she weighed nothing. She wrapped her legs around his waist, his hands sliding to her ass, holding her aloft. She wrapped her fingers around his thick, hot cock, positioning the head of it at her wet, slick entrance. Steaming water beat down on them as she slowly, slowly sank down until his cock was embedded deep inside her, stretching, filling her completely.

"So good." His voice was a strangled flash flood of need. He dropped his forehead to hers, breath dragging in and out of his lungs like a bellows. "So hot and tight," he groaned, as if the sensation of being inside her was almost more than he could handle.

She shifted.

He gripped her hips. "Hold on . . ." he choked out. "Please . . . Don't move. I gotta —" His jaw clenched. "Don't want to finish too soon." He huffed out a breath. "You're so damn sexy, Eve . . . I can't take it."

The fact that Rhys needed all movement to cease and was struggling for control made Eve feel powerful. As if she were channeling a magnificent sex goddess from ancient times.

"Don't stop," she ordered. "Fuck me." Her arms entwined around his neck, she pounded her fist against his taut back. "Deep and hard."

"Oh God, woman," he groaned. He took a deep breath, then shifted their bodies so she was pressed against the cool marble wall. He braced her against it, then withdrew slowly, teeth gritted, and thrust deep.

"Yes." She moaned. He felt so damned good. "Like that." Hot water cascaded over them, a counterpoint to the coldness against her back.

She fisted her hands in his hair, pushed his head downward, forcing his mouth to meet hers. Tongues met and danced, tasting each other, as his thick cock drove into her again and again. He cradled her in one arm as his free hand slid between them, started stoking her *there,* circling her wet clit in the most delicious way, while everything in her tightened around him. She was moaning now, panting, as he spiraled her higher and higher. His knowing fingers, his hard cock driving in and out . . . in and out . . . The tingling, edgy tension, the voracious need, was building and building.

His mouth left hers, his tongue tasting its way down her neck. He fucked her hard while he placed a gentle kiss at the base of her neck. The kiss morphed into a light bite, and then his mouth latched on, sending an intoxicating mixture of pleasure and pain swirling through her. *He's marking me as his. Everyone will be able to see what he's done.* And the thought of this drove the tsunami of pleasure that was building inside her to peak. Energy flew outward from her core in a million shimmering pieces, as wave after wave undulated through her.

Tremors of the earth-shattering orgasm were still coursing through her body when Rhys thrust into her one final time, his face strained, neck arched, teeth bared. Untethered, undone, his fingers dug into her buttocks. Her name burst forth from his lips, an exultant roar dragged from the very depths of his being.

Thirty-Eight

The old bat is sure to be asleep, but no need to court trouble. Once the car had climbed over the hump, he switched off his headlights, cut the engine, and coasted the final thirty yards down the driveway. He tapped his brakes lightly to keep from picking up speed on the slight descent, then slowly eased to a stop by the darkened house. His hands glistened in the moonlight, slippery, sticky wet. Reminded him of gutting and scaling fish with his dad, the coppery smell of fresh blood. He missed his father — the quintessential man's man — missed the camaraderie, the hunting, fishing, visiting whores.

His dad probably would have enjoyed this little undertaking of his.

Too bad he wasn't here.

Although, then he would've had to share. Dad always got first dibs and he got the leavings.

A surge of long-buried anger erupted like a volcano, causing his vision to blur. "It's good that he's dead." Dead and buried in an unmarked grave. "Gone, gone, gone," he sang, because truly, his dad had deserved it.

The vehicle lurched. "Whoopsie." He laughed softly, yanking hard to get the right tires out of the shallow ditch and back onto the asphalt drive. "You gotta focus, man. Keep a grip on that steering wheel, or it'll get away from you." The lurch was a wake-up call that brought him back to the present. For it was his show now. He was in charge.

He eased the vehicle alongside the house and set the parking brake, leaving the door slightly ajar. He'd return, silent as a ninja, to wipe down the steering wheel, the door handle, and gearshift with his special solution.

It wasn't until he switched on the light in his underground bunker that he realized what a messy boy he had been. Discovering his ladylove wasn't cowering under the bed or hiding in the closet or bathroom had been a trifle disappointing, to say the least. Perhaps he'd been overzealous in his impromptu dismembering of the body, but boys will be boys, sometimes rough in their play.

It had helped alleviate a modicum of his frustration.

"Ah well," he said, his voice bouncing off the concrete walls. "Better clean up."

He laid the ukulele on the floor and started to strip. Everything was soaked from the rain and blood. He lifted his arm and sniffed. Perhaps the contents of a few intestines were also included in the mix. He had been rather . . . vigorous. Unschooled. Naughty boy.

He giggled. Even his toes inside his shoes were slipping around in the muck.

Once he had stripped down, he gathered his clothes and stepped into his gum boots to protect his feet. He picked up the red plastic gas can and lighter and headed aboveground.

Douse anything in enough gasoline and it will burn, he thought, enjoying the heat and the merry glow of the orange and yellow flames leaping and dancing in his rusty burn barrel.

"What the hell do you think you're doing?"

He whirled to face her, startled. Torn from a daydream of Eve and him whiling away the blissful hours, him strumming his newly acquired instrument, her serenading him with her dulcet tones.

There was a crease along the old bat's right cheek, an impression from her pillowcase. She looked sleepy, a little angry, but mostly scared.

Scared was good. "None of your business," he said, making his voice cold and dismissive. "Go back to bed."

She didn't return to the house. Stubborn bitch. She started crying. Noisy, unattractive, gulping sobs. Apparently, she'd waited up all night, was disturbed to find him standing by the burn barrel, wearing nothing but gumboots and covered in blood.

The therapist had told him he needed to work on his empathy, on seeing things from her point of view.

Fine. He would have preferred to practice his empathy fully clothed, but he closed the distance between them, even though it was bloody cold that far from the flames, and patted her on the back. "There . . . there," he said. "Enough with the tears. It's not all bad. Hey, I got an idea. Why don't I cut us some roasting sticks, and we can toast some marshmallows." But that just made her cry harder.

THIRTY-NINE

Eve's lungs momentarily stuttered to a stop when she pulled her car into the Intrepid parking lot and saw a shadowy hulking figure of a man. His shoulders hunched, hands cupped around his eyes as he peered through the back window of the building.

"Hey!" Rhys yelled, yanking the passenger door open and vaulting from her car before she'd come to a complete stop.

The man whirled, hands up. "Not doing nuthin'," he said, backing up against the door, the light over it illuminating his face.

"Larry. What the heck?" Eve snapped, adrenaline running through her. "Why are you lurking around the building at this ungodly hour?"

"I — I work here," he stammered, looking guilty as hell.

"Not for two hours, you don't."

"I just thought" — he kept his head down, unable to meet her eyes — "with Maggie gone and all that, you might need a little extra help setting up."

"We've got it covered," Rhys said, his face a granite mask and his voice sharp enough to cut glass. "Why don't you tell us the real reason you're here."

Larry flushed. He mumbled something, but Eve had no idea what it was.

"What's that?" Rhys demanded, getting in Larry's face.

Larry's gaze darted over Rhys's shoulder to her. He took a big breath, looking embarrassed but determined. "I had a . . . feeling," he said. "I get them sometimes, and when I do, I've learned not to ignore them. Like that other day when someone broke into your apartment — I had a feeling then, too. It's sorta like a flash." He puffed out a breath, his cheeks filling with air and then deflating.

"And what did this *feeling* say?" Rhys asked, steely-eyed, jaw set. "I think it would be a good idea to break into Ms. Harris's apartment? To stalk and harass her?"

"No!" Larry said, glaring at Rhys in outrage. He turned back to her. "It was nothing like that. You gotta believe me."

"No. She doesn't," Rhys countered.

Eve put a hand on Rhys's forearm. "I'll handle this." Miraculously, Rhys snapped his mouth shut and took a half step back. "Go on, Larry."

"I was uneasy all evening, couldn't sleep. Didn't know why. And then this voice told me I needed to come to the Intrepid. That something was wrong. That I need to stay close to you, Eve." Larry nodded his head at her, his fists clenched. "Need to keep you safe."

"Larry," she said, keeping her voice calm. "I appreciate your hard work and your dedication to the Intrepid. However, it is not appropriate for you to continually be on or around the premises after hours."

"But —" Larry started to speak, but she raised her hand and forestalled him.

"I don't want it to happen again," she said sternly. "If it does, I'm afraid there will be consequences."

"Con— consequences?" Larry asked, eyes wide, bushy eyebrows shooting upward.

"That's correct," said Eve briskly, stepping forward and unlocking the door.

The minute she crossed the threshold, there was a sense of wrongness. As if somehow the place had been violated. Invaded. Unease lifted the fine hairs on her arms and on the back of her neck.

She heard Larry moan behind her. "Quiet," she said, a little sharper than was warranted, slipping her keys into her palm. She closed her fist so that the individual keys protruded from between her fingers like porcupine quills. Her other hand flicked on the light.

Everything seemed normal.

Nothing was out of place.

She exhaled and stepped into the kitchen.

"You okay?" Rhys asked, catching sight of her face as she turned to hang her jean jacket on the coatrack.

"Sure." She smiled ruefully as she slipped her apron over her head and tied it at the waist. "Seem to be jumping at shadows this morning."

Once Rhys was settled at the ovens and Larry was sweeping the leaves off the front walk, Eve went into the utility room. Between the furnace and the hot water tank they'd had a broom cupboard built with a false back, where the safe was housed. She opened it. The cash from the week was still neatly stacked inside.

"Thank God." She closed the safe, spun the lock, and shut the false back. She straightened, allowing the relief to trickle through her. Larry had spooked her. Everything was fine. It was time to get to work. She grabbed the mop and bucket.

She filled her bucket with hot soapy water, put Adele's *19* CD on, and started mopping. She left Rhys's work area untouched. Didn't want him to slip on the wet floor. Once he had all the ovens going and took his coffee break, she'd give that area a thorough washing.

By the time she'd finished mopping the kitchen, Larry was back inside and unloading the dishwasher. She dumped the dirty water from her bucket, refilled it with clean, and headed to the front of the house. Working hard and fast, singing along with Adele, she kept her head down and focused on the work. She could feel the burn in her muscles more than usual. *Probably on account of our nocturnal activities,* she thought, a smile cajoling the corners of her mouth upward. A feeling of contentment spilled through her at the memory of the taste and feel of Rhys's skin. She dragged her forearm across her face to wipe off the sheen of sweat gathering there.

Eve had a system for washing the floors. She liked to work her way backward through the room. Once she got to the front door, she'd walk around the building to the back entrance and reenter, where the floor would've dried.

It wasn't until Eve straightened to stretch out her lower back that she noticed the gaping empty spot on the wall.

She must have screamed. Didn't remember doing it, but both Rhys and Larry burst through the swinging doors, faces pale.

"What is it? What happened?" Rhys demanded.

"My . . . my —" She couldn't get the words out, pointed at the wall.

"Her painting," Larry roared, charging over to the blank wall. "*Midnight Moon.* Someone stole it." He slammed his palms on the wall as if somehow that would bring the painting back, and that's when Eve noticed the money.

A neat stack of bills tied with a red satin ribbon was sitting on the table underneath where the painting had hung. There was a red rose and a foil-wrapped chocolate kiss resting on top of the cash.

"What the hell?"

Rhys must have seen it, too.

"I think," Eve said, feeling a little nauseous, "I've just sold my first painting."

Forty

Rhys crouched down by Eve's seat, tucking her cold fingers around a mug of hot coffee. "How you doin'?"

She smiled weakly. "Been better." She noticed the mug in her hand. "Thanks."

"Drink up," he said. He could see slight tremors running through her. "The warmth will help settle you."

She took a sip. "What did Luke say?"

"He agrees with me that Larry should go."

She stared down into her mug. "It's going to break his heart."

"A temporary suspension until Jake has run Larry through their systems. Maggie weighed in as well. It is clear you have a stalker, so ensuring your safety is of paramount importance, until we get the green light on Larry."

"He's just so sensitive . . ."

"He was found at the scene of both break-ins."

"I know," she said, waving her hand wearily. "You're right. Better safe than sorry." She sighed heavily. "It makes me sad is all." She placed her coffee mug on the table, rose to her feet, and squared her shoulders. "I'll go tell him."

Eve dashed through the swinging doors loaded down with dishes. Glanced at the clock on the wall and groaned. It was only 11:15 a.m., and she was already exhausted. She wasn't sure how much of the fatigue was the extra workload created by sending Larry home and how much was guilt weighing her down. To say Larry was distraught would be a massive understatement. "But I'm your A-one worker," he'd sobbed. And then his mom, Rose Shumilak, dropped by on her coffee break, still wearing her smock. She'd pretended she'd had a sudden craving for a dozen jam-dot cookies, but really, it was to plead Larry's case. That had been difficult. Eve hated disappointing her. Rose had looked so tired and worn. She'd had Larry late in life, an only child, and the apple of her eye.

"Order's up," Rhys called.

"I know." Eve scraped the plates, stacked them in the dishwasher, which was already stuffed to the gills, added soap, and started it. "If you could unload this when it's done," she said, drying her hands and hustling over to pick up her order.

"No problem." Rhys removed a pan of brownies from the oven. "Damn. Slight charring around the edge."

"The icing will cover it, no worries," she said, adding a scoop of potato salad and a sprig of parsley to the club sandwich.

"Also, Luke called. He booked a private jet. They'll be heading out as soon as they're packed and have settled their accounts. They'll be home tomorrow afternoon."

"Oh dear." Eve plopped coleslaw and a pickle next to the pulled pork sandwich. "I didn't want them to cancel their vacation."

"They wouldn't be able to relax worrying about you," Rhys said.

Eve sighed, picked up the plates, and pushed past the doors to the crowded café.

She *was* sorry her sister had cut her vacation short, but if she was being totally honest, she was relieved, too. Luke had specialized in international security before he'd moved to Solace Island. He'd know what to do. Would find whoever was behind all of this and stop them in their tracks.

Lavina and Ethelwyn were huddled over a teary-eyed Irene, patting her on the shoulder. "Food's up," Eve said, setting the dishes down at their table.

"Could we get a sharing plate?" Lavina asked.

"I couldn't," Irene said, her voice quavering. "I . . . I have no appetite."

"You have to eat." Ethelwyn dragged a spare chair to their table. "No asshole of a man is worth losing your health over."

"Men are dogs," Lavina added, looking up at Eve. "She's just found out that her husband is in love with someone else."

"Oh dear," Eve said. "I'm so sorry." But her words of comfort didn't seem to help the matter; they just triggered a renewed bout of tears.

"Another set of cutlery, too, please," Ethelwyn said.

"Absolutely," Eve replied.

She gathered another place setting, along with a piping-hot pot of Afternoon Blend, a fresh mug, and a dainty creamer of half-and-half. Irene preferred it to the traditional milk. "Here you are." She placed the items on the table. "Tea is on the house." She gave Irene an encouraging pat on the shoulder, then headed back into the fray.

It would've been hard enough managing the workload without Larry on a normal day, but today the crowds swarming into the restaurant were unprecedented.

"What in the world is going on?" she said as she passed a slightly harried, flushed-faced Dorothy, who was scooping vanilla ice cream onto slices of warm pie.

"You didn't *hear*?" Dorothy said, the tail end of her sentence a surprised squeak. "A movie star was spotted at the pharmacy yesterday afternoon. Everybody's come into town hoping to run into him. This movie star is apparently a super big deal. Marjorie says all you gotta do is look at him once and you're ready to rip off your undies." She waved her hand for emphasis, apparently forgetting that she was holding a scoop. The ice cream dislodged and went sailing in the air. "Not that I wear them," Dorothy continued, happily oblivious. "Undies, that is."

Dorothy's blob of ice cream landed on the floor with a *splat.*

Great, Eve thought, scooping the melting glob of ice cream up and plopping it in the sink. *Some weirdo is stalking me. I've got Larry's tearstains on my shoulder, an undies-less waitress, and there's a scavenger hunt on for Rhys —*

"Not that my lack of underwear —" Dorothy boomed.

Eve squeezed her eyes shut and counted to three. God forbid the woman moderate her tone when speaking of undergarments.

"— would suppress my natural urges. If anything, it just adds to them." She punctuated this unwelcome information with an exuberant belly-dance undulation of her hips for emphasis, eyes twinkling. "A good healthy breeze up the hoo-hah is very good for vaginal health. Speaking of vaginal health . . . If this ac*tor* is as hot as they say" — Dorothy cackled happily, her thick gray eyebrows waggling — "I'd better start attending the *cin*ema!" She nudged Eve hard in the ribs. "Maybe if we combined forces we could convince Mackenzie to start showing action movies at the theater, instead of that artsy-fartsy Academy Award shit. Hot men running around half-naked, wielding big guns . . . sounds like a hell of a lot more fun than hanging out Friday nights with my vibrator —"

"Dorothy," Eve interrupted, before any more unwanted confidences could emerge from Dorothy's mouth. "You need to serve those pies before they get cold."

"Right," Dorothy said, turning back to her work. She paused, confused. "Hey, where'd my ice cream go?"

Table three flagged Eve. "Excuse me, miss? Uh . . . we've been waiting on our food for quite some time now."

"So sorry. We're a little backed up. We're short-staffed right now. Let me go check on it."

Eve dashed into the kitchen.

Rhys wasn't there.

"Rhys?" she called.

No answer. Which was weird. If he was going on break he usually let her know. What if he'd been right about Larry and Larry had snuck back to the café and taken Rhys into the alley and was . . . "Rhys!" she yelled, panic rising.

Big mistake.

A gaggle of squealing women burst through swinging kitchen doors, necks craning, heads spinning around as if they were auditioning for a role in *The Exorcist.* "Oh my God! Where is he? Did you see him?"

"Who?" Eve said, momentarily confused.

"Rhys Thomas, of course!" "The sexy movie star!" Their voices tumbled over one another like wiggling puppies.

Oh shit. That's right.

"Which way did he go?" "Is he as hot in person as he is on the screen?"

"So sorry. False alarm!" Eve yelled over their giddy chatter. "There is no — I repeat — no Rhys Thomas back here. I yelled 'ice,' not Rhys. I've run out of ice. Please, ladies." She shooed them toward the swinging doors. "Please, I *need* you to return to your seats. I am *not* insured for you to be back here."

Once she corralled the ladies through the swinging doors, Eve sprinted over to the cook's station. Rhys must be in the washroom. She found the order slip for table three and scanned it quickly.

"You can do this," she muttered as she ran to the fridge. "Food is already made. You just have to assemble and warm them." She grabbed the cheddar cheese, ham, and the pan of quiche and sprinted back to the counter. She cut an extra-generous wedge of quiche to make up for the delay and plopped it on a baking sheet. Then she sliced open a chive-and-cheddar scone, smeared butter on both sides, laying them butter-side-up on the pan. She added thick slices of cheddar on one side and carved a nice slice of ham and placed it on the other. "Did it," she said, feeling rather proud. She picked up the pan, opened the oven —

"This mean I'm out of a job?" Rhys's amused drawl came from over her shoulder.

"Where were you?" She whirled around. Must have moved too quickly because the quiche and sconewich skidded off the baking sheet and onto the floor. "Dammit!"

"Not to worry." He wrapped his arms

around her and dropped a kiss on her head. "I can take over." He scooped the food off the floor and tossed it in the compost.

"They know you're here," Eve said, her arms wrapped around her solar plexus. She didn't want their idyll to end, but he needed to be warned.

"Who?" His competent hands assembled the sconewich. Gorgeous long-fingered hands that knew just how to make a woman's body sing.

"The women of Solace Island."

"Here?" he asked, cutting into the quiche. "At the Intrepid?"

"No, but it's only a matter of time before somebody shows Dorothy a photo of you, and then all hell will break loose." She smiled apologetically. "Dorothy has a bit of a big mouth."

"Really?" Rhys grinned at her. "I hadn't noticed." He didn't seem too upset by the news that his cover was blown. Maybe he wasn't aware of just how enthusiastic the women looking for him were.

"When word gets out, it's going to be impossible for you to work here."

He leaned over and kissed the tip of her nose. "I know you don't want to hear this, but you're so adorable standing there, looking so worried. I just want to gobble you up." He reached past her and slid the baking sheet in the oven. "I would, too. Set you up on this counter and have my way with you, but it's going to have to wait because we're a little backed up."

"I know. It's crazy out there. Better go take care of the hungry hordes." She turned to leave.

"Wait." He snagged her hand. "Eve, I'm flying to LA when we close."

Her stomach plummeted. "You're . . . going to LA?"

He nodded.

"Today?" she managed to croak. She shook her head, suddenly angry with herself. She'd known it was going to be short-term, but this must be some kind of record.

"Yeah." He was already working on the next order and acting completely casual, as if he hadn't just dropped an enormous frikkin' bombshell. "I was planning to zip down by myself and to be back around midnight, but with all that's been going on, I think it'd be best if you came with me."

"To LA? Tonight?" All her grouchy thoughts came screeching to a halt. "You want me to come with you?"

"I know it's short notice, but we could make it fun. Stay overnight. You could see my place." His thumb was gliding back and forth on the inside of her wrist, sending tingles up her arm. "It'd mean a lot to me if you'd come. I'd like you to meet my mom."

"That's your big Thursday-night date? Your mom?" *And he wants me to meet her?* Her gaze snapped from her wrist to his eyes, her lungs feeling as if they'd forgotten how to draw air. *Holy cow!*

"I think you'd like each other, and more important, you'd be with me. I wouldn't have to worry. Would know you were safe."

Forty-One

Eve leaned back in the luxurious leather armchair. *I'm going to take Maggie's advice and enjoy every second of this lovely adventure,* she thought as she watched through the Cessna Citation jet's window as Solace Island dropped away from view.

It had been a mad dash, racing to the house after the café closed, packing an overnight bag. Luckily, Lavina and Ethelwyn were able to take care of Samson.

On the way to the private airfield, Eve had called Maggie and let her know about the change in plans. She didn't want her sister and Luke to freak out if they arrived on Solace Island before she and Rhys returned.

"I'm glad you're going to LA," Maggie said. "Since it will take you out of harm's way until Luke can sort everything out. And don't waste your time away by worrying. Enjoy yourself. We'll figure out this stalker thing." There was a slight pause on the other end of the phone, and then Maggie laughed. "I still can't believe my big sister is *dating* Rhys Thomas." With her eyes shut Eve could imagine Maggie sitting beside her in the car as it whizzed down the road, beaming her wide-open smile. "The man is *gorgeous*, Evie. Super *hot*!"

Luke had growled in the background, which had made Maggie laugh again as she covered the phone with her hand. Her voice was muffled, but Eve heard her murmur something to her husband, love evident in her tone.

When they'd arrived at the private airfield, Rhys had driven his truck onto the tarmac, right up to the gleaming white jet that was waiting for them. He handed his car keys to the ground personnel. The two pilots and the steward introduced themselves. Eve's overnight bag was stored in the baggage compartment at the back of the plane.

"All right, Mr. Thomas, we're fueled and ready to go," one of the pilots said. And that was it. No lengthy lines to check in, no security. Arrive at the airfield, and five minutes later you're in the air. Unbelievable.

"Ms. Harris, would you care for a blanket?" Before takeoff, the steward had settled them in with drinks. Once altitude minimums were reached, he unbuckled his seat belt and started moving about the plane again.

Eve wasn't cold, but he had gone through the trouble of taking the blankets out, and maybe the cabin would get cold later on. "Thank you. That would be lovely."

He opened the blanket and draped it across her lap, then returned to the galley.

"Oh dear." She smiled ruefully across the glossy burl wood table at Rhys as she smoothed her hand across the whisper-soft cashmere blanket. "A girl could get used to this."

She took a sip of champagne. "Yum . . ." The bubbles were frolicking in her mouth. There were hints of ripe fruit, a woody earthiness, the delicate floral note that lingered on her tongue. A slight moan escaped from her lips. "I don't know if this is the best champagne I've ever tasted or if the gorgeous crystal flute affects the flavor."

Desire gleamed in Rhys's dark eyes. "We can run a couple of experiments if you'd like." His voice was a low growl as he shifted in his seat.

Eve let her gaze wander languidly down his body and was rewarded by the sight of a massive erection straining against the confines of his jeans. She smiled, suddenly ravenous for him. "You're incorrigible," she purred. *Who knew that simply enjoying my drink would bring him to such a state of arousal?*

She traced the rim with her tongue, enjoying the flavor as well as the texture of the smooth, cool crystal.

"You're killing me," he said.

She tipped her head back and took a long last sip, her gaze locked on his hungry eyes. "Mm . . ."

She became aware of a droplet of champagne trickling down the side of her flute. "Oh my," she murmured. "I'd better get that." The tip of her tongue captured the droplet, then began a slow, sensuous ascent as she followed the droplet's pathway back to the rim of her champagne flute.

"That's it," Rhys said, energy crackling through the cabin like an electrical storm. He ripped off his seat belt, lifted the polished burl wood tabletop, and slid it into its slot in the wall. "You are in trouble, woman," he growled, rising to his feet in a smooth, predatory manner, one hundred percent focused on her.

She felt powerful causing this raging need in him and was laughing up at him as he loomed over her. Then suddenly the world shifted and she was upside down. *How did he get me unstrapped so fast?* She couldn't stop laughing as he slung her over his broad shoulder.

She saw Rhys's hand snag the bottle of Perrier-Jouët Belle Epoque, and anticipation joined the hot-blooded dance coursing through her veins.

Polished men's shoes and black trousers stepped into her view. "Can I interest either of you in a bite to eat?" The steward's voice sounded smooth, unperturbed by the sight of Rhys with Eve slung over his shoulder. "An iced-prawn cocktail, perhaps? Or —"

"Privacy," Rhys barked, on the move, his arm firmly around Eve's thighs, her ass in the air as he headed toward the back of the plane. "You can interest us in some privacy until further notice."

"Very good, sir," she heard the steward reply.

"Rhys," she said, trying to sound stern, but the laughter didn't help. "I am not a sack of chicken feed that you are hauling to the barn. Put me down."

"I'm happy to accommodate your request."

He took two more steps and then she was soaring through the air before landing on a —

"A bed!" Eve pushed up onto her elbows and gazed around, enraptured. She was lying on an actual bed, fully decked out in crisp white linens with caramel piping. There was a cashmere throw blanket at the base of the bed and an abundance of plump pillows. "They have a bed back here. This is amazing!"

He set the bottle of champagne on the bedside table, then turned and yanked a set of folding curtains shut, closing off the rest of the plane.

"Curtains! I hadn't noticed those —"

Then he was on her, and she was surrounded, caged in, captivated, mind and body. His mouth descended on her, a match to dry summer grass, engulfing her in the fierce flames of desire.

She could hear the steward moving around beyond the curtain, the clink of glasses being cleared as Rhys was slowly unbuttoning her blouse, christening each newly exposed inch of flesh with a kiss, a stroke, a gentle bite. "Rhys," she moaned softly, writhing beneath him.

He spread her blouse open so she was exposed to his gaze. She could feel her nipples tighten under her black lace and mesh bra. "Nice," he said, his thumb gliding over the material, the taut peak of her breast, his mouth descending, a swirl of his tongue.

"Rhys . . ." She couldn't speak as heat

spiraled through her. He'd barely touched her, and already her undies were soaked through. He reached for the champagne, drizzled the ice-cold bubbly liquid along the center of her body. It trickled downward, pooling in her belly button.

"Mm . . ." he murmured. "Very nice." He set the bottle down as he followed the champagne's path with his gaze and then his mouth. The contrasting sensations from the ice-cold champagne and the silky heat of his tongue forced her heartbeat to take up residence lower in her body, in her labia, her pulsing clit.

"Please . . ." Eve was torn between thrusting him away and yanking him closer. "We can't."

A low guttural laugh rumbled from the back of his throat as he slid up her body and tugged the delicate black fabric down with his teeth. Her right breast was now fully exposed. The cool air from the overhead vent caused the aching tip, wet from his mouth, to tighten even more.

"He'll hear," she gasped, as Rhys's tongue traced its way to her other, still-clad breast, his hand cupping her exposed breast, his clever fingers causing her body to jolt upward toward the low ceiling.

He lifted his head, eyes gleaming. "Not if

you're quiet," he said, watching the effect on her as his fingers squeezed her nipple. Taking her to that point where pleasure dances on the razor's edge of pain, causing her body to buck as she craved, wanted more.

A high-keening cry of need erupted from her lips.

He braced his weight on his elbow, still caressing her breasts. "Shh . . ." he whispered, his voice a sensuous tease, as he placed a finger on her lower lip. "Be quiet." His finger glided along her lip, then dipped inside. "Here," he murmured. "Suck on this."

She did, but it didn't help. His mouth was on her nipple again, his fingers on her other breast, driving her need higher and higher.

The more she sucked, the hornier she got. It felt good to have part of him inside her.

"Jesus, woman," he groaned, removing his finger from her mouth. "You're driving me crazy." He was breathing hard now, as if he had just completed a five-hundred-meter dash.

He lowered his body. His button-down shirt chafed her sensitized skin; he was fully clothed and she was undone. It was so damned erotic. He made her feel wanton, beautiful, desired.

Her hips writhed against his jeans-clad erection, the hard heat of him winding her tighter and tighter. She tucked her pelvis upward in small circles, wanting contact *there.* Right *there.*

His hand traveled downward, undoing the button on her jeans, her zipper. He shoved her jeans down, peeled her panties back. His hand cupped her mound, laying claim to all the energy rocketing around at her core. He dipped the tip of one finger inside her opening, barely penetrating her. Slid his finger out again, then gently swirled it along the outside rim. "You're so wet for me," he whispered with his breath warm behind her ear, his lips following his breath in a kiss before capturing her earlobe between his teeth.

Another moan escaped from her lips. "Oh shit. I can't —" She clapped a hand over her mouth, trying to stop words, noises from escaping.

She heard the sound of a door opening. Two male voices, talking low, words indistinguishable.

"That's right," he murmured, languidly dipping his finger again, then gently trailing his forefinger along her slick wet folds. "One of the pilots has come out of the cockpit. For coffee, a chat." He barely skimmed her clit, causing her to buck upward. She muffled her wail with her hand, wanting, needing more.

"Maybe they're going to eat some dinner." He circled his shimmering wet finger on the hood of her clit, slow, languorous circles that wound her need tighter and tighter.

"I gotta . . . I need . . ." She wailed soundlessly into her palm.

She could hear male laughter. Did they know what was going on?

Higher and higher. Body undulating, no control. Her world narrowed down to his hand, her pussy, the men right outside the curtain.

She could hear a cupboard being opened, liquid being poured, Rhys's breath harsh and fast against her neck near her ear. So wet. So damn wet, tremors building, building. She could feel the juices from her pussy saturating the duvet beneath her. She would leave a wet spot for sure. No way to hide what they'd been doing back here. "Oh, sweet Jesus," she moaned.

"Gotta keep quiet." Rhys's voice was a low, barely there growl. "Everyone's gonna hear," he whispered as her orgasm roared through her like a runaway train.

FORTY-TWO

The limo sped down the Pacific Coast Highway, a high, craggy embankment on their left, the ocean on their right, glittering like a multifaceted sapphire in the setting sun.

The color of the water was quite similar to the starbursts and the deep blue that encircled the outer rim of Rhys's iris. Her thought was followed by a rush of tenderness, a desire to lie in his arms and gaze into his eyes until they both were old and gray and covered in cobwebs for not having moved for years and years.

He'd grown quieter since the plane had landed, as if he were gathering his inner resources, bracing himself.

"If you change your mind and want to see your mom alone, I totally understand. I'm happy to grab a coffee somewhere."

He placed his hand over hers. "I want you with me," he said. There was a wistful smile on his face, a trace of sadness in his eyes. Then he turned to gaze out the window again.

The residence his mom lived in was a Spanish hacienda high on a bluff overlooking the ocean. Beautiful antique hand-painted tiles were on the risers of the stairs leading to the arched doorway of the lobby. Inside, large Saltillo tiles made up the gleaming floors.

The setting sun cast a warm glow that seemed to bounce off the white stucco walls and ceiling, making the lobby look quite magical. The exposed wooden beams and a stunning wrought-iron and crystal chandelier gave the place a rustic, elegant charm.

As they traveled through the lobby, Eve noticed several residents in quiet conversation, ensconced in comfortable sofas and chairs, a few in wheelchairs. An elderly couple were duking it out over a chessboard. Eve had the sense that they'd been playing chess together for years. The friendly staff moved among the residents with a calm competence and a caring demeanor.

Rhys led the way through another arched doorway and onto a pathway that meandered through the lush, fragrant garden. He held the homemade fudge he'd purchased on Solace Island carefully in his hand. An abundance of flowers were blooming, such a contrast to Solace Island, where the leaves had already started to change color. "It's a lovely place, Rhys," she said softly.

He stopped in his tracks, turned, looked at her. The vulnerability in his face was heartbreaking. "Really?" he said, as if wanting, needing to believe that placing his mom here had been the right decision. She could see the struggle in his eyes.

"Truly," she said. "There is a lovely feeling about this place."

"Please, God, I hope so." He squeezed his eyes shut as he exhaled shakily, then shook his head and tried to smile. "You know, every night I say a prayer. Not for me or for little things like whether I'll get a particular job or not. I pray for her. That she's safe and happy, that I made the right decision moving her here." He opened his eyes, his expression bleaker than anything Eve had ever seen. "That she knows that she's" — his voice broke — "loved."

He kept his head bowed as he fought for control over his emotions. "You know, I used to have her staying with me. I thought that would be what was best for her."

A self-loathing half laugh fell from his lips. "Best for her," he said bitterly, kicking a fallen twig off the walkway with his foot. "See" — he whirled to face her again, his expression ferocious — "I was gone, being the big hotshot movie star for huge chunks of time. I wasn't there, overseeing the caregivers I'd hired."

His jaw clenched, his mouth a harsh straight line, then his shoulders slumped, as if the weight on them had gotten too heavy to bear.

"I was in Mobile, Alabama" — the words came slowly — "shooting *Caught.* A location fell through." He scrubbed his hands across his face. "There was a scramble to find a new sports arena, a rearranging of the shooting schedule. I had three days off. Enough time to fly home, check on her, and then fly back. I didn't bother calling as I usually do. Came home unexpectedly."

Her heart was breaking for him. He looked so tortured, pale tension lines around his nose and mouth, his breath shaky.

"I could hear my mom crying before I even opened the door. Found the couple I'd hired to take care of her — who had glowing references, by the way — in the den, feet up, munching on popcorn, a half-eaten bucket of ice cream melting on the coffee table, the TV blaring. Totally ignoring my mom's cries. When I got to her room, she was tied to the bed like an animal, her face swollen from crying so long and so hard. Her teeth hadn't been brushed probably since the last time I'd been home. Her hair was uncombed, her diaper, soggy and soiled. I wanted to kill them. Might have, if my mom hadn't been there." He blew out a breath. "So that's how she ended up here. I know it's not perfect, but I feel safer, knowing there are checks and balances while I'm away."

"I think you made the right decision," Eve said, gently wiping away a tear that was sliding down his cheek. She slipped her arm around his waist and placed her head against his chest, giving silent comfort.

A few minutes passed. Shadows lengthened across the lush lawn. Crickets chirped. A broad-winged condor lazily circled above.

Rhys straightened, cleared his throat. "All right," he said, rolling the residual tension out of his shoulders. "I'm good now." He seemed lighter as he tucked her hand into the crook of his arm, like a weight had been lifted. "Let's go see my mom."

She was sitting in her favorite spot, on the glider swing. Her head was tilted up, her eyes shut, an expression of absolute contentment on her face. She was humming softly.

"What are you doing, Mom?" Rhys said, keeping his voice gentle so as not to startle her.

"Catching the last rays before the sun says its sweet farewells until tomorrow," she replied, her eyes still shut.

"Sounds like a good plan," Rhys said. "Mind if we join you?"

"Not at all." She gestured to the empty seats beside her. "It can be a farewell party."

He sat beside his mom. Eve sat on his other side. Their bodies settling into the swing caused a deeper glide, forward and back, forward and back.

He didn't speak. Was happy to bask in the quiet peace surrounding his mom at the present. *A farewell party for the sun.* He smiled at the thought. She never said things like that when he was growing up. Always seemed to be surrounded with a miasma of bone-weary depression. Had she always had such whimsical thoughts? Or was it a new pathway that had opened after the brain damage had occurred? For a flash he got a vision of his mom when she was young, six or seven years old. A freckle-faced child looking up at him with a gap-toothed smile, unruly brown curls tumbling into her sparkling eyes, a cotton pinafore, and a skinned knee. Had she believed in magic and happily-ever-afters?

The sun dipped beyond the horizon, its rays no longer caressing their corner of the garden.

"All done," his mom said, opening her eyes and dusting off her hands. "Bye-bye."

"Bye-bye, sun," he said. "See you tomorrow."

His mom turned, a beatific smile lighting her face. "Rhys. You came," she said. "I knew you would. I was so worried. But you're here now. You're safe here. I'm so glad."

Rhys exhaled. She was having a good day, knew who he was. "Hi, Mom." He put his arm around her shoulders and dropped a kiss on her head, where her hair was more white now than gray. "I'm big and strong. You don't need to worry about me. I can take care of myself."

"Don't let him hurt you," she said, her expression perturbed, eyes round. She must be mixing up time. Thinking he was young again, in Howie's power.

"Mom," he said, taking her cool hand in his, patting it soothingly. "Howie's dead." When had the skin on her hands gotten so wrinkly? Had it been a gradual process and he just hadn't noticed? "He can't hurt either one of us anymore."

"No. Not him . . ."

He could see she was starting to get agitated. Remembering Howie and the past would do that, so he changed the subject. He had become quite deft at that.

"I brought you some fudge," he said, shaking the box so the fudge bumped enticingly against the sides. "Four different flavors. I also brought someone I'd like you to meet."

"Fudge!" she cried happily, her face clearing. "Four flavors!" She reached for the box.

"Not now." Rhys laughed, holding the fudge in the air and out of his mom's reach. "First I want to introduce you to someone." He stood, pulled Eve to her feet, and tucked his arm around her. "Mom, I'd like you to meet Eve Harris. Eve, this is my mom, Lorelai Thomas."

"Lorelai *Margaret* Thomas," his mom said. "You're awfully pretty. Are you his girlfriend?"

"Um . . ." Eve said, unsure what to say.

"Yes, she is," Rhys said, enjoying the surprise flickering across Eve's face.

"Is it serious?" his mom asked, tilting her head to the side like a curious baby bird. "Are you in love and going to get married and make millions and trillions of beautiful little babies?"

"Whoa, now, Mom. Let's not scare her off," Rhys said, laughing, trying to make light of his mom's questions and mask the deep pang of longing that had roared to the forefront of his emotions.

"But you've never brought anyone to see me before."

How in the hell does she remember that when she can't even remember what day it is? "How about," Rhys said, cutting her off, "we take this fudge inside, cut it up, and set it on a plate for easy access?"

"Oh boy!" his mom said, rising to her feet and tucking her hand in his. She leaned across him. "I love fudge," she told Eve. "It's my absolute favorite!"

Forty-Three

He was sitting in the leather armchair, a vodka on the rocks in one hand. He had the living room to himself. She knew better than to disturb him when he was in one of his moods.

He stared out the big plate-glass window. The dramatic plunging view was obscured by the inky-black nothingness of night. A fire was burning in the hearth, but it did little to alleviate the ice-cold that had seemed to encase him.

The matrix had once again changed. Shifted course. Another flare of anger surged. He suppressed it. *Empathy,* he told himself. *Empathy.*

He could see her reflection in the window as she approached the living room wringing her hands. *Don't. Even,* he thought, his back teeth clenched so hard they were in danger of shattering.

She paused in the doorway, hovering, one

second, two seconds, her hand rising to her throat. Then she silently returned the way she had come.

Good. He had work to do. New plans to formulate, implement. He did not need the added burden of her fluttering around.

Forty-Four

As the vehicle turned the bend, the glare of the limo's headlights illuminated a few die-hard paparazzi parked in front of his house.

"Keep going," he told the driver.

A few heads turned as the limo glided by them, but they were unable to see past the dark-tinted windows.

He was relieved to see the progress that had been made on the stone wall. It appeared to be around three-quarters of the way built.

"Turn right into this driveway, please," he instructed the driver.

Once the limo driver had unloaded Eve's suitcase, been tipped, and disappeared into the night, Rhys grabbed her small suitcase and took her hand.

"Follow me," he said, keeping his voice low so it wouldn't carry over the noise of the automated gate swinging shut. He led her along the side of the house. They followed stone pavers to a curved wooden gate with an iron peekaboo window. They entered another yard and walked past the pool.

"Your neighbors don't mind you traipsing through their yards?" Eve whispered.

"They would," he answered. "That's why I bought them out."

"What?" she said, eyes wide.

"Yeah." He shrugged, feeling a little self-conscious. "I know it seems wasteful, but it helps me maintain a modicum of privacy. And the rise in property values more than pays for the maintenance. I like to think of it as diversification."

"Mortgage payments must cost an arm and a leg," Eve said.

He shrugged. "I know there is a tax advantage to carrying a mortgage, but" — his mind flashed to coming home from school and finding his mom weeping over red-stamped overdue notices — "I prefer not to carry debt. Call me old-fashioned, but I won't purchase something unless I can pay for it in cash."

"Must be nice," Eve said. There was an undertone of something buried in those three words. But before he could sort it out, she stopped in her tracks, tilted her face to the sky, and inhaled deeply. "Do you smell that?" she asked. "Vanilla . . . and jasmine?"

He breathed in, enjoying the scent of the blooming Cestrum nocturnum and heliotrope.

"The smell makes me feel," she said, turning to him, her face aglow, "like I'm *really* on vacation. Somewhere different. Magical."

What she doesn't know, he thought as he placed her suitcase down, wrapped his arms around her, and savored the taste of her sweet mouth, *is it's her who makes our surroundings so magical.*

When they arrived at his house, he didn't bother with the lights. There was no need. The moonlight streaming through the windows lit the way. They walked in silence, hands clasped, to his bedroom. He undressed and made love to her, slow and sweet, with the cautious optimism of the first flowers of spring making their way through the still frozen ground. There was a fragile, just-born quality imbued in every touch, every kiss — a tenderness that had been lacking in his life.

Ah, he thought with a sense of wonder as he withdrew and then slowly sank back into her warm, welcoming body. *This is what making love is.*

Eve lay next to Rhys, his arm snuggling her

close. Her head was on his chest, her hand, too. She could hear the steady thump of his heart. Feel the rise and fall of his chest, the slow, soft inhales and exhales as he slept. The duvet was pulled over her shoulder. The warmth emanating from his body should have been enough to keep her toasty, but she felt chilled.

Scared.

She wasn't sure why exactly.

She flipped through various reasons, checking in with her gut, riffling through the obvious ones first.

In the last week someone had broken into her apartment, stolen her sheets, and purchased *Midnight Moon.* Normally she'd be happy that someone had bought one of her paintings, but the creepy way they did it . . . And if all three incidents were connected, even creepier.

She blew out a breath. Thinking about that series of incidents made her stomach clench and her throat burn as if bile were threatening to overflow into her mouth.

It made sense that those incidents were what was causing this unease.

But that's not it, is it? No, it wasn't. It didn't explain the chill, the slight feeling of dread.

She sorted through a few more thoughts.

There was guilt about sending Larry home, but that wasn't the cause of this feeling.

Maggie and Luke coming home? No, she was thankful they were.

It's crazy to be feeling this. You are tainting the present with worries that may or may not have any bearing on you. You're in no danger now. You are safe and sound, lying in the arms of a wonderful man who is funny and kind and sensitive and oh so lovely to his mom. What's not to love?

Oh shit. She stared into the darkness. *You've gone and fallen for him, haven't you? Dammit!* She gently extricated herself from his arm around her shoulders, then lay on her back, glaring at the ceiling. *There is no way your heart is not going to end up broken. He's a movie star, for fuck's sake! This is a recipe for disaster.*

Rhys shifted, his hand moving up as if to caress her shoulder, only to find she had moved away. He rolled to his side. She could feel him studying her profile.

"You okay?" Although sleep-roughened, his voice was gentle.

"Yeah," she said, but even she could hear the tension in her tone.

She felt the air around her shift as he reached out, his knuckles skimming her cheek, a barely there touch. "Eve," he said softly. "We made a pact. Remember?"

She turned to face him. "Fine," she snapped. She was unsure why she was so angry, which didn't help matters. It just made her madder, at herself, at him. "You want the truth. I'm scared shitless about this stalker —"

"Me, too —"

"Stop interrupting!" she shouted, slamming her hands on the mattress. She knew she wasn't being fair, that she was being a bitch, but she didn't care. "If you want me to tell you how I feel, then you've gotta shut up."

"Okay," he said, totally calm, not judging.

"I like you more than I should and that makes me mad! I saw that. Stop smiling. It's not funny. I'm going to get hurt."

"Eve," he started to say, but she flipped over and straddled him, her hand over his mouth.

"My turn," she said ferociously, her face up close to his. "You think you know me, but you have no idea. I have debt. Did you know that? No, of course not! I have *major* debt. Three hundred and seventy-six thousand, five hundred and twenty-three dollars, and eighty-nine cents! And I don't know how the hell I'm ever going to pay it. I can't sleep at night. Do you know what that's like, not being able to sleep because you are worrying about the bills? Of course you don't, Mr. I-Like-to-Pay-for-My-Multitude-of-Homes-in-Cash! I've got debt! Big debt with no way out. Stick that in your pompous pipe and smoke it." Then, like a summer squall that rises sudden and vicious and finally blows on by, all the anger and fury drained out of her.

"Oh, honey," he said, sitting up, wrapping his arms around her trembling shoulders. He tucked her head against his solid, broad chest, then snagged a tissue from the bedside table and gave it to her. His large hand traced slow, soothing circles on her back.

"I'm . . . so ashamed," she said.

"There's nothing to be ashamed of. It's not healthy to hold things in. Gotta let it out, or the stress will kill you. There you go. That's right, honey. Cry it out."

FORTY-FIVE

Eve woke a little discombobulated. She was in a massive bed. The room was flooded with morning light streaming across a pure white linen duvet cover and rumpled sheets. *Where . . . ? Oh. That's right.*

Rhys's side of the bed was empty. When had he slipped out? Last night? This morning? Did he regret bringing her there?

She wouldn't blame him after last night's histrionics.

She felt her face heat up. What the hell had come over her?

She sat up and glanced around. The man had gorgeous taste. His bedroom looked like it belonged in the pages of an interior design magazine. The wooden bedframe was the same warm wood tones as the floors, just a hint darker. The walls appeared white, but she could see a tinge of unbleached titanium mixed in that warmed and softened the color. A stunning wooden and glass arched double door led to a covered outdoor area with comfy sofas and an armchair covered in rich rust, golden, and brown chenille. There were cushy pillows to nestle in, and beyond the private seating area was the lush garden. So different from Solace with orange and lemon trees, flowering trumpet trees, lilies, lavender, a thick verdant grassy lawn. She wanted to sprint barefoot across that grass and dive into the sparkling blue tiled pool beyond. Hoping the cool water would wash away the embarrassing memories of her late-night confession.

Instead, like the grown woman she was, she showered, dressed, and followed her nose to the kitchen, where she could smell coffee brewing.

She entered the kitchen looking like a modern-day Aphrodite having just risen from the sea. She was finishing a loose braid in her long dark hair, which was still damp from her shower. Her gaze was cast down, a delicate peach flush high on her cheeks, her luscious lower lip caught between her straight white teeth.

He envied those teeth and their proximity to her mouth, her lips. The sight of her sent heat rushing through him like a double shot of whiskey downed.

"Morning," he said, pleased with how normal he managed to sound, given that he wanted to leap upon her like a ravening beast. "Coffee?"

"Please."

He poured her a mug of steaming coffee, could feel her watching him, but when he turned and handed her the mug, her eyes met his for a split second. Then she leaned her hip against the counter, took a careful sip, and gazed around the kitchen.

"Well," she said. "If you ever dump acting and decide the cooking gig is just too damned difficult, you could always pick up some extra dough as an interior decorator. This place is gorgeous. I love your use of color and contrast."

"Whoa. Hey now," he said, taking a step back, his hands up and palms out. "You think I did this?" He couldn't help it. He started laughing. "Eve, there is no way in hell I could pull off something like this. I hired a decorator. The place cost me a goddamned arm and a leg."

"Well, it was worth it," Eve said.

"You think?" Rhys looked around. "I'm not sure. It looks perfect and all, but it feels like a movie set. You know, as if I'm acting out the life everyone thinks I'm supposed to have. All these decorative touches?" He gestured dismissively at the table, at the tasteful old-fashioned cream-colored roses in a clear crystal vase with a dainty tendril of ivy curling down the outside. His gaze wandered over the napkins the color of summer wheat, tucked into antique acorn napkin holders, then moved on to the silver and crystal salt-and-pepper shakers. "I wouldn't know how to put this assortment together to save my life."

"Do you like it?" she asked, looking at him now with her intelligent, sea-green eyes that seemed to see right down into the core of him.

He sighed. "Sure. It looks nice. And I know how lucky I was that Mavis — the designer — took me on. She books up years in advance. But a big job fell through, and the producer's wife of the movie I was working on convinced her to do my house. She told Mavis it was an emergency, that I was living like a heathen."

Eve laughed. Her shoulders seemed to lose some of their tension. "A heathen?"

He nodded. "Yup. I guess I was. Had this gorgeous house, a dual-purpose beat-up leather sofa bed, a matching beanbag chair — they were on sale the day I ambled into the store — a couple pots and pans, a couple plates, a couple towels, and a pillow."

"That was it?" She was grinning at him.

"Yup," he said, feeling rather pleased with himself at having entertained her.

"Where'd you put your clothes?"

"Oh, that's right. I forgot. I had one more item. My suitcase. Just left it sprawled open on the floor, easy access."

"Huh," she said, looking around again. "Well, you can think of this place — the interior design work she did — as a great starting-off point. Now all you need is a few personal items scattered around to make it yours. That's easy to do. The hard part has already been done for you. Why are you chuckling?"

"I just love the way you are, the way you dive into problem-solving mode, the way you attack your painting, the way you sip your coffee . . ." He needed to rein himself in. He was getting *way* too mushy. He cleared his throat. "Speaking of coffee, I don't have much more to offer. Haven't been home for a few months, so the proverbial cupboard is bare." He walked to the pantry, opened the door. "A couple cans of soup? Oh, I found some salted cashews. Want some?" He scooped up a couple and jingled them around in his cupped hand, then popped them in his mouth. "Ick!" He spit them out. "Never mind. Stale." He saw a large gift basket stuffed in the corner. "Eureka," he said, as though he had just stumbled across a pirate's treasure trove. "Gotta be something edible in here!"

It was a glorious breakfast. In the basket Rhys had unearthed a bottle of that delectable Perrier-Jouët Belle Epoque champagne, French brandy truffles, and a large tin of duck confit from Paris!

Rhys might not know how to decorate, but the man knew what to do with a tin of duck! He found a couple of wrinkly old potatoes and an onion in the fridge and whipped up a delicious duck hash. He topped the whole mess off with an egg simmered in butter, which they divided between them, the soft yolk adding a buttery goodness to the mix.

"Now," he said, pushing back from the table, picking up their plates, and walking them over to the dishwasher. "About your debt . . ."

Eve's stomach lurched, the duck confit hash turning into a congealed lump of lard in her gut. "I don't want to talk about it."

"Eve," he said, turning toward her, his eyes dark with compassion. "Clearly you need to."

She didn't reply. Couldn't. Just watched him as he rinsed the plates and silverware and placed them in the dishwasher.

"You wouldn't have gotten so upset if it wasn't bothering you. I've found it's best to talk things out. Makes them lose their power over you." He dried his hands, returned to the table, and sat down. His long legs stretched out, bumping gently against hers, the warmth of him infusing her with cautious courage. He didn't seem perturbed by her late-night confession. He wasn't running in horror or regarding her any differently, even though he knew about her massive debt. He reached out and tilted her chin up so her eyes met his. Then he took her hand. "Tell me about it."

There was something about his straightforward tone, the caring expression in his eyes, that suddenly made her want to tell him. Need to. She took a deep breath and began. "I have a good FICO score. Have always been crazy careful not to overspend, not to buy things I couldn't pay off, but when Maggie's fiancé dumped her last year, she was so broken up. I'm her —" Eve paused. She was going to say "big sister." The lie had slipped off her tongue for so many years, but somehow, to this man, she didn't want a lie between them. "I've . . . I've always looked out for her. Protected her. I wanted to help, needed to erase that bruised look from her eyes." She looked down at their hands, where his thumb was gently gliding across her knuckles. "We decided to go into business together. I had enough money to cover my portion of the down payment, but I had to borrow from the bank for my share of the renovations. And I have a mortgage."

"You both are on the mortgage."

"No. Just me. Maggie was able to pay her share of the expenses outright."

"How?"

"She got an inheritance from her" — she caught herself just in time — "from my aunt Clare."

"And presumably *her* aunt Clare as well? What kind of aunt leaves money to only one of her nieces?"

She clamped her mouth shut. Damn the man. He noticed too much.

"Eve?" He was looking at her inquiringly.

"I can't," she said. She could feel the shutters slam over her eyes, her heart, decades-long loyalty refusing to let her speak. *We are sisters,* she thought, suddenly angry — at herself, at the situation, and inexplicably at him — because she wanted, so very much, to share the secret with him. *We are! In all the ways that matter.*

"Fair enough," he said, as if she had spoken her thoughts out loud. The fingers of his other hand drummed on the table once, twice. "See, the thing is, Eve, there is nothing to be embarrassed about. You have debt. So what? So does most of America. The difference is, your debt is what I think Suze Orman — finance guru to the world — would call 'good debt.' You haven't mindlessly blown money on things that lose their value. You took on debt to purchase a property and outfit it for what appears to me to be a very thriving business. Does the Intrepid earn enough to cover expenses? Are you making any profit?"

"Sure, but —"

"No buts about it," he said firmly. "Do you know how rare it is for a start-up business to be profitable in its first year? Generally it takes years, if *ever,* to achieve profitability. You should feel very proud of what you and your sister have accomplished."

And just like that, the tension in her chest and behind her eyes dissipated. She felt lighter. Hopeful. Clean again.

Forty-Six

"Are you okay?" Eve asked. Rhys looked pale beneath his tan. He hadn't spoken for much of the flight, and when he did, there was something unusual in his tone. As if it took a while for her words to penetrate whatever it was he was stewing on.

"Yeah," he said.

"Rhys." She reached across the table, hands upward, needing contact. "Pact."

He exhaled. "I'm worried," he said, placing his hand on hers. The solid warmth emanating from it comforted her. "I don't know what we're flying back to. I want to keep you safe, to be the hero, but I'm an actor, for Christ's sake. I feel so ill equipped. I can't figure out where the dots connect." His hand tightened around hers. "There's something we aren't seeing. Last night, after you fell asleep, I kept turning it over and over in my brain. I feel as if I'm trying to chart a course with blinders on — like the ones they put on the horses pulling buggies through Central Park. I'm plodding down the road in front of me, but there are millions of vital details I'm missing. I know they are there. I can sense them, smell them, but I can't bloody well see them. It's frustrating."

She traced the pale scar between his knuckles with her thumb. "Rhys," she said softly. "It's not your job to keep the world safe. You can do what you can, and so will I, but neither one of us is God. For what it's worth, I am a fighter. I know how to defend myself. I will not go quietly into the night."

"You don't have to convince me of that," he said, a rueful smile flickering across his face. "I was the one hog-tied and facedown on Luke's kitchen floor. Incapacitated with a damned toaster cord, of all things."

"So," she said, her gaze rising from his hand to his beloved face. "If by some freak accident something untoward happens to me, I don't want you to waste your life blaming yourself" — he opened his mouth to argue, but she placed her fingers over his mouth — "like you do with your mom," she whispered. "It would hurt my heart to be the cause of such sorrow."

"Eve," he said, his eyes dark, tortured. So

she did the only thing she could, rose from her seat, leaned over the table, and silenced him with a kiss. A gentle, barely there kiss, slow and tender and full of all she was feeling but wasn't ready to say.

Forty-Seven

"I will not," the old biddy said, her voice harsh with suppressed emotion, "allow you to bring that hussy's things into my dining room."

He ignored her. He draped his napkin across his thighs, then opened the oblong blue velvet jewelry box and lovingly removed Eve's spoon.

"I mean it." Her voice was growing more and more shrill.

"Enough, woman!" he shouted, slamming his hands palms-down on the table. "Stop nattering at me. *You* are the one who inserted yourself into my affairs. Did *I* ask you to go snooping around? *No.* So shut. The *fuck.* Up."

She did. Sat there, pale-faced, like she was a ghost already. Sat there silent, fists clenched, and watched him eat his Greek yogurt and bran. Watched him slide Eve's spoon in and out of his mouth over and over.

In and out.

In and out.

Tears falling in her uneaten food.

Best breakfast he ever had. It made it so much better to have an audience. The two of them witnessing what he was doing. Knowing what it meant.

If he had known how good it was going to be, he'd have encouraged her to snoop sooner.

Forty-Eight

By the time the Cessna Citation X was approaching the landing field, the migraine had its claws firmly into him. The dark spots and zigzags in his vision were gone, but now the pain rampaging through the left side of his head was excruciating. The change in air pressure wasn't helping.

Nausea was also walloping him big-time. He hadn't brought his damned migraine medicine. *Idiot.* His eyes flickered open. Luckily, Eve was enraptured by the gorgeous landscape out the window, seeing it up close, the sparkling ocean, tall evergreens, the ground rushing toward them.

"It's so beautiful," she said, her face luminescent, as if lit from within.

"Mmm," he said, managing a smile, then let his eyes drift shut again as his hand fumbled in the pocket of his jacket for his sunglasses.

"Minimums . . . minimums . . ." over the

speaker systems. Loud. Too loud, as if someone were clapping his head between two twenty-two-inch crash cymbals. A moan escaped. He couldn't help it.

Eve swiveled to face him.

Damn.

"You aren't well," she said. "You should have told me."

He opened his mouth, tried to respond, but his words weren't cooperating.

She put her hand on his arm. She was trying to help, but it pulled his focus from managing the pain. His impulse was to shake her hand off, but he didn't. Couldn't. She wouldn't understand. It would hurt her feelings.

She was talking to him. "Can I get you something? Water? Some crackers?"

Oh shit . . . The mention of food pushed him over the edge. He yanked off the safety belt and bolted down the aisle to the bathroom at the back of the plane.

"Mr. Thomas, please, you need to be strapped in!" the steward called.

No way in hell that's going to happen. Rhys wrenched the bathroom door open, threw the toilet cover up, and spewed out the contents of his stomach while the plane's wheels hit the tarmac hard. A couple of bounces, and then gradually the plane came to a stop.

He heard the pounding of footsteps running toward him. *Great. Just what I need, the woman I'm trying to impress witnessing me doing this.*

"Rhys, are you okay?" Her hand settled on his back. The movement caused another bout of vomiting, but his stomach was empty, just dry-heaving acrid air now.

"Mr. Thomas," the steward said. "Can we get you anything? Some ginger ale? Dry crackers?"

"Does he have motion sickness? The flight was bumpy," Eve said. "Didn't seem to bother him on the way to LA, but —"

"Please . . . don't," he tried to say, "talk . . . so loud."

But they must not have heard him, or maybe he was garbling, because the steward was talking, too. "No, miss. It can't be that. According to his chart, Mr. Thomas doesn't suffer from air sickness."

"The duck, then," said Eve. "Must be that damned tin of duck we had this morning. Food poisoning. Didn't affect me, because I have a cast-iron stomach, but poor Rhys." She bent down. "So sorry it made you sick."

"Migraine," he croaked.

"Pardon?" She bent closer. "What did you say?"

"Not . . . food poisoning . . . Migraine."

"Oh!" the steward exclaimed, his voice shrill with excitement.

I aim to entertain, Rhys thought wryly as another wave of nausea overtook him.

"I should have guessed! What a dodo brain. My husband, Mike, gets them." The steward was still yammering on. "Honey, this is what you gotta do. Get that man of yours home. Tuck him in bed, shut the blinds, curtains, whatever. Main thing is to get that room dark."

"Okay," Eve said. Rhys could hear the worry in her voice. "Anything else?"

"And quiet." The steward dropped his voice to a stage whisper. "They need absolute quiet when they're like this. There's migraine medicine they can take, too. Let me text my husband and get the name of it for you. It works like a charm."

"How long will it last?"

"It's a mystery," the steward replied. "It can run the gamut — a couple of hours to a couple of days. But the medicine will help. Trust me. You want to pick some up."

Forty-Nine

She settled Rhys in his bedroom, blackout blinds down, his phone on vibrate, a glass of water and a plate of crackers on the bedside table. "Text if you need anything," she whispered so as not to jar his head. "I'll check in on you every now and then to make sure you're all right."

"Thanks," he mumbled. His thick lashes flickered open for a second. He gave a ghost of a smile, a wince, and then shut his eyes again. His breath was slow and labored.

She left the room on silent cat feet, shutting the door quietly, carefully behind her.

Once in the living room, she called Ethelwyn, explained the situation.

"No worries," Ethelwyn said in her growly voice. "We love Samson. Hell, we'd keep him full-time if we could."

"Thanks so much. I'm not sure if it'll be Maggie, Luke, or myself, but one of us will pick him up by dinnertime at the latest."

After she hung up, Eve went into the kitchen, scribbled a note for Rhys, and left it by the coffeepot so he'd be sure to see it. Then she grabbed her car keys, reset the house alarm, and slipped out the door.

Eve was pulling into the pharmacy parking lot when her phone rang. *The glories of Bluetooth,* she thought as she pressed answer. "Rhys?"

"Hmm." Maggie's familiar voice came over the speaker. "Sorry to disappoint you, but it's just the old Magster."

"Hi, Maggie." Eve's heart filled with gladness at hearing her sister's voice. "What time are you getting in?"

"Well, we got a little delayed. There was a huge lineup at the refueling station in Honolulu. Took forever to get back in the air. Anyway, I wanted to let you know, we'll be landing on Solace in around three and a half hours. I've *so* much to tell you, Eve! Luke gave me the best present *ever*!"

"Your hubby is so darn generous. What did he give you this time?" Her sister sounded good. Relaxed. Happy.

"I'm not going to tell you. I want to see your face for the big reveal. That's half the fun, but I can tell you this . . . You are *not* going to believe it!"

"Maggie, I'm *dying* of curiosity. Give me a hint at least."

"Nope," her sister said gleefully. "You're going to have to wait. Where are you, by the way? Your voice keeps disappearing on me."

"In the pharmacy parking lot."

"Figures." Maggie snorted. "Notoriously terrible cell reception there."

"Well, at least you were able to get through. Anyway, wish me luck. I'm going to try to wheedle a couple of migraine tablets out of the pharmacist. Rhys is at the house with a bad headache."

"You're by yourself?" Maggie said in a stern, lecturing tone that no little sister should ever have access to. "Eve, you really shouldn't be. Not until we figure this thing —"

"Maggie darling, I'm parked in the middle of one of Solace's most happening parking lots. I will walk into our pharmacy, be surrounded by people —"

"You don't know that."

Eve laughed. "Magpie, the *pharmacy.* Seriously. You know how many old people we have living on this island. The pharmacy is *always* hopping. Anyway, gotta get Rhys some medicine. See you soon. Love you tons." Eve made a kiss-kiss noise, disconnected the call, and exited her car.

FIFTY

A couple of hippie kids were sitting at the foot of the steps that led from the parking lot to the pharmacy and a small cluster of shops. They were strumming their guitars and singing Leonard Cohen's "Take This Waltz," their hat on the ground. They actually sounded pretty good. Looked skinny, hungry. The two of them sang so earnestly, it flashed Eve back to Levi in the early days, when music and love were enough.

So, even though she was counting her pennies, she scooped some coins from the bottom of her purse and dropped them in their hat.

The young men gave nods of thanks.

Eve nodded back, wishing she had more to give. She pushed down a nostalgic wave of sadness, for Levi and her younger self. "But he turned himself around. Got clean," she murmured as she pulled the door open and entered the pharmacy. "So that's a happy something."

The place was hopping. As luck would have it, the first person she bumped into was Rose Shumilak in her blue employee's smock, restocking the shampoos in the hair care section. She had forgotten Larry's mother was working part-time at the pharmacy to supplement her retirement income.

"Hi, Rose. Nice to see you," she said, trying for a breezy, nothing-wrong-here tone as she attempted to ease past her.

No such luck. Rose Shumilak's hand darted out faster than a snake's tongue and landed on Eve's forearm. She had a surprisingly strong grip. "He's still crying," she whispered, furtively glancing around, not wanting to be overheard. "Wouldn't touch his buttermilk pancakes, even though I made them special. You gotta let him come back." Her face was sweaty with desperation.

"He'll be back at work soon. I'm sure of it," Eve said, sending up a prayer that she wasn't lying. "If it were up to me, he wouldn't have needed to take a break. However, I'm only part-owner of the Intrepid. You know how protective Maggie's husband, Luke, is. Why, if the Blessed Mother Mary herself showed up on my doorstep, he'd need to run a security check on her before he'd let her in for tea. It's just his way."

Her words didn't seem to soothe the woman. If anything her grip tightened. "My boy got into trouble in his teens, early twenties, but you know that. Right? Larry said he'd told you."

"He did tell me. Don't worry. I'm sure it's going to be —"

"He's a good boy now. He is." The woman's eyes were filling up. "He's worked so diligently to clean up his act."

"I agree. He's a good man, hardworking, conscientious — now, if you'll just let me get by. I have to get medicine for a sick friend." Eve disengaged her arm. "Luke's going to be home this evening," she said, slipping past. "And hopefully we'll have this whole mess cleared up before Monday's workday. See you later, and please give Larry my regards." Then she headed to the back of the store to stand in line for the pharmacist.

"I'm sorry." The pharmacist did not look sorry at all; he looked like a self-satisfied automaton. "I cannot give you this migraine medicine" — he pushed the crumpled piece of paper Eve had handed him back across the countertop — "without a prescription from his doctor."

"But he can't. Get. To his doctor," Eve said, trying to keep the frustration out of her voice. "As I said before, he's from out of town. He's incapacitated." The line behind her had been steadily growing, which didn't help matters, as now she had an audience. Eve leaned in, lowered her voice. "He is really in a bad way. Perhaps you could give me one pill to help alleviate his pain enough to get him to a walk-in clinic. Then we can come back, prescription in hand . . ." Her voice petered out. The expression on the pharmacist's face was one of intractability. "Please," Eve said, hating the begging note that had crept into her voice.

"No. He's going to have to make do with over-the-counter." He looked past her to the next person in line, his fingers drumming impatiently on the counter. "Yes, Mr. Withers, what can I do for you today?"

Eve wanted to give him the finger, hoist it high. Might have when she was younger, living in the big city, even though she knew it was unfair. He couldn't help that he was an unbending marionette. The man was just doing his job.

Maggs would be proud of you for resisting, she told herself as she marched to the first aid aisle and grabbed a couple of varieties of over-the-counter headache pills. *You are a business owner. Solace Island is a small community. No telling how many potential customers the Intrepid will lose if you behave impetuously.* She pulled out her cell phone to research which over-the-counter medicine had the most positive reviews.

"Excuse me."

Someone tapped her shoulder. Eve turned. Irene Dawson was standing before her, face flushed, slightly winded. *Reminder to self,* Eve thought. *I need to stay active as I get older.*

"I'm sorry for intruding," Irene said. She seemed tentative, unsure. "But I overheard your conversation with Stanley . . ."

"Stanley?"

"The pharmacist." She shrugged a little self-consciously. "My brother. He always was a pompous rule-adhering prig. I was going to be the pharmacist. He copied me. Always had to do everything I did, but better. Then I fell in love, got married, gave up my career. Fool that I was." Storm clouds rolled across her face. "So I guess Stanley got the last laugh, because here I am holding a bag of empty promises. But that is neither here nor there," she said, looking at Eve, her head cocked to the side like an inquisitive Golden Laced Wyandotte hen. "What matters is you need migraine medicine, and I have it."

"You do?" Eve felt a lightening of her heart that this woman, whose own life was coming apart at the seams, would be so thoughtful. Would volunteer to do this random act of kindness.

Irene nodded. "I suffer from migraines myself. Horrible, debilitating things. Stanley can be such a tight-ass sometimes." She started rummaging through her purse. "I might have a spare migraine tablet in here. If not, for sure I have some at home. I live super close, three or four minutes tops. You might as well put those back." She gestured to the pill bottles in Eve's hands. "From what you told my brother, the migraine already has your friend deep in its grips. Those piddly medicines won't do the trick. Believe me."

Fifty-One

Eve eased her car to a stop behind Irene. The woman clearly had no awareness of time. The drive had taken at least twenty minutes, maybe twenty-five. Her home was in a ritzy part of the island. A lot of ta-da homes owned by part-time residents. Five-acre lots was the minimum, a way to ensure privacy for the owners. However, many homes far exceeded the required five.

Eve got out of her car. The wind had picked up and was whipping her hair around her face. She tugged her jean jacket together and fastened the bottom two buttons, a ripple of unease lifting the tiny hairs on the back of her neck. *City girl,* she scoffed. *You watched too many horror films in your youth, expecting to see some guy in a ski mask wielding a chain saw explode out of the woods.*

Still, she wouldn't have taken Mrs. Dawson up on her offer if she'd known it was this far out. Hopefully Rhys was still asleep and didn't need her.

"Brrr . . ." Irene said, all tentativeness gone. She was back to being the society butterfly. "Fall has definitely descended. Better come inside and keep warm while I get your medicine."

Eve followed her up the steps and into the living room. The home surprised her. It was super sleek and modern, floor-to-ceiling windows, the furniture low-slung, in steel gray and slate blue. A solitary white potted orchid sat in the center of a glossy black coffee table. Not at all what she would have imagined Irene Dawson's home would look like. The place was beautiful, cold though.

Eve shivered. She was glad for her jacket and found herself reaching up to skim her fingers across her grandmother's brooches. Her good-luck charms, which made her feel as if her grandmother was watching over her.

She hadn't realized when standing in the driveway at the front of the house that Mrs. Dawson's home had been built right along the cliff's edge, or how far up Mount Morden they had driven. The residence felt precariously situated, as if the smallest nudge might send it plunging over the cliff to smash on the jagged rocks far below. Just looking toward the enormous windows made her feel slightly anxious. *However,* she told herself, *the engineers must have known what they were doing and the views are drop-dead gorgeous just as long as a person isn't prone to vertigo.* She could see down the mountain, past the inner harbor to a multitude of small islands scattered like fairy dust, and the Olympic Peninsula beyond.

"What a stunning house you have," Eve said as she followed Irene through the living room to the large kitchen beyond.

"Take a seat." Irene patted one of the kitchen chairs as she passed. "I'll get you a nice refreshing glass of iced tea."

"Sorry. I can't stay," Eve said, not wanting to be rude but unwilling to get suckered into a tea party either. "I have to get back. Attend the patient."

"Sit, sit." Irene wafted a hand at Eve as she opened the fridge. "A sip of iced tea won't kill you." She laughed merrily as she removed a crystal pitcher from the fridge. "It might take me a minute to sort through my meds. I'll need to dig up my reading glasses from wherever I left them last. The print on the damn bottles is so small nowadays."

"I can come with you, read the labels if that would help?"

Irene's eyebrows shot up to greet her hairline. "Good gracious, no! Our bathroom is a mess! Absolutely not. Sit down. Have a drink. You're going to hurt my feelings."

Reluctantly, Eve lowered herself into a chair. "Okay, but I can't stay long."

"That's a good girl." Mrs. Dawson smiled approvingly at her. "Do you like sugar? A wedge of lemon?"

"No, thank you."

"Oh, come on. You're slender. You can take it. Live a little."

Eve heaved a sigh, snuck a look at her cell phone under the table. Rhys hadn't texted. He was probably still sleeping. "Sure," she said, because Irene wasn't going to take no for an answer. "Give me the works."

"The works it is," Irene sang gaily.

At least someone is happy, Eve thought, feeling a bit like Eeyore in *Winnie-the-Pooh.* She could hear the clinking of ice cubes, the sugar bowl opening, the tinkling of the teaspoon hitting the side of the glass as Irene stirred the sugar in.

Irene set the glass of iced tea in front of Eve, the sugar bowl in her other hand. "Take a taste. Let me know if you need a touch more sugar."

"Thanks," she said. The tea looked very refreshing, condensation beading and trickling down the side of the glass, the wedge of lemon among the ice. She took a sip. "No, it's perfect," she said, drinking some more.

"I grate a bit of fresh ginger into my iced tea, the juice from two lemons, drop some whole cloves in the pitcher as well," Irene said, looking pleased. "It gives it a little bite."

"Ah . . . It's quite tasty." She hadn't realized she was thirsty. Had been so busy worrying about Rhys.

Irene beamed. "I'll drop the recipe off at the Intrepid next time I'm in town." She placed the sugar bowl back on the counter. "Once Maggie tastes it, she'll love it so much she'll want to add it to the menu, and in gratitude, she'll name the tea after me!"

"Mm . . ." Eve said, lifting her glass and drinking heartily to avoid making any promises.

"Irene's Solace Sensation!" Irene said, her hands spreading in an arc before her as if creating a banner. She smiled, all teeth. "Be right back with the migraine medicine. And not to worry, the pills are individually packaged in hermetically sealed blister packs," she tossed over her shoulder as she left the room. "The company's information is printed on it, so your friend can read about it online." She was still talking even though she had disappeared from sight.

I'm glad Irene's feeling better.

Eve stifled a yawn. The sleep deprivation of the last few days must've caught up with her. She patted her hands against her cheeks in an attempt to keep alert. Her hands felt a little floppy.

I am tired, she thought. *Maybe I'll rest my eyes for a second.* Her elbows slid outward on the table, and her body pitched forward until her head was resting on her hands. *That's better.* She shifted in her chair, felt her cell phone slide off her thigh and clatter on the floor. *I'll pick it up in a minute,* she thought, another yawn overtaking her. *I need to take a little nap first, or I won't be able to drive down the mountain. Tired. So tired.*

Footsteps approached. She must have drifted off. Mrs. Dawson was returning. Eve knew she should remove herself from the kitchen table, but she felt as if she'd been filled with wet sand. Her body, her head, too heavy to lift. "Sorry," she tried to say, but her mouth was uncooperative.

"Ta-da!" Mrs. Dawson's voice sounded like it was coming through an incredibly long vacuum hose.

Eve could hear someone else entering the kitchen. From the sound of the footsteps, it was someone large and male. She felt vulnerable splayed across the table and tried to rise, but there seemed to be a disconnect between her muscles and her brain. *The tea. Must be —*

"What is it?" He sounded brusque, impatient. "You'd better have a damned good reason for interrupting me."

"A present." Irene's voice, high-pitched and filled with an anxious excitement. "I brought you a present. See?"

"Please . . . help," Eve tried to say. "She's . . . drugged me. She's crazy." But her lips weren't cooperating either.

"It's her," Irene said, reaching out, shoving Eve's hair back to reveal her face. "The slut. I brought her home for you. You happy? Say something, Timmy. Tell me you like my prezzie."

Eve heard his sharp inhalation. *He must be horrified, too.* "Please," she tried again, but only a faint moan came out.

There was silence, only the sound of him jiggling spare change in his pocket and Irene hyperventilating.

Then he chuckled, a sound of pure evil that raised the hair on the back of Eve's neck and arms. "Irene, dear one," he said, his voice almost a breath, rough with emotion. "You spoil me so."

She knew that voice. Had heard it before. *Where?* Her mind was scrambling, trying to make sense of things, but everything was jumbled, panic rising to a crescendo. *Get up!* She could feel tears sliding down her face. *Run!* But her body refused to yield to her commands.

She felt herself detach from her physical body and drift toward the ceiling, looking down as if observing a crime scene. She could see her slumped body in the chair, the top half of her sprawled across the kitchen table, convulsions rippling through her torso. She could see Irene Dawson fluttering about her husband, wringing her hands, a grotesque smile frozen on her face. She could see him moving toward her limp body, reaching out and stroking her head, softly, gently, as if she were a sleeping dog.

Fifty-Two

Reluctantly, Rhys's mind tugged him back to the land of the living. He hesitated for a second, waiting for the waves of crippling pain to crash over him. When they didn't materialize, he cautiously opened his eyes. The bedroom was dark, the shades drawn. Razor-thin lines of gray light were sneaking past the blackout blinds, so either there was dark cloud cover overhead, or it was dusk.

The pain had receded to a dull ache. Thank God. Still, he felt like he'd been run over by a Mack truck. He'd sweated through his shirt. Needed a shower.

He pushed the covers back. Swung his legs so he was sitting on the side of the bed. Knew from experience not to rise instantly. Waited for the wave of dizziness to abate.

As he waited, he became aware of a repetitive chime. He glanced over at the smart panel on the wall. Someone was at the gate.

The panel chimed again.

Whoever was there was not going away.

"I'll get it," he called, his voice rusty. He pushed to his feet. *So far so good.* Four steps to the smart panel. Didn't barf. Progress.

He tapped *front gate,* which activated the camera and intercom.

Shit. His stomach dropped. It was rarely good news when the men in blue dropped by. Although maybe they had news about Eve's break-in. "Yes? Can I help you?" The cop was backlit by the car's headlights, and it was hard to make out his face.

"Luke? It's Detective Joe Mackelwayne from Solace Island Police. We were told we could find Eve Harris at this residence. We'd like to speak with her."

"I'm a houseguest of Luke's. Hold on. I'll be right out." Rhys disconnected and ran into the hall. "Eve," he called.

Nothing.

"Eve!"

The house was silent and dark.

Shit. Shit. Shit. He had a very bad feeling in his gut. "EVE!" he bellowed, yanking open the door to her bedroom, sprinting to the living room, then the kitchen.

The smart panel chimed again. The damned cops at the gate.

He activated it. "Sorry," he said. "Be right there."

He ran outside. Her car was gone. The house alarm started chiming. *Shit.*

He backtracked, turned off the alarm, shoved on some shoes, because that gravel drive was hell on the feet. Sprinted to the gate, punched in the code, and stepped out of the way as it slowly swung inward.

He could tell by the way the two cops were standing this was not a casual call. He'd mimicked that body language during the *Stung* years. "She's not here," Rhys said. He wasn't sure what this visit was about, or why they were looking so grimfaced. Until he did, he'd keep his answers succinct.

"Do you know where she is?" Detective Joe Mackelwayne, the heavyset cop, asked.

"I don't actually."

"When do you expect her back?"

"Sorry. I can't help you. I have no idea. What's this about?"

The cops exchanged a look. "When did you last see her?" the younger cop asked, his Adam's apple bobbing.

They didn't answer his question. Not good.

"Tell you what," Rhys said. "Give me your card. When I see her next, I'll make sure to pass it on."

The older, heavyset cop's eyes narrowed slightly. "Luke or Maggie Benson home?"

"No, sir," Rhys said, keeping it polite. No sense pissing them off. "Won't be back until later tonight. But I'm happy to pass your card on to them as —"

"Wait a minute." The young cop stepped forward, his face brightening. "I know you! It's Rhys Thomas! The frikkin' movie star!" he exclaimed. "I love you, man. You're the bomb." He turned to his partner, who was looking at Rhys as if he were a bug that had just crawled over his shoe. "Joe, you seen any of the *Stung* movies? This guy's the star in it. He is a*maz*ing!" He turned back to Rhys. "Hey, man. Mind if I grab a selfie with you?"

Out came the cell phone, the arm slung around Rhys's neck. Close quarters, physical contact. It was worth another try. "So, why do you wanna talk to Eve?" Rhys asked softly, both of them looking into the cop's cell phone.

"Found a disme—"

"Ben . . ." There was a warning note in the older cop's voice.

"Joe. This is Rhys-frickin'-Thomas. He's cool. Spends half his life around cops, the FBI, CIA." He grinned at Rhys. "Gotta say, you got it down pat."

"Thanks." Rhys kept the easygoing expression on his face. "You were saying . . . ?"

The younger cop opened his mouth, but Detective Mackelwayne cut him off. "There's an incident we're checking into."

"Yeah, an incident," the younger cop said, a shadow falling across his face. Then he brightened. "Hey, I'm hanging with Rhys Thomas. It's a good day. Smile."

The cop's cell phone flashed. *Click . . . click . . . click.*

"And you want to talk to Ms. Harris because . . . ?" Rhys made sure to keep the internal tension that was coiling tighter and tighter from being outwardly visible.

"She was the last person seen . . ." the young cop said, lowering the cell phone and swiping through the photos. "Wow! These are fantastic. What a thrill running into you, dude. Here's my card. Let Ms. Harris know we'd like to talk with her. Call if you need anything, or if you'd just like to grab a few brewskis and hang out." His eyes reminded Rhys of the overeager puppy his friend Ken had snuck into their elementary school. They'd managed to keep the pup hidden until fifth period, and then all hell had broken loose.

"Will do," Rhys said, keeping his smile in place. "So, you were saying, she was the last person seen —"

"Tell Ms. Harris we need her to drop by the station." Detective Mackelwayne's voice was a brick wall as he steered the younger cop to their car.

"Okay. Thanks for dropping by." Nothing more was going to be forthcoming. Rhys activated the gate, gave a wave, maintaining his relaxed nonchalance while the gate closed, then headed to the house at a dead run.

Fifty-Three

Rhys was pulling on his coat and was half-way to his truck when his cell phone rang. His heart leapt into his throat. *Let it be Eve,* he prayed.

"Rhys? Hi. It's Maggie, Eve's sister. Is she with you? I got your number from Luke. Look, I'm sorry to bother you, but I'm kind of freaking out. I've been trying to get ahold of Eve, but she's not answering her cell phone."

"I know." Frustration was making his throat tight. "I tried calling her as well."

"So, she's not home yet?"

"No."

"Damn. I knew something was wrong. Felt it in my gut — Luke, she's not there — I spoke to her around an hour ago. She was just about to go into the pharmacy."

"The pharmacy?" Trying to push coherent reasoning through the residual dull throb from the receding migraine was making his thought process sluggish.

"To get you some migraine medicine. That was more than an hour ago. She should have returned by now. It's possible she got side-tracked, dropped into the grocery store, but why isn't she answering her cell phone?"

"I'll go to the pharmacy now. Maybe she had car trouble, a flat tire or something. Also, heads up, the police dropped by, wanting to talk with her about an 'incident.' I'm not sure what the hell that's about. Wouldn't tell me what kind of incident. Were very tight-lipped. If you could have Luke do some digging, see if he can shed some light on it. I'll let you know if I hear from her."

Fifty-Four

Eve became aware of a *drip . . . drip . . .* the sound steady and consistent as a metronome. She pried her eyes open. She felt groggy, disoriented. *Where am I?* Her eyelids were heavy, wouldn't stay ajar.

Drip . . . drip . . .

She was lying facedown, something soft against her cheek. What was it? *A bedspread, maybe?* Her eyes flickered up, then shut again. *The fabric's a pretty color, dark crimson crushed velvet. And soft, like a kitty.* She tried to stroke it, but her hand wouldn't work. It was secured to something. Both her hands were. That realization yanked her out of the drifty zone and plunged her into full-blown panic.

Her eyes snapped open.

She was on a bed, her arms over her head, her hands affixed together, and the rope was tied to the bedpost. She crawled to her knees, her legs weak and wobbly. Where her belly had been resting there was a large gold cross embroidered in the center of the crimson bedspread. A green spray of leaves and a sprig of delicate white snowdrops were interwoven over and under the cross. The handiwork was beautiful, expensive, and it made Eve feel slightly nauseous. As if God were saying, *I haven't seen you in church recently, and now look what has happened.*

Drip . . . drip . . . drip . . .

What is making that infernal noise? She jerked her gaze away from the bedspread. Hunching her shoulders, she was able to see under her arm to the room beyond. A looped black garden hose was attached to a concrete wall. It hadn't been shut off completely. *Why would someone need a hose inside?*

From what she could see, the floor, the walls, and the ceiling were all made of concrete. No windows. A lightbulb hung from the ceiling. The room was cold, damp. It felt like she was underground. Panic rose. She stuffed it down.

Where was she and how did she get there? It was as if there were a gray curtain of fog between her and her memory.

Rhys. She could remember Rhys. He was sick. Needed medicine.

Fifty-Five

Rhys pulled his truck into the pharmacy parking lot. The small town of Comfort was closing down for the night. Most of the boutique shops were already dark and locked. The pharmacy and Becca's Italian Gelato were still lit, but the neighboring storeowners had already shuttered their storefronts and gone home.

There were a few cars and trucks in the parking lot, but Eve's was nowhere to be seen.

He peeled out of the lot, the smell of burnt rubber from his back tires singeing his nostrils. He swung into the large parking lot by the grocery and liquor store.

Her car wasn't there either.

Shit! He slammed his fist on the steering wheel, a growing sense of fear and helplessness sucking the air out of his lungs, panic rising.

Think, man. Think! You are not a helpless

child anymore. This will not be a repeat of your mom. He exhaled slowly, centering himself. *Go back. Trace her steps. Maggie says she was going to the pharmacy. Start there.*

Rhys expanded the snapshot he had taken of Eve and his mom until Eve's smiling face filled the frame. His goddamned hands were shaking. "Did you happen to see this woman this afternoon?" He showed the image on his phone to the young homeless couple setting up for the night.

"No," the young woman said, eyes lowered to the blanket she was spreading on the sparse patch of green between the wall and the parking lot. As if by not looking at him, at the image on his phone, she would make herself invisible. Make him less of a threat. She could probably feel the tension pulsating off of him, no matter how much he was trying to tamp it down. Her animal instinct could tell that his adrenaline was running hot.

"Abby," the young man said, jerking his head to the side.

She dropped the blanket instantly and darted to stand behind her skinny young man, his chest thrust out, gaze hard as glass, a hunting knife suddenly appearing in his hand.

"Leave her alone."

"I mean you no harm," Rhys said, turning his hands palms-up, Eve's face on the screen of his phone glowing in the dark. "My friend is missing."

"We don't got her —"

"I didn't think you did. I'm hoping you could help. Maybe you noticed her. Saw something that triggered alarms." He took a careful step closer, the phone in his palm outstretched. "I'm worried. I think she's in danger." He took another step, slowly, as if approaching a feral dog. He was close enough now for the defiant young man to see the image. "Have you seen her? Was she by herself?"

The young man stared at him, eyes narrowed, jaw jutted out. Rhys held still. He knew he was being measured, judged, and if found wanting he would feel the sharp edge of the knife.

There was a flicker in the guy's eyes, a slight softening of the stance. He didn't relax the grip on his knife, but he glanced down. Paused. "Yeah," he said. "I saw her. She went into the pharmacy. Came out with some lady. Hopped in her car and followed her out of the lot."

"What did the other woman look like?"

"Middle-aged, stick up the ass, rich."

"Hair color? What was she wearing? What kind of car did she drive?"

"Sorry, man." The young man turned back to setting up camp. "Wasn't paying much attention. That's all I got."

"Thank you," Rhys said, setting a hundred-dollar bill on top of their backpack, which was propped against the tree. "I appreciate your help."

Fifty-Six

The lights were still on, but the pharmacy door was locked. Rhys glanced at the time. Three minutes after eight. *Damn.* He could see the staff moving around inside, an elderly woman pushing a large dust mop, the cashier closing out the till. *Is she the one who recognized me?* He couldn't tell. It had been a blur of giggling faces.

He knocked on the glass door. The occupants didn't look up. Must happen all the time. People wanting to slip in to purchase "one last thing." He knocked a little harder. The old woman straightened and looked at him.

Please, he mouthed.

She shook her head, waggling an admonishing finger at him, then pointed at the store hours that were posted on the window.

He knocked again, mimed it was urgent.

She frowned, shook her head again, then

bent to her work.

He saw the pharmacist in the back of the store, a dark overcoat slung over his arm. He must have said something to the older woman and cashier, because they both looked up and nodded, then went back to work as the pharmacist disappeared through a door.

Of course! An employees' exit. Rhys sprinted around the building. Heard a steel door slam shut. Got to the parking lot just in time to see the tall, cadaver-like pharmacist fold his body into a hybrid Camry.

"Wait!" Rhys put on a burst of speed. "Could you help me? Please!" He was almost abreast of the car when it reversed quickly and squealed out of the lot.

"Bloody drug addicts," the pharmacist yelled, shaking his fist out the window. "They should lock you up."

Rhys heard the door behind him open, along with the sound of women's voices. *Don't blow it,* he told himself as he turned to face them.

"Hi," he said.

The cashier with the ponytail glanced over. The older woman tugged on her arm. "Come on," she said.

He made his feet stay put. *Try to put them at ease. Let them know you aren't a threat.* "I was in your store a couple of days ago. Don't know if you remember me? Rhys Thomas. I'm an actor."

"Oh my goodness." The younger woman smiled and stepped toward him. "Rose, this is the movie star I was telling you about."

"I'm sorry to bother you, but my girlfriend's gone missing. She was last seen at the pharmacy." He held out his phone. "Here's a photo of her. I was hoping one of you might help me. Perhaps noticed something unusual, had some information."

"Sure." The younger woman snapped her gum. Held out her hand. "Lemme see." She looked at the photo, then shook her head. "Sorry. Don't remember her. Do you?"

She stepped back to the older woman and showed her the phone.

"Oh dear," the woman murmured.

"Did you see her?" It was an effort to keep his voice steady, calm.

"Yes," the woman said, looking shaken. "That there is Eve Harris. She was in the store this afternoon."

"Did you notice who she spoke to?"

"Well, we . . . we exchanged words," she said, her face paling.

"What about?"

"My boy, Larry. But he didn't have anything to do with her going missing. I swear.

He's a good boy. Besides, I put him on the ferry during my lunch hour. He's gone to visit my sister on the mainland. Gonna help with the yard work, clean out her gutters. Figured that was better than letting him mope around the house all weekend."

Rhys nodded. "Did you notice Eve speaking with anyone else?"

"She had a lengthy conversation with Stanley, our pharmacist."

"The young couple outside said she left with a middle-aged woman," Rhys said. "Do you have any idea who that would be?"

"I saw her talking with Irene Dawson," Larry's mother said. "Didn't notice if they left together."

"They described the woman she left with as 'middle-aged, stick up the ass, rich.' "

Both women snorted. "That would be Irene," the cashier said. "My sister had the dubious pleasure of being a server at one of her shindigs. Treated the catering staff like shit, and no tip when the evening was done."

"You know where she lives?" Rhys's heart had lodged itself in his throat.

"No." She shook her head. "Sorry."

"Perhaps you could call your sister . . ."

She shrugged. "I'll give it a go." She dug her phone out of her purse and dialed.

Rhys could hear the phone ringing, then

came the faint, "I'm unable to answer the phone right now. If you —"

The cashier hung up. "Yeah. Sorry about that. She rarely has her sound on. If you give me your cell number, I could call when —"

"Hang on," Larry's mom said, thinking hard. "I remember Larry telling me about making a big delivery at some fancy mansion on Manzanita Heights. A lot of lugging back and forth. No tip. Could have been Irene. Not sure, though. I imagine Maggie would keep a record of large delivery orders on file."

Fifty-Seven

Rhys flipped on the light, illuminating the closet that Eve had repurposed for the Intrepid office, his breathing harsh, overly loud in the small space. He strode to the metal filing cabinet next to the small desk and tugged on the handle.

It was locked.

Dammit.

He yanked the top desk drawer open only to find pencils, pens, Scotch tape. *No help there.*

The next drawer proved to be more fruitful. Large paper clips. Perfect.

Fred, the prop master on *Stung,* had shown him how to jimmy the lock on a variety of objects during the interminable hours of waiting while the sets were lit. Fred had come from a long line of locksmiths, and it had broken his pa's heart when he'd run away and joined the circus that was Hollywood.

At the time, learning how to jimmy locks had been an idle way to pass the hours, but now Rhys was grateful. "If this works, Fred my man," Rhys muttered as he prepped the paper clip, "I'm buying you that fifty-nine Chevy you were lusting after."

He carefully inserted the clip into the small round lock. His fucking hands were still shaking. *Get your shit together, Thomas. Every second you screw up is another second that asshole has her.* On the third try, the damned lock finally gave way.

He found the orders file neatly labeled and in alphabetical order. He flipped through the pages. *Bingo!* There was the information he was looking for. He pulled the order form out.

DAWSON, IRENE —
Address: 983 MANZANITA HEIGHTS.

Quiche: 1 potato-leek-bacon with Parmesan and cheddar, 1 classic, 1 goat cheese with shallot and chives.

Pies: 1 lemon-lime meringue, 1 apple, 1 peach-apricot.

Toppings: 1 qt. of lemon-drop ice cream, 1 qt. vanilla ice cream, 1 Lg. whipped brandy cream, 1 Lg. plain whipped cream.

Cookies: 3 doz. sugar cookies. 3 doz. chocolate-caramel.

*Aug 28th, 4 p.m. delivery.

Rhys plugged the address into his phone's GPS and sprinted out of the building.

Fifty-Eight

Eve managed to flip her body over and pull herself to a sitting position, using the restraint securing her hands for leverage. Her shoulder sockets ached from the maneuver, but at least she wasn't facedown and vulnerable. Her back was pressed firmly against the headboard. Yes, her hands were still tied. There was nothing she could do about that. However, sitting against the headboard instead of being sprawled in the middle of the bed had created some leeway in the restraint. She was able to move her arms.

She had a clear view of the room now. There was a shrine, a photo of her exiting the church after her sister's wedding.

She swallowed hard, her gorge rising. For months he had been there. Watching. Waiting.

She forced herself to look further. Knowledge was power. She needed to learn all she could about her abductor, and hopefully somewhere in the rubble, she would find the key to her escape.

Her pale blue sheets, stolen from her apartment, were draped across a wall. They were carefully arranged, like a work of art. The sheets were stained.

She jerked her gaze away from them, refused to contemplate what had put those stains there.

Her red scarf was lying in a silken puddle next to the framed photo. All those hours spent searching for her scarf only to come up empty-handed. Her gaze moved on, past the bar with its crystal decanters of liquor, the dark leather armchair and side table, with Levi's ukulele propped against it. *How the hell did he get that?* And then she saw her painting, her beautiful, dark, moody painting of moonlight, night sky, trees in silhouette and shadow. How had she not noticed it right off the bat, her painting hanging on the wall?

And that was the thing that undid her. That he had stolen and tainted even her art.

She clenched her eyes shut, her jaw aching as she tried to force the nausea to subside. Tremors coursed through her like BB gun pellets rattling around an old soup pot. She clutched her tied hands hard against her chest, trying to stop the ache, trying to will the shakes to stop.

Tears rose. She angrily dashed them away. "Not now," she told herself sternly, her barely there whisper sounding loud, too loud. She forced herself to take a long centering breath. *Your job,* she told herself, slowly exhaling and placing her hand over her grandmother's brooches, *is to corral all this fear that is rampaging through you and convert it into concrete action.* She could feel her heart pounding like an off-centered washing machine. She took another deep breath, filling her lungs, her fingers tracing the wings of the jeweled dragonfly. She exhaled slowly as she moved her fingers onto the diamond stem of the flower, slid them up over the leaves. So many times her fingers had traced over them, finding comfort and solace. It felt as if her grandmother's energy was flowing through them, watching over her. Keeping her safe.

From the center of the flower, her fingers started to travel outward. As always, she counted the sapphire petals, then slid her fingers underneath, exploring the bottom of the brooch. *What is hidden, kept private, is as important as what you show the world.* Her grandmother's voice echoed in her head. And that's when she snagged her finger on the sharp pin.

"That's it." Eve breathed a short prayer of thanksgiving, then unpinned her grandmother's brooches. A difficult maneuver with her wrists bound. However, she managed to detach them and tuck them into her right palm, positioned so the sharp pins were barely visible as they protruded from between her fingers.

"You're gonna get a big surprise, buddy," she said, a grim smile on her face, the brooches gripped tight in her hand.

Fifty-Nine

"She's what?" Irene Dawson stared up at him bleary-eyed. The smell of gin and Opium perfume permeated the air around her.

"Missing," Rhys repeated patiently. The temperature had dropped quite dramatically, and the wind had picked up, causing the tall trees that surrounded the house to sway and groan, small branches snapping off and plummeting to the ground.

"Oh dear." She wrung her plump, bejeweled hands, drunk and distraught. "I'm so sorry. This is very disturbing indeed. I wish I could help, but I haven't seen her."

"You were seen conversing with her at the pharmacy this afternoon."

She blinked once, twice, owl-like, her body swaying as if on a boat, her mouth slack and slightly ajar. "I was? Are you sure?"

He nodded.

"Oh my." She shook her head. "At my age the days blur together —"

He cut her off. "Another witness saw her follow you out of the parking lot in her car."

"Well . . ." She gave a slight laugh, which contradicted the tight sadness around the corners of her eyes. "I have no control over whose car exits the parking lot after mine, do I?"

Rhys didn't answer. As an actor, part of his training was to observe people, to look for and understand the subconscious clues. She was dissembling. He was sure of it.

Irene shifted, glanced to his hand on the doorframe, then back at him. "Oh, silly me." She giggled. "I just remembered. She did drop by, only for a second. It was so inconsequential, I forgot all about it. The dear girl was looking for migraine medicine." She shrugged in a bemused sort of way. "I gave her a couple of mine, and off she went, happy as a bug in a rug."

"Then you wouldn't mind if I came in, took a quick look around?"

It took only a split second for her befuddled, distressed expression to morph into something that caused the hair on his arms to rise. "Are you threatening me, young man?" Her voice was sharp, cold. Eyes suddenly lizard-like.

"Where," he bit out succinctly. "Is. She?"

"How should I know? I'm not her keeper. But she's not here." There was a hint of mockery lingering under her innocent act. "If she'd decided to stay for a visit, wouldn't her car be here?"

He hesitated.

Her lips twisted into a bitter smile. "That's right. You are barking up the wrong tree, and if you don't vacate the premises immediately, I'm calling the police."

"Do that," he replied, but it was bravado. Was it possible he'd read the signs wrong? Maybe Eve had returned home and was wondering where he was.

The door slammed shut. He heard the dead bolt being thrown. He could feel in his gut that time was running out.

Sixty

Eve heard a *snick,* possibly a key turning in a lock, then a metallic *clunk* and a *scrape,* the sort of noise a padlock makes when yanked down and removed from a locker.

There was a long *creak,* and then a waft of fresh air. Footsteps descending. They sounded heavy — it must be the man.

She was listening hard, but she couldn't tell whether he was coming down wooden stairs or a wooden ladder.

There was a slight grunt, then another *clunk.* The door had been shut, cutting off the outside world and sealing him in. With her.

Her heart thrashed in her chest like a wild bird in a cage. *Stay calm. Stay calm.* A silent incantation as she gripped her grandmother's brooches tight for courage. Her mouth was dry as chalk. *You're going to have one chance to catch him off guard. Play along until you see your opening.*

Footsteps. Leather-soled shoes. A soft tuneless whistle, more breath than sound.

Her throat constricted, as if a large hand was wrapped around it, cutting off her air.

He appeared in the doorway, at first as a hulking dark shape, and then he moved into the room. The overhead lightbulb cast shadows across his face, distorting his features, but there was no mistaking who he was.

"Eve, darling," the coffee-only customer said, holding a mangled bit of metal and glass in his hand. "I found your cell phone under the kitchen table. You must have dropped it when you were drugged. Not to worry. I've disabled it, so no one can trace you here and burst in on us at an inopportune moment." He giggled, the sound like a fistful of spiders crawling up her spine. "Sledgehammers are *so* much fun."

"I'm sorry, remind me of your name?"

His mouth tightened. "Timothy," he said as if she had disappointed him.

"Timothy," she repeated softly, trying to appeal to his human side. "Clearly you're rich and successful, have a beautiful home and a devoted wife. Don't throw it all away to fulfill some sort of misguided fantasy. I'm not for you. Let me go."

"Number one," he said, holding up a finger. "Possessing you is totally worth the risk.

If anything, the risk will heighten my satisfaction quotient. Number two —"

"You will never possess me," she said, trying to keep the shakiness from her voice. "Rhys will find me and —"

"Are you kidding?" Timothy laughed as if she had said something funny. "And how's he going to do that? Hmm? No one but my wife has ever discovered my little predilections. What makes him different from the rest of mankind? Not to mention, the chief of police and I are like *that.*" He held up two entwined fingers with a smirk. "We went to grade school together. He would never suspect me. As far as letting you go? No," he said ruefully, shaking his head. "So sorry, but I've never been one to share my belongings."

The airy way he implied she was a belonging of his made her want to punch him in the face, but she kept her expression blank.

He ambled to the desk, slipped off his gray suit jacket and draped it over the back of the chair. "By the way, speaking of . . . Rhys? Is that your *ex*-boyfriend's name?" His conciliatory tone made her want to spit. "He did drop by. My wife, bless her soul, sent him on his way." He unbuttoned the cuffs on his crisp white shirt and rolled them up. "She's useful that way. A good-looking young man. Too bad I'll have to kill him. Can't have someone asking questions, snooping around, complicating our straightforward arrangement. Anyway . . ." He smiled and spread his arms outward in a congenial manner. "Enough of the small talk. I won't bother you with the pesky details. Suffice it to say that I'll deal with him later tonight. Perhaps I'll bring you his head on a platter. A silver one! That would be fun, huh? No. Silver-plated! That would be funnier. But we'll deal with that later, the construction of our future plans." He bowed with the flourish of a Shakespearean actor. "Welcome to our humble abode, my love."

Sixty-One

Rhys turned right at the end of the long driveway, keeping the truck's high beams on. He scoured the winding mountain road for a place to park that wouldn't attract attention.

There.

The neighboring property had a fancy entryway with substantial stone gateposts. Beyond that was a turnout with additional parking for overflow. There were two beat-up cars already parked there — probably staff. He slid his truck into the vacant parking space between them, shut the engine off, and got out.

Swiftly and silently he made his way back to Irene Dawson's property. He turned left into her drive, slipping past the apocalyptic-looking gateposts, jutting jagged shards of steel thrusting upward. The full moon shined bright, like a beacon, covering the world in a silvery-blue light. The driveway was lit up like the road to Oz.

Rhys could see without the aid of a flashlight, but so could Irene if she glanced out the window. *And if I were a betting man I'd say the woman has a pistol in her bedside table,* Rhys thought as he made his way toward the house. He kept his body crouched low, using the luxuriant rhododendrons that lined the driveway as a shield.

His phone buzzed, causing an additional jolt of adrenaline to shoot through him. He stepped behind a massive Douglas fir tree, using his jacket to contain any ambient light. "Yes?"

"Luke here. We've just landed. Any word from Eve?"

"No. However, two eyewitnesses saw her leave the pharmacy with Irene Dawson. I spoke with Irene, and something's off. Eve's car isn't here, which would point to the fact that Eve already left. That's all I've got, but my gut is telling me not to leave. So I parked down the road. I'm making my way back to Irene's house to suss the situation more thoroughly."

"Good. Always listen to your gut. I believe we pick up cues intuitively that our logical mind can't absorb. Give me the address."

"It's 983 Manzanita Heights."

"We're on our way over."

Rhys slipped his phone back in his pocket, relief causing him to drop his knees to the ground. Luke was on Solace Island and was heading over. Thank God, because he was a fucking useless actor who was in way over his head. He had no idea how to find a missing person or how to keep them safe. His characters did, but that was all smoke and mirrors, with pretend weapons and pretend blood and a director to yell "cut." The real Rhys Thomas was a failure as a man. He hadn't kept his mother safe, and now history was repeating itself with Eve.

Eve. His eyes felt hot, his throat constricted. *Thank God Luke is coming.* He pushed himself to his feet and dragged his arm across his eyes to mop the salty wetness that had streaked his face. *Luke will know how to find Eve and will decimate the person who's been harassing her.*

And that's when he saw — through the gap between the rhododendron bushes — the paper-thin rectangle of shimmering light. It was around thirty yards from the house and seemed to be emanating from the forest floor.

Sixty-Two

"No. Please," Eve was sobbing, but it was to no avail. Timothy Dawson had already removed her shoes and was dragging her jeans down over her hips, exposing her pale flesh to his hungry eyes and the cold, damp air. She was trying to choke back the tears, but they wouldn't stop. The acrid taste of fear burned the back of her throat.

His cool fingers lightly skimmed her skin as he drew her pants down past her thighs, her knees, her calves, her struggling feet.

She was freaking out. Yes. But there was a part of her brain that was removed from emotion. That was coiled and waiting like a cobra for the right moment to strike.

He stood, admiring his handiwork, her jeans dangling from his fingers. "Beautiful." His eyes were glazed, eyelids at half-mast. He released her jeans, and they fell to the floor. "And now, for the pièce de résistance." He climbed onto the bed and straddled her hips, grinding his pelvis into her groin, laughing low and deep in his throat. "You're shaking like a leaf, dear one." He reached out and stroked her hair. "Don't worry. You'll experience the glory of my magnificent dick soon enough. But you're going to have to be patient." He smiled. "I want to take my time, savor possessing you." He ground his pelvis into her again. She could feel his small, rigid dick rubbing against her through his gray wool slacks. The smell of his body and his overpowering cologne were making her gag. He was sweating profusely. Dark wet patches had soaked through the fabric under his arms.

He leaned forward, covering her mouth with his wet, clammy lips, his tongue jamming against her teeth, trying to find entry but unable to. Her jaw clenched shut. His nose smashed against hers, eliminating her flow of air. She couldn't breathe.

Now, her inner voice shrieked. *Now! Slash the bastard's eyes out.* But something made her wait. She felt a better opportunity was going to present itself.

He pulled away, his hands closing around her throat, squeezing slightly. "Open your mouth," he ordered.

So she did, choking on spit and tears. And

down he swooped, his fat tongue plunging into her mouth. His hands at her throat, compressing slightly, cutting off part of her air supply.

Now? Can I do it now? Claustrophobia threatened to overwhelm her. Her body wanting, needing to vomit. But still she waited as his slimy tongue thrust in and out.

His hands left her neck and moved to her cheeks to hold her flailing head still, as his thumbs slid back and forth, gathering her tears. "That's better . . . so much better," he murmured. "When you stop fighting me, you get to enjoy so much more." He kissed the tip of her nose. Lapped the salty wetness from the corner of her eyes. "Now it's time for your panties to come off."

He swung his knee around so he was straddling her in reverse, then bent over. She felt the scrape of his chin as he gripped the silken waistband of her panties in his teeth, his wool-clad ass and package hovering around two inches above her face.

This was the blessed opening she had been praying for. She moved her tied fists to the center of her chest, pulled them in close to her body to give her strike more force. More momentum. She clenched her fingers tight together so the pins would strike true. Fear gone now, vanished like a summer squall, leaving in its place a warrior woman ready to rumble.

The dipshit started to edge her panties down.

Now! her inner voice commanded. She slammed her fists hard into his exposed groin. She could feel the brooch pins driving deep through fabric and flesh, hitting bone. She heard his high-pitched scream ricocheting off the concrete walls as he toppled off her, doubled over, and clutched his junk. An unearthly roar erupted from her mouth as she flipped onto her side. Using her bound hands as ballast, her bottom leg bent under her at a right angle to ground the weight of her body into the bed. Her other leg soared into the air, foot flexed. Then she slammed her leg down as hard and as fast as she could, her heel smashing into his head over and over, each impact accompanied with a volcanic "NO!"

Sixty-Three

Rhys tore through the underbrush at a dead run. Sometimes he could see the sliver of light and sometimes not. Every time it flickered out of sight, his chest felt like someone had kicked it hard with steel-toed boots.

There it was, almost indiscernible among the detritus of the forest floor, a camouflaged trapdoor leading into the ground. A large padlock lay open beside the door.

Whoever had her was down there now.

The faint sounds of a muffled commotion filtered out through the wood door. No time to lose. He yanked the door open, the sound of the battle bursting outward, filling the night air. No time to use the ladder, he swung his body down, dropped to the floor, and tore down the narrow, dank hallway toward the lit room beyond.

He burst into the room, squinting in the bright light, ready to tear her stalker into a million pieces. But the moment he laid eyes on her, it was clear Eve — even with her hands tied — had taken care of the problem. The guy was out cold. His body limp, his face a bloody mess, and still Eve was roaring at the top of her lungs, her leg crashing down on him, an enraged thunderbolt of fury.

"Eve. Eve, honey." Keeping his voice soothing, calming, so as not to startle her, even though he wanted to sob for joy. "You can stop now. You saved yourself. Everything's okay."

She looked up at him as if awakening from a dream. "Rhys?"

"Yeah. It's me, sweetheart," he said, going to her, gathering her in his arms. "You're safe now, you magnificent woman. He can't hurt you anymore."

And that was when the tears came, his and hers. Clinging to each other like life preservers, unable to let go.

Rhys broke the crystal decanter and used the jagged edge to free Eve's hands. He ripped strips off the sheets and made sure the assailant was securely bound, while Eve pulled on her jeans and slipped her shoes back on.

"Ready to get out of here?" he asked, holding out his hand.

Eve hadn't spoken since saying his name. She was clearly in shock. All the color had leached from her face, but she nodded and placed her hand in his. She was trembling, her teeth chattering.

He took off his jacket and wrapped it around her shoulders, rubbing his hands briskly up and down her arms and her back, attempting to warm her. Then he put his arm around her shoulders. "Let's go," he said, guiding her toward the hall.

She made a distressed noise and pulled free, running back to the bed where the guy's limp body was lying.

"Eve, what are you doing?"

She was scrabbling frantically around the bedcovers. Trying to lift the guy.

"Eve?"

"My brooches . . . my grandmother's brooches. I can't leave without them."

He was heading toward the bed to help when he heard someone descending the ladder into the bunker. *"Eve,"* he whispered.

She whirled around. "What?"

He jerked his head toward the noise, touched his fingers to his lips, then stepped back, pressed against the wall, blending in with the shadows.

Footsteps approaching. *Is another man involved?* He could hear his pulse thundering loudly in his ears.

When Irene Dawson's frumpy, floral-clad body stepped into the room, some of Rhys's tension drained away. Between Eve and him, they would be able to handle whatever this matron could throw at them.

"How dare you hurt my Timmy," Irene roared. Why was Eve looking so terrified? She could take Irene down with her little pinkie. She must be in shock.

He pushed away from the wall, took a step toward Irene, and that's when he saw the deranged smile on her face and the gun in her hand leveled on Eve. "Time to die, bitch!" Irene shrieked, the noise and her rage amplified as the sounds in the chamber bounced off all the hard surfaces. He heard the *snick* and knew exactly what had made that sound. He saw her finger tightening, starting to compress the trigger.

No time to think. No time for negotiations. A bellow erupted from his lips as he charged, trying to pull Irene's focus from her intended target.

Irene whirled. *"You,"* she spit out, her mouth twisted into a sneer.

He heard a loud *pop* a split second before he crashed into Irene. His right shoulder jerked back as if someone had slugged him hard, his forward momentum knocking both of them down, him pinning her to the ground. Burning pain sliced through his shoulder as he yanked the gun from Irene's hand and sent it skidding across the room.

"The sheets," he shouted, his voice sounding far away, odd to his ears.

Eve ran over. Strips of sheets fluttering behind her. Once she had secured Irene's hands and feet, Rhys pushed himself off the bound woman and to a sitting position.

"Goddamn you —" Irene was shrieking, writhing around. "You ruined everything! You fucking — cocksucking —"

Eve made the executive decision to apply a gag, effectively stopping the onslaught of swear words and spit.

"Good job," he murmured. He felt odd, light-headed.

Eve turned and smiled, her face radiant. "You saved my —"

He was trying to stay upright, but gravity won the battle, and the cool concrete floor rose up to greet him.

Then Eve was beside him, pressing wadded-up fabric into his shoulder, the pain making the room spin. Her other hand patted his pockets, yanked out his phone. Punching in a number. "Oh please, God, no. Honey, Rhys, sweetheart, there's no frikkin' cell service down here," she said, tears streaming down her face. She lifted his hand to his shoulder. "I need you to press here. Press hard. I have to go aboveground to call nine-one-one. I'll be right back."

He heard her run down the hall and scramble up the ladder. "Help! Please. There's been a shooting . . . The address? I . . . I don't know . . . I don't know. It's on Manzanita Heights. Left-hand side of the road, just past Cranberry Road. Long driveway. Supermodern, twisted stainless-steel gateposts. Yes! That's the one! The Dawson residence. Hurry! Please."

And then she was back, applying pressure to his shoulder, cradling his head. *If this is death,* he thought, *it's not half-bad.* Eve crooned loving words he couldn't quite make out, her blessed face like an angel gazing down on him with such love in her eyes.

The darkness at the outer edges of his vision was seeping inward. Only a pinprick of her was left. *I love you,* he mouthed before she slipped away completely. *I love you so much . . .*

Sixty-Four

Eve was pressing down on his shoulder as hard as she could, but still his blood, sticky and warm, seeped out from under the wadded-up fabric beneath her palm. Trickles of blood ran along the seams of her fingers, the curve of his biceps, staining his jacket and the concrete floor beneath him.

She heard a vehicle tear up the driveway, doors slamming, voices calling her name. "We're here!" she yelled. "Over here. Underground!" The sound of pounding feet headed their way. There was the faint wail of sirens approaching in the distance. *Thank God Irene left the trapdoor open. The light spilling out is creating a beacon for rescuers.*

"Hold on," she told Rhys. "Help's on the way." His face was pale beneath his tan, the color drained out, his lips turning a bluish tinge.

She could hear footsteps descending, running down the narrow hall.

"Eve!" Maggie burst into the room, Luke on her heels. "Thank God." Her sister flung her arms around Eve. She could feel Maggie's warm tears falling on the nape of her neck. "I was so damned scared."

Luke dropped to his knees beside her, ripped a strip of fabric off the sheets and applied a tourniquet just above the bullet wound. "Let me," he said, his voice calm, strong, as he removed her hand and took over the compression on Rhys's shoulder.

The sirens were loud piercing howls now, the emergency vehicles screeching to a halt outside.

"Be right back." Maggie pressed a kiss on her head, then disappeared down the hall and up the ladder, hollering instructions to the emergency personnel.

Sixty-Five

Sitting in the hospital waiting room, her back against the wall and her stomach in knots, Eve watched the minute hand jerk forward. "Why is it taking so long?" she murmured. "Why?" She had a death grip on Maggie's hand. "Do you think he's okay?"

"I don't know, honey," Maggie said, her eyes dark with worry. "I hope so."

"Why did he throw himself into the bullet's path? Who does that?"

"I'd take a bullet for Maggie," Luke said, "any day of the week." Luke had been a godsend in the aftermath of the abduction and rescue. By the time the paramedics had Rhys in a cervical collar and strapped to a backboard, Eve could hear the blades of the medevac helicopter Luke had arranged for overhead. When the helicopter landed, the paramedics and Luke had Rhys waiting on the circular driveway, attached to a heart monitor, two large IVs in place. The police were still drilling questions at her about all sorts of weird, unrelated topics. For a moment, it looked like they weren't going to let her travel to the hospital with Rhys, but Luke worked his magic. Promised to personally escort her to the police station for further questioning once Rhys was in the clear. On the flight to Seattle, Luke had roused his friend, who happened to be an eminent orthopedic surgeon, from her bed. By the time the helicopter landed, Dr. Shawna Soon was already at the hospital, scrubbed and ready to operate.

When Eve had thanked Luke, he'd nodded like he hadn't just moved heaven and earth. "In situations like these," he'd said, "every second counts."

Eve watched the minute hand jerk forward again. Another sixty seconds gone. Another sixty seconds slipped past. Were they the crucial sixty seconds that meant the difference between life and death?

The doors at the far end of the room swung open, and Dr. Soon stepped through, her eyes scanning the occupants in the waiting room. Eve was suddenly frozen in her chair, wanting to know yet scared to know.

Luke stood. "Doctor's here," he said, stepping forward.

The tug of Maggie's hand, her upward momentum, broke through Eve's momentary paralysis. She shot to her feet. "How is he?" she said, stepping forward, searching Dr. Soon's face for clues. The surgeon looked fatigued. Was that a bad sign?

"Rhys Thomas is a very lucky man," Dr. Soon said, a faint smile crinkling the corners of her eyes. "The bullet didn't hit bone. Missed the brachial nerve plexus by a millimeter. The axillary artery was untouched. It could have been so much worse. That being said, he's not out of the woods yet. There is always the possibility of a reactionary hemorrhage, acute myocardial infarction, pulmonary embolism, a secondary infection, fever . . ."

"But the surgery was a success?" Eve asked. "He's okay?"

Dr. Soon nodded. "Yes."

"Can we see him?"

"He's in the post-anesthesia care unit for recovery. It will be a couple of hours before you can see him. If you want to visit the cafeteria, maybe grab some breakfast. Or" — Dr. Soon glanced at Eve's and Luke's blood-caked hands and splattered clothes — "you could check into a hotel, have a shower, take a quick nap."

"Are you saying we stink?" Luke deadpanned.

"Just giving you some options, Luke," Dr. Soon said with a laugh. "Just giving you some options."

Sixty-Six

Rhys drifted in and out of a pain-fueled fog. Whenever his eyes flickered open, Eve was there, sometimes sitting in a chair beside his hospital bed, sometimes reading, sometimes not. Sometimes she would be standing, stretching her back as she gazed out the window at the bustling city beyond as the night bled into day and back into night again.

Nurses and doctors would come and go, prodding and poking, the thrum of machines by his bed beeping and spitting out data.

Sometimes her sister would be in the room and the two women would talk in quiet undertones. Other times he'd hear Luke's voice, too, gruff and steady. But it was Eve's voice that kept him tethered to the earth, as if it were an indestructible golden thread connecting his heart to hers.

"I love you," she'd whisper. "I love you so much . . ."

Sixty-Seven

Eve snapped a rubber band around the stack of twenty-dollar bills and wrote down the amount. Their monthly intake had been more than thirty percent higher. The café had been hopping. *Nothing like a couple of murders and a kidnapping to bring the customers flooding in,* she thought wryly. She paused momentarily, shut her eyes, and sent a prayer for safe travels for Levi's soul. Whenever he popped into her mind, she would do this, hoping that in some way it helped. *Poor Levi.* It didn't seem fair, cut down in his prime by a madman just as he was getting himself sorted out.

Once her prayer was finished, she slipped the various rubber-banded stacks of cash and the deposit slip into the interior compartment of her purse. She zipped her purse and shut the cash register door.

Eve closed her eyes and exhaled slowly, letting her residual sadness flow through the floorboard and into the earth below her. *Be in the now,* she reminded herself. *Be in the present. Each day is a gift to be savored.*

When she felt centered, she reopened her eyes and glanced around the room. She liked the satisfied stillness of the café, when all the customers had gone. She could feel the weight of their earnings in her purse. It was a good feeling to have the week's take tallied up, her purse stuffed full of money, both from the till and the safe in the office. The clouds had blown out and the afternoon sun had already started its descent and was partially tucked behind the roofs of the shops across the street.

She pushed through the swinging doors to the kitchen. "Be back in fifteen," she told Maggie, who was elbow-deep in pie dough. "Going to the bank." She grabbed a delicate sugar cookie to nosh on her walk. "Oh, and good news on the art front. I queried an art gallery in Seattle and they've asked to see my portfolio."

"Eve, that's wonderful," Maggie said, smiling over at her. "Hey, Luke said Art Expressions Gallery near the boardwalk is really well respected."

"Tell me about it. Any artist would be over the moon to have their art hung there. But there is no way in hell they'll take me on."

"Luke said the owner, Zelia Thompson, is really nice."

Eve laughed. "You're so cute, Maggie. I love you to bits. But the fact of the matter is, Zelia Thompson represents established artists from around the world. Some of her artists even have pieces in the Museum of Modern Art in New York. There is absolutely no way she is going to waste her gallery space on a newbie like me. Don't look so crestfallen. It's the way things are in the art world."

Eve removed her black vintage coat from the coatrack and slipped it on. "Maybe someday," she added, to cheer Maggie up. "In ten years or so, once I'm established, I can approach her, head held high. Gives me something to aim for."

A feeble ray of sun darted through the upper window, landed on her precious brooches, and created the familiar dancing rainbow flecks. "Hello, Grandmother," she whispered, running her fingers lightly over them, then pushed the door open and stepped outside.

"Beautiful day, huh?" she said, stepping around the large pile of autumn leaves that Larry was sweeping off the sidewalk in front of the café. What she really wanted to do was leap into the middle of them. Crunch them underfoot, throw huge armfuls of them into the air, and let their colored crisp beauty rain down on her.

If it had been Rhys doing the sweeping, she totally would have. It would make Rhys laugh, and then he'd join in the fun, one-armed, of course, as the other was still in a sling.

However, Larry was always so serious about doing things right. She might hurt his feelings by diving into the leaves. He'd think she was making fun of him.

"Wow. That's a huge pile of leaves," she said, taking a generous bite of her cookie. The buttery goodness crumbled in her mouth, the crunch of the sugar adding sweetness and texture. *Maggie is a cooking genius,* she thought, wishing she had grabbed another. "Good work, Larry."

He just grunted, but she could tell that he was pleased. "Gonna be an early winter," he said.

Larry was probably right about that. There was a definite chill in the air. By the time she arrived at the bank she could feel that her cheeks, nose, and ears were a bright red.

"Well, I was able to make the deposits in the Intrepid Inc. account . . ." Jennie Schmitt tapped a few more keys on her keyboard and peered over her bifocals at the screen. "However, I'm having trouble with your mortgage. Appears to be shut down or something. It won't accept payment."

"That doesn't make sense." A low-grade anxiety was starting to build in the pit of her stomach. "I know I owe hundreds of thousands of dollars. There's some sort of mistake, and it needs to be sorted out, because otherwise I'm pretty sure I'm going to be stuck with late-payment interest-rate hikes, and I can't afford any extra expenses."

Jennie held up a finger. "Can you hold on a minute? I'll talk to my supervisor," she said, pushing away from the counter.

Eve waited. She forced herself not to glance over her shoulder. She didn't want to see the disgruntled faces of the customers waiting in the teller line. The line that was considerably longer than it had been ten minutes ago. The palms of her hands were starting to feel clammy.

She glanced down. There were a few sugar cookie crumbs clinging to the breast of her coat. *Great. You're a class act, Harris,* she thought, discreetly brushing the crumbs off.

When Jennie returned a few minutes later, a middle-aged balding man in a suit accompanied her. "This is our consumer loan manager, Wayne Dabney. He's going to figure out what's going on."

"Nice to meet you, Ms. Harris," he said, shaking her hand with his smooth, squishy one. "If you would come this way?" He had a radio announcer's voice, which totally didn't match his appearance.

He led the way to a corner office in the back. "Now, let's see what's going on, shall we?" he said, settling in behind his desk. "Could I have your client card, please?"

She handed it over. He glanced at her name, his eyebrows rising. "You the Evelyn Harris that was splashed all over the news? The one involved in that sordid mess with the Dawsons?"

"I was stalked and abducted by them, if that's what you mean," she said firmly. There were some people in town who had been friends with the Dawsons for years and refused to believe the facts.

"I was on the hospital board with Irene. Played the occasional round of golf with Timothy." He shook his head. "Guess you never really know what darkness lurks inside people."

"No," Eve said, keeping her face a polite mask. "You don't."

When it was clear no salacious details were going to be forthcoming, the loan manager reluctantly swiveled his chair to face his computer and punched in her data. "Well, they are both in prison now. Hard to imagine."

Eve didn't respond. She was not interested in prolonging the conversation. The less she thought about the Dawsons the better. She just sat there with her spine ruler straight and her chin set.

Mr. Dabney read through her file. "Hmm." He leaned toward the computer screen, eyes intent, brow furrowed. "This is odd. Let me just . . ." He typed a little more.

She watched as if her focusing on him would help sort things out, the knot in her stomach intensifying with every keystroke.

"Huh." He leaned back, the chair creaking slightly, and regarded her through steepled hands. "It appears, Ms. Harris, that you paid your mortgage off."

For a split second she was tempted to say, *Thank you very much. So I did. Silly me. Bye-bye!* and scamper out of the bank, cackling like a madwoman.

Eve sighed. "No," she said, shaking the impulse from her head. "I wish I had, but I didn't. There must be some mistake. A wrong number inputted. Someone has paid off their mortgage, but it wasn't me."

Mr. Dabney rolled his chair closer to his

desk and typed a bit more. "Nope," he said, angling his computer screen so it faced her. "See right here?" He jabbed his stubby finger at the screen. "Three weeks ago. October sixteenth. Paid in full."

"Wasn't me," Eve said firmly.

"You sure?" He looked at her, mouth pursed to the side, like he was trying to figure out if she were pulling a fast one on him.

It took a great deal of self-restraint not to roll her eyes. *Hellooo? What kind of idiot pays for her mortgage in full and then forgets about it?* She nodded politely. "Yes, I'm sure."

"Okay, then. Thanks for your honesty, Ms. Harris." He quickly rotated the screen away from her, as if worried she might have a photographic memory and was memorizing secret bank stuff. "I'll . . . ahem . . . dig a little further and get back to you."

Sixty-Eight

"You are never going to guess what just happened," Eve said, unbuttoning her coat. "I was at the bank, making our deposits." She hung her coat, inhaling deeply, filling her lungs with the warm, cozy smell of home baking that permeated the place. Her stomach grumbled, so she ambled over and leaned against the counter by Maggie, snagged another sugar cookie and bit into it. "Mm . . . so good. I could eat these delectable bits of tasty goodness until the cows come home." She paused. "What does that mean, 'until the cows come home'? Seriously. Is that supposed to imply that the cows never come home of their own free will? That you have to go out and get them? Or does it mean that the cows come home when the sun sets? Meaning I could eat these cookies until nightfall?"

Maggie didn't bother commenting, just smiled softly and kept rolling her pie crusts.

A wave of sisterly affection rushed over Eve. She flung an arm around her sister's shoulders. "I love you so much, Maggs," she said, then released her quickly, because Maggie had a certain rhythm she liked to get into with her cooking, and it was best not to disturb it. Eve took another bite of her cookie. "So, I tried to make the payment on my mortgage and . . . Now, hold on to your hat, Maggie, because this is the funny part. They wouldn't let me." She laughed. "Some computer glitch. Thought I'd already paid the thing in full. I have to admit I was sorely tempted not to correct their mistake. But then I worried that someone else had scrimped and saved, or perhaps they'd received an inheritance, thought they'd gotten the old debt monkey off their back. Couldn't do it. Damned morals!" She laughed again and popped the last bit of cookie into her mouth. "Anyway . . ." She turned and looked at her sister, who was standing stock-still, hand to her mouth. Clearly Maggie was in total shock. The expression on her face was so funny. "I know," Eve said, shaking her head. "It's hard to believe, but I do have them. Morals, that is."

"Eve," Maggie croaked, carefully placing her rolling pin down. "We need to talk." She took Eve's hand with her floury one and led her over to the faded celadon sofa against the back wall.

"What is it? Is everything okay? You look so serious."

Maggie looked down at their clasped hands. "Eve," she said, her voice tentative. "Remember how Great-Aunt Clare left me her estate?"

"Yeah." Eve swallowed, but the clogged feeling in her throat didn't abate.

"Didn't you ever wonder why she left everything to me?" Maggie's gaze rose from their hands to her face. She looked troubled.

"Well, she liked you best." Eve patted her sister's hand, prevaricating. "You were such a sweetheart of a child, with sturdy little legs, rosy cheeks, and lungs louder than a foghorn. Who wouldn't love you? It didn't bother me one bit that she gave it all —"

"Eve . . ." Maggie blew out a long, slow breath, as if she was bracing herself for something. "I was actually her biological daughter." Maggie's eyes filled up. "I didn't know. I swear to you." Words tumbled out now. "I wasn't trying to pull the wool over your eyes. I didn't find out until last year, when I had my stuff moved to Solace. I was sorting through old boxes and I came across a copy of her will. It was in a sealed envelope. I'd never opened it. I mean, why would I? Mom and Dad handled it all. I was practically just a kid when she died."

She was crying hard now. Eve rubbed slow circles on her sister's back, trying to sort out what to say.

"Maggie, it's okay."

"No, it's not. And I wanted to tell you. Truly, I did. But I was scared, too. Worried that you wouldn't want to be my sister anymore."

"Maggie, you *are* my sister. You'll always be my sister."

"It was a horrible feeling to have my whole sense of self — of who I thought I was — ripped away. All these years I never understood why she left everything to me and nothing to you. The guilt was overwhelming at times. I was worried that deep down you'd resent me for it."

"Maggie, honey, I'd never resent you for it. I kn—"

"Eve, please." Maggie interrupted, holding up a hand, her face tear-streaked. "I need to get this out. Then you can talk. Okay?" She blew out a breath. "So, that's why — when we were holidaying at Laucala and Luke asked me what I wanted most in the world — I told him about Great-Aunt Clare, and about you. The guilt I felt. The stress you've been under trying to pay your mortgage. And so he paid off the remainder of your mortgage."

"Wha . . . ?" Eve felt as if she'd been hit over the head with a two-by-four. "I . . . I don't understand."

"We paid off your debt. You have a clean slate, Eve!" Maggie's tearstained face glowed so brightly, it was as if the moon had taken up residence.

"Maggie, honey," Eve said, trying to find the right words. "That's so sweet of you to even think to do that. I am so moved." *Humbled, actually.*

"Don't say 'but,' " Maggie wailed.

"But I . . . I can't accept." She felt shaky, overwhelmed. "It's my debt, Maggie. I took it on. I just . . . I wouldn't feel comfortable letting Luke pay my mortgage."

"He's a multi-*multi*millionaire, Eve!" Maggie's hands rose to Eve's shoulders, attempting to shake sense into her. "It's a minuscule amount to him."

"But it's not to me."

"Anyway," Maggie said quickly. "The money wasn't from him. It was from me. It was his gift to me. You have to let me do this, Eve. Please."

"First off." Eve wiped her eyes with the back of her hand, then gently removed her sister's hands from her shoulders and clasped them in front of her, holding tight and gathering the words she wanted to say. "There is no reason for you to feel guilty about Great-Aunt Clare's estate. I knew why she'd left everything to you."

Maggie studied her face. Eve could see the inklings of cautious hope dawning in Maggie's eyes. "You did?"

"I've known she was your birth mother for years."

"You have?"

Eve nodded, glad that she was finally able to talk about it, but cautious, too. "Do you remember the summer there was a terrible heat wave? You were eight and a half and I was almost twelve. Grandmother had rented a beach house for the summer."

"Great-Aunt Clare was there. Mom was, too. Was Dad there? He must have been."

"No. Dad had to stay in town on the job, and it was too far for him to drive back and forth on the weekends. He missed us something fierce." Eve glanced down at their interlocked hands, shoring her strength, hoping that Maggie wouldn't be mad that she'd kept something so important a secret. "I woke up one night, and Mom and Great-Aunt Clare were arguing. That's how I found out. Grandmother found me at the top of the stairs crying."

"You've known for" — Eve could see Maggie doing the math in her head — "nearly twenty years?"

Eve nodded. She could feel the prickles of heat rising up her neck, flooding her face.

"Why didn't you tell me?" Maggie said. Her face was usually so easy to read, but in this instance Eve had no idea what she was thinking. Was Maggie feeling angry and betrayed, outraged, or simply sad and disappointed in her?

"Grandmother made me promise not to," Eve said softly. "You were such a happy child, so secure in your place. I'd always protected you, looked out for you. I didn't want anything to ever cause you harm. You were — and always will be — the sister of my heart."

Maggie was silent, digesting what she had just heard. Eve knew there were a million thoughts churning through her sister's head.

"So," Maggie said slowly. "You say I'm the sister of your heart . . ."

"You are," Eve said, suddenly feeling fierce. No one, not even Maggie herself, was going to take away her sister. "Absolutely, one hundred percent."

"Does family help family?"

"Of course. I'll always be there for you, Maggs, no matter what. You know that."

"So, this whole Great-Aunt Clare thing doesn't change anything? I'm family?"

"Yes!" What the hell was Maggie getting at?

Maggie nodded decisively and stood, smacking her hands together, sending little dust clouds of flour swirling into the air. "Great. I'm glad we got that sorted out. As family, I claim my familial prerogative to help you out, aka, dispense with your pesky mortgage." A triumphant smirk appeared on her face.

"Maggie . . ." Eve protested weakly.

"Am I your sister or am I not!" Maggie demanded, tipping her nose in the air imperiously.

"You are. You know you are." When had her sister become this fierce, tricky Amazon queen?

"Good. Then our problem is solved. Your mortgage and line of credit have been paid in full. I don't want to hear another word about it!" With that final pronouncement, she marched over to the counter and returned to rolling out pie dough, humming happily to herself.

Sixty-Nine

Rhys heard the clatter of Eve's feet racing up the metal stairs leading to her apartment above the café. He quickly rolled up the brochure he'd been reading, threw himself on the sofa, sliding the leaflet under the pillow beneath his head.

Eve burst into the living room, the door slamming shut behind her. "You are never going to guess," she said, her face glowing, "what just happened to me!" She laughed breathlessly. "Goodness, I hardly believe it myself." She spun in a circle, hugging herself, then flopped on the sofa beside him.

Luckily, I have good reflexes, Rhys thought as he uncurled his legs and draped his knees comfortably over Eve's warm thighs.

"Maggie knew!" Eve exclaimed. "She found the old will buried in a box. She *knew*! She's still my sister. Oh, Rhys, I'm so happy I could spit!" She flung herself on him, careful not to jostle his shoulder as she hugged him fiercely.

He wrapped his good arm around her, breathing her in with all his senses. Rhys wasn't sure what it was Maggie *knew* about, but it was important to Eve, so it mattered to him. And whatever it was, it was more important than dealing with the ever-ready erection that always seemed to arise when she was in close proximity. "That's wonderful," he said.

"Not only that, but she paid off my *mortgage,* Rhys. My mortgage *and* my line of credit!" She was excited, her words tumbling over one another like a basket of kittens. "She wouldn't take no for an answer. I tried, Rhys. I really tried. I'm her big sister." She bumped her fist on her chest. "I'm supposed to take care of *her.* But she insisted. Trapped me with that interminable logic of hers. Refusing her gift wasn't an option."

She sat up, her gaze flying around the living room with unseeing eyes, her hand rising to her mouth. He wanted to kiss the slight tremble from her lips, but that would need to wait, too.

"Oh, Rhys." She shook her head. "I can't believe it. My crushing, suffocating, overwhelming debt has been wiped clean, and I . . ." She had the stunned look of a child whose first tooth had been yanked out. "I . . . I just feel so damn grateful . . . but guilty, too. I don't want to take advantage of her good nature . . . her good fortune. Yet she wouldn't *let* me say no. Oh God, Rhys, I love her *so* much —" And then no more words were able to come out because she was sobbing too hard.

He held her, his heart and arms full of the most remarkable woman he'd ever met. He held her and let her cry and then laugh and then cry again.

He wondered for a second if perhaps she was pregnant, with her emotions seeming to swing from one extreme to another. He was shocked to realize that if she was indeed carrying his child, it wouldn't freak him out. The idea of having a child with her actually caused a warm glow to take up residence in his chest.

After she had run the gamut of emotions, he made her a pot of Darjeeling tea and set her favorite teacup on the table. The teacup was a delicate bit of whimsy. With a pale robin's-egg blue exterior, white interior, and the rim and dainty handle, gold.

That teacup was imbued with magical properties. It never failed to shore Eve up and had gotten a lot of use since they had arrived back from the hospital. He could tell when she was thinking about Levi or the events in the underground bunker because she'd march to their little kitchen area. Out would come the pot of Darjeeling, her favorite teacup, and his mug. He'd drop whatever he was doing, and they'd sit at her small Formica table from the forties and sip tea, holding hands. Sometimes they'd talk, and sometimes they'd be silent, letting the warm liquid and the delicate, slightly flowery scent of the tea wrap around them and soothe their jangly senses.

When the Darjeeling was sufficiently brewed, Rhys poured some in her cup, added a half teaspoon of sugar, and handed it to her.

"Thanks," she said, smiling at him. Her eyes were puffy and pink from all the weeping. Her nose was red, and her hair was falling out of its tortoiseshell clasp.

I've got it bad, he thought, smiling to himself, because she'd never looked more beautiful.

SEVENTY

Eve's throat was getting sore, her voice rocking a huskiness that it sometimes got when she'd been overenthusiastic at a concert or was recovering from a cold.

She'd talked long into the evening, told Rhys all about their Great-Aunt Clare, that long-ago summer when her life had tilted on its axis. She told him about her brooches, their significance in her life. How she'd used them to stop her attacker and how it had felt as if her grandmother were there, fighting alongside her. She'd told him about Maggie, too. And as she spoke, the burden of that secret gently detached itself from her shoulders and floated up and out the window like a helium balloon.

Finally, hunger forced its way through the deluge of memories, their stomachs growling like ravenous beasts. It was after eleven o'clock, so going out for dinner wasn't an option. The restaurants in Comfort had closed hours ago. Even the kitchen at Toby's Pub was locked down by ten.

"Wait," Eve said, remembering the pies Maggie had been rolling out that afternoon. "Come on." She tugged his hand. Out the door they went, the night air cold and crisp, the crescent moon high in the sky, their bodies wrapped around each other for warmth as they dashed down the metal open-rung stairs. Neither of them had bothered with a coat.

She unlocked the door, flipped on the lights, both of them blinking for a moment under the bright fluorescents.

"Right," she said. "Let's see what we have." She strode over to the fridge and swung the door open. "Hmm . . . Looks like some kind of berry and . . . apricot-apple maybe. Not sure."

"Let's try the mystery pie," Rhys said, switching on the oven. "I love how fast these industrial ovens heat. We're going to have to get one installed at our place."

Eve laughed. "Honey," she said, picking up the pie and swinging the fridge door shut with her hip. "I hate to break it to you, but there is no way one of these monsters is going to fit in my little apartment." She put the pie on the counter and removed the plastic wrap.

"What?" she said, because he had gone still. "You okay?"

He blinked, looking a bit dazed. "I can't believe I forgot," he said, a slight smile tugging the corners of his lips.

"Forgot what?"

"Hold on one second," he said, his index finger rising into the air, and then he was gone.

He returned a couple of minutes later, the night air rushing in with him. He carried rolled papers in his hand. "All right, now, don't freak out. I don't want you to feel any pressure whatsoever . . ." He ran his hand through his hair, rumpling it even more. "But I went house hunting today."

"You went what?" she squeaked.

"I know. It was ballsy of me. We haven't discussed me moving here. But in my defense, I was just kicking tires. I was bored being laid up with this stupid shoulder, unable to help, listening to the hustle and bustle down below. I thought it would be fun to look at some real estate. What I didn't expect was to find a home that I totally love . . ."

"Rhys, you live in Los Angeles."

"I don't have to. I'm at the point in my career where I can live anywhere I like."

Her mind was spinning. *Rhys might buy a*

home here? There's a possibility this could become more than a short-term fling?

"I could totally make it work. It's easy to fly down and visit my mom. The jobs come to me . . ." The indigo blue in his eyes was almost black with suppressed emotion, his face wide open and vulnerable. *This must be what he looked like as a boy,* she thought. *Before life knocked him around.*

"Now, I am fully aware" — he was pacing now and wringing the hell out of the papers in his hands — "that you might not feel ready to move in together . . ."

Move in together!

"But I want you to know I am committed to you one hundred percent. I'm willing to wait for you, to do whatever it takes for you to feel comfortable."

The oven *ding*ed. He laid the crumpled papers on the counter and smoothed them out. "Here's the brochure for the house." He shrugged like it was no big deal, but she could tell that it was. "No pressure," he tossed over his shoulder as he strode to the oven and put the pie in. "Just something to consider." He shut the oven door and turned to face her, nervous tension tightening the corners of his eyes. "I know we've got brunch scheduled at Luke and Maggie's tomorrow, but I was hoping you'd be willing to swing by the property with me beforehand. Take a look at the place, give me your thoughts?"

"Rhys," she said, going to him, sliding her hands around his waist and leaning in. His heart was pounding against her cheek. "I would love to check out the house with you."

She felt him exhale, the tension leaving his body with her touch. His arm wrapped around her tightly as he pressed a gentle kiss on the top of her bowed head. "Thanks." His voice, his warm breath, felt like a blessing alighting and dropping into her heart.

SEVENTY-ONE

Eve hovered on that delicious precipice between consciousness and sleep, her head nestled on Rhys's chest in the slight dip between his pectoral and biceps, her thigh flung over his thighs. She smiled sleepily, her fingers gliding through the pale golden hairs that were lightly scattered on his chest.

Sometimes, lying in his arms, she wondered if God had been taking a coffee break from dealing with all the war and heartache and pestilence and had looked down and seen Rhys and her bumping around, lost, lonely. If God had said to himself, *Look at these two people, both good-hearted and kind, perfectly suited. I wonder what would happen if I . . .* Was that how Rhys had been plucked from his movie set and plopped next to her in Luke and Maggie's house?

Eve smiled. *I'll never know, I guess.* What she did know was all the darkness they had just battled through had made the sacred nectar of life so much sweeter.

Rhys loved her. He was thinking of putting down roots on Solace Island.

She snuggled in closer, breathing in the good, clean smell of him. She turned her head slightly and tasted the faint saltiness of his skin.

"Hey, now," he said, his voice a low rumble under her ear. She felt his flaccid penis start to stir under her thigh.

"You gotta be kidding me," she said, a hint of laughter in her voice. "We just finished up." She reached down between his legs and nestled his penis in her hand. "Don't get hard, okay?"

"Impossible not to when you've got your hands on me."

"But I'm just cupping gently. Not doing anything fancy. Don't get me wrong. I love it when you're hot and hard and ready to go."

"Woman," he groaned, his cock swelling a little more. "You're killing me."

"But I also enjoy holding you like this. After we've made love, when it's soft and wee —"

"My mighty, massive penis is *not* wee," he said in mock outrage, his voice dropping an octave.

"You know what I mean," she said, chuckling softly. "When it's like this, it seems even more intimate than the other somehow. Vulnerable." She kissed his chest. "Sweet." She kissed him again. "Trusting." She slid her hand down to cup his balls — they were warm and heavy in her hand — then moved back up to hold his cock. "Oopsie."

He was fully erect now. She hadn't meant to awaken the beast, but clearly she had. "I have to confess, Rhys, I do love having you in my bed. My own private furnace keeping the autumn chill at bay."

She felt him shift as his arm reached out, heard a foil pack ripping. She smiled. "I love how our bodies fit together. I love the sleepy aftermath of our sweet, tender lovemaking. I love that today was a day well spent."

"And *I* love *you,*" Rhys said, his large warm body now on top of her, gazing into her eyes. She could feel the heat and the taut, swollen head of his thick cock nudging past the slick wet folds that guarded the entrance to her core. "My God, Eve," he said as he pushed into her, his expression fierce and tender. "I love you so damned much."

Much later, drifting in and out of sleep, Rhys's finger lightly traveling the length of her spine, Eve thought she heard him murmur something about getting married . . .

little children tumbling around their house . . . But she wasn't sure. It could have been part of a dream.

Seventy-Two

The Realtor had done most of the talking on the ride over. Rhys and Eve were tucked into the back seat of the Realtor's silver Range Rover, both of them still groggy with sleep. Eve took a bracing sip of her coffee, enjoying the earthy, rich flavor, the hint of smooth chocolate providing contrast for the bitter hot liquid. Fragrant steam rose like a misty belly dancer, undulating, leaving in its wake minuscule droplets of moisture on her upper lip and around her nose.

She passed the mug to Rhys, who took a large slug, then handed it back. His long fingers skimmed hers in the handoff, causing warmth to pool in her abdomen.

She still couldn't wrap her mind around the fact that he was considering making Solace Island his home.

"Here we are," the Realtor said, pulling into a driveway.

Rhys's hand tightened around hers.

The Realtor lowered his window and punched a code into the keypad, and the gorgeous wrought-iron gate with the large bronze sun at its center swung open.

"There were bigger homes," Rhys said, keeping his words soft, meant only for her ears. "More impressive ones, with all the bells and whistles. I saw a spectacular waterfront mansion with a walk-on beach, but . . . I don't know, Eve . . . This one called to me. There was a sweetness about it that reminds me of you."

"Twenty acres, around two-thirds of it pristine first-growth forest, with your own private trails to hike," the Realtor said, gesturing to the majestic woodland they were driving through.

"Rhys," Eve whispered, tingles running through her. "It's gorgeous."

"There's a gate at the end of the trail," the Realtor continued, "on the south side of the property. It leads to parkland and a huge network of trails. The property used to belong to Rebecca S. Flynn, the author of the renowned Rabbity-Tabbity books."

"Oh my gosh. Rhys, I loved those books growing up! They were my favorites. Daddy read them to me so many times that he joked he didn't even have to look at the pages anymore. I love her. I can't believe we get to see where she lived."

"Well," the Realtor said, his eyes twinkling in the rearview mirror, "she wrote those books right here on this land, a lifelong Solace Island resident."

"I had no idea she . . ." And then words failed Eve because the vehicle had come out of the woods, and ahead, nestled in the crest of a rolling hill of fragrant meadow, was the most beautiful home she had ever laid eyes on. Gray cedar shingles, with cheery white trim around the windows and doors, lots of windows to let in the light. It had one of those thick cedar shake roofs, a chimney, which meant a cozy fireplace, and a cupola with a series of small square windows, which added whimsy to the exterior and more light. There was a wide welcoming covered porch that would offer shade during hot summer afternoons. "Oh, Rhys," she murmured. "It is absolutely the most perfect house."

He laughed low in his throat. "But you haven't even stepped out of the car."

I don't need to, she thought. *I already know.*

The Realtor pulled up to the front of the house, and they got out, the pea gravel crunching underfoot. "I'll open the door," the Realtor said, heading down the flagstone walkway lined with flowerbeds and mature rhododendrons, "turn on a few lights, and let you wander."

"Over there by the garage," Rhys said, "there is a peach tree that apparently has the sweetest and juiciest peaches on the island." He gestured toward a fenced garden area. "There are also a couple of apple trees, a pear tree, and an Italian plum tree. And if you follow that path there, it winds back through the woods to another little clearing, and there's a gorgeous studio. It's where Rebecca wrote. There are skylights and huge windows, tons of light. When I stepped into that studio, I could see you there. Literally. It was like for a split second I could see the future. I saw you painting. You had music blaring, and the rain was thundering down. I could feel the creativity pouring out of you. You seemed so content, unfettered, and that's when I knew for certain that I should make an offer on this house . . . Oh dear . . ." He pulled her into a one-armed hug, his chin resting on her head. He exhaled shakily. "Damn. I wasn't going to tell you that. Look, Eve, we don't have to do this. I haven't signed the contract. It was just an idea. Don't cry, sweetheart. Please. Don't cry."

"I'm not crying because of that, you goofball," she said, whacking him on the chest.

"I'm crying because I'm so damned happy. I *love* this home." She leaned back, tipping her head up so she could see his beloved face more clearly. "It's the most beautiful place I have ever seen in my life. It's the dream home I never knew to dream. But what *makes* this place so magical is the idea of you and me at the center of it. Because where *I'm* the happiest, where I feel the *most* at home, is when I'm with *you.*" She took a deep breath, centering herself. "So, yes, Rhys," she said softly, her heart overflowing, reflecting back the love she could see radiating from his deep blue eyes. "I would be honored to create a life with you. Be it here, at my apartment in town, or even in LA. I love you, Rhys Thomas. You are the magic at the end of my rainbow."

Seventy-Three

"You all right?" Eve asked as she turned her car onto Sunset Drive. Rhys had been a little quiet on the ride over.

"Sure," Rhys said, but there was a slight hesitation before he answered. A minuscule one, but Eve caught it.

She glanced over. He smiled at her reassuringly, but she could see strain lurking just under his skin. They were only a couple of minutes from Maggie and Luke's home. If something was bothering him, it was best to get it sorted out before they arrived.

Eve swung the car into a turnout, switched off the engine, and turned to face him.

"What's going on?" she asked.

"Nothing," he said. "Truly."

"Rhys, I know you better than that. Look, if you're having second thoughts about the house, moving in together . . ."

"God no." He looked a little indignant. "Absolutely not. It isn't that."

"Then what?"

He stared out the windshield. Sighed deeply, his cheeks puffing out and then deflating again. "I'm . . ." He cleared his throat. "A little nervous." His eyes shut briefly as if the admission pained him.

"Of what?"

"Meeting your sister."

"My sister? Rhys, that's crazy," Eve said, relief rushing through her. "Maggie is the sweetest person in the whole world."

"I'm sure she is. That's not what's worrying me."

"Besides, you've already met her. She was at the hospital with me."

"Doesn't count. I was delirious, all hopped up on painkillers. She couldn't tell if I was a nice guy or a dickhead. Wouldn't know if I was worthy of you or if I could string a coherent sentence together."

Eve would have laughed if he hadn't looked so distraught. The idea of Rhys being apprehensive about meeting Maggie blew her mind. "Rhys, you're talking crazy talk. She's gonna —"

"I know it's crazy. Hell, I have to meet people all the time. Famous actors, rock stars, directors, studio heads, dinner at the White House. I've even met the Queen of England, for crying out loud. No problem.

Gave them all the old razzle-dazzle. Any nerves? Nah. Not really. At least not on the scale of this . . ."

She opened her mouth, but he kept talking.

"Eve, I know how important your sister is to you. And if she doesn't like me, I'm well and truly screwed."

"Rhys," Eve said, placing her fingertips against his lips to stop the torrent of tortured words that were spilling out. She slid her hands outward to cradle his beloved face. "It's going to be fine. You'll see." She kissed him gently, then pulled back so she could gaze into his beautiful blue eyes. "You have *nothing* to worry about. I am *so* proud to introduce you to my sister. I am looking forward to the pleasure of you meeting my parents someday, too, because I *know,* one hundred percent, they *all* are going to *adore* you."

"You sure?" His face was still a little pale and the look in his eyes so vulnerable.

"I'm positive," she said softly.

He must have felt her absolute conviction, because some of the tension left his body. He exhaled slowly. "All right, then," he said, squaring his shoulders and facing forward once again. "Let's get this show on the road."

■ ■ ■ ■

Brunch was amazing. Maggie had outdone herself. Eve had eaten way more than she should have, but she'd worn a long sweater and was able to discreetly undo the top button of her jeans. After everyone had eaten their fill, the dishes had been plopped in the dishwasher. The pans were soaking in water waiting to be washed. And yet they were having such a good time they were reluctant to leave the table. So they lingered, enjoying the November sunshine that was slanting through the windows. With winter closing in fast, they knew to relish the light and warmth as heavy wind and rain could sweep in at any moment. Sipping mugs of café mocha with generous dollops of Kahlúa, whipped cream, and shaved chocolate on the top, they sat savoring the contented aftermath of a delicious meal, family and friendship, love and laughter.

"All right. I've got one. We were shooting in the south of France," Rhys said with a grin.

Maggie reached over and squeezed Eve's hand. *I love him,* she mouthed. *He's your perfect match.*

I know, Eve mouthed back. *I am so damned lucky.*

"The cast," Rhys was saying, "and some of the key members of the crew were staying at this gorgeous, *very* posh old hotel. Summer. Hot as hell. We'd been shooting outside, baking under the sun all day. We entered the grand lobby of the hotel. We weren't looking for trouble. All we wanted to do was stagger upstairs and collapse face-first onto our beds. Several members of the crew were dressed for the heat, wearing shorts and T-shirts.

" 'I'm sorry, sirs!' the manager said indignantly, hustling over. He was an old guy, but boy he could move fast. 'We have a very strict policy. No shorts allowed!'

" 'Right,' Alwyn, the sound mixer, said. He was Welsh and had a wicked sense of humor. 'A trifle inconvenient, but rules are rules and must be obeyed.' He dropped his shorts and continued up the staircase bare-assed naked. Of course the others thought this was great fun. Off came their shorts, too. A great contingent of large-bellied, hairy-assed men marching naked up the grand staircase of that fancy hotel . . ."

Luke busted out laughing, shaking his head as if trying to dislodge the unwanted image from his mind. Maggie was laughing, too. Laughed so hard she needed to wipe her eyes. And there was Rhys, tipped back in his chair. He gave Eve a wink, a cocky grin on his face. He looked so pleased and relaxed and happy.

"Did you?" Eve asked.

"No!" Rhys was pretending to be shocked, but the twinkle in his eyes laid waste to the pompous, dignified expression he had settled upon his face. "I was wearing trousers. My goodness, woman, what a wild imagination you have."

"You goofball," she said, still chuckling.

"*Your* goofball," he said, capturing her hand in his, lifting it to his mouth, and dropping a gentle kiss on her knuckles.

"I love you so much," she whispered, her heart full.

"Love you, too," he replied.

My dear readers,

I grew up in a large family. Our mom somehow managed to support all of us children on her teacher's salary. My stepfather had worked sporadically for the first two years of their marriage, but after that it all rested on our mom's shoulders. We had to be very careful and manage money wisely to make sure there was food to last us to the end of the month. Therefore, there was no money for restaurants, fancy boxed cake mixes, store-bought candy, sugar cereals, potato chips, or things like that. If we wanted candy, cookies, or cakes and such, we had to figure out how to make them ourselves.

I was four years old when I attempted my first cake. It came out of the oven looking more like a large cookie instead. A very hard cookie. We had to break it with a hammer. I managed to eat some of it, but it was hard on the jaws. My brothers and sisters were laughing their guts out. They thought it was funny. Me? Not so much. I remember staring at my toes, feeling embarrassed. I had been so proud that I was baking and wanted it to be good.

As the years passed, I got more proficient in the kitchen. When I was six, my little sister and I were responsible for making all the school lunches — and also for keeping the family bathroom clean. Yes, "bathroom," as in singular. There was only one bathroom for seven children and two adults! At age seven I graduated to breakfasts. At age eight another baby arrived, along with more chores and another mouth to feed.

In the beginning, I stuck with recipes. Checking them over and over to make sure I didn't make mistakes. As I got older I found I liked to mix things up, became more of a free-flowing cook. I find it fun to figure out how to make exactly what my taste buds feel like eating.

The following oatmeal cookie recipe is one that I've continuously morphed and changed over the years to make what I think of as the perfect oatmeal cookie. Crisp, with a slightly soft inside, a tasty treat, and not too sweet. Seriously, when I bake these cookies I'm in trouble, because if they are sitting on the counter, I can't help but eat them all.

When I mention Maggie's oatmeal cookies in this novel, these are the ones I am describing. It's my recipe, and I am *so* happy to share with you a tasty treat from the Intrepid Café!

THE INTREPID CAFÉ'S DELICIOUS OATMEAL COOKIES

Ingredients:

1 cup salted butter, softened
1/2 cup granulated sugar
3/4 cup light brown sugar
1 teaspoon vanilla
1 egg
1/4 cup raw almonds
1/2 cup pecans
1 1/2 cups unbleached white flour
1 1/2 cups old-fashioned oatmeal (don't use "instant" or "quick")
1 teaspoon baking soda
1/2 teaspoon salt
2 slightly rounded teaspoons cinnamon
5 to 8 shakes nutmeg (depending on your preference)
3/4 cup to 1 cup raisins (depending on your preference)

Preheat oven to 375 degrees Fahrenheit. (If you have a convection oven, you can use it to make the cookie edges even crispier.)

Mix together the butter, both sugars, vanilla, and egg. Using a blender, combine the almonds and pecans. Zap the nuts until they are around the size of barley. (If you have one of those pain-in-the-ass blenders with a million parts that take forever to clean, then you can just mince with a good old-fashioned large knife on a cutting board.) Add mixed nuts to the butter mixture and stir.

In a separate bowl, combine the flour, oatmeal, baking soda, salt, cinnamon, and nutmeg. Then blend the dry ingredients into the butter mixture. When it's completely blended, sprinkle in the raisins. (You could forgo the raisins altogether, leave out the cinnamon and nutmeg, and stir in a cup of semisweet chocolate chips. Personally, I prefer raisins. However, that's the joy of being the cook. You get to decide these things.)

Mix in the raisins (or chocolate chips) so they are evenly spread throughout the dough, then drop rounded teaspoons of the cookie dough onto a greased pan (greased with butter of course!). Smoosh the rounded balls slightly with the palm of your hand and bake for 8–12 minutes. (The time all depends on how hot your oven runs. I have two ovens. Both take different amounts of time to cook with the exact same dough.) The cookies should be golden brown all over, crisp on the outside, and have a slightly soft chewy center.

Cool slightly on a cookie rack if you have it, just until they firm a little. (If you don't have a cookie rack, not to worry; they will still taste yummy. They just won't have quite the same crisp on the bottom.)

And then gobble a couple of them while they are still warm, with a nice cold glass of milk! Don't feel like you have to eat the whole batch in one sitting; they are really delicious cold, too.

** Another trick I use — now that the children have left home and I am baking cookies only for my husband and me — is I bake only what we will eat that day. The rest of the cookie dough I store in the fridge. This way, every day I can make a couple of freshly baked cookies for each of us to devour.*

ACKNOWLEDGMENTS

I have been very blessed to have help and input from my wonderfully talented editors, Cindy Hwang and Kerry Donovan, who helped make *Cliff's Edge* shine.

My thanks to the design teams who created the wonderful cover and the interior look.

I am grateful for the dynamic marketing team at Berkley. Erin Galloway, Jin Yu, Ryanne Probst, Jessica Brock, and Fareeda Bullert, thank you for your superhuman efforts in getting the word out about my novels.

My thanks also go to Nancy Berland, Cissy Hartley and the Writerspace team, as well as Kim Witherspoon and Jessica Mileo at InkWell Management for all that you do and have done.

I feel so fortunate that three extremely talented *New York Times* bestselling authors, Jayne Ann Krentz, Kat Martin, and Mariah

Stewart, carved time out of their busy lives to read my novel. They then gifted me with glorious blurbs. My profound thanks to these amazingly generous women, and to my friend Mary Bly for her friendship and writerly encouragement.

An enormous thank-you to my husband, Don, who encourages me, makes tasty food, and cheers me on every step of the way, and to my beloved sisters and my family and friends. I love you all very much.

And last but not least I'd like to extend my heartfelt gratitude to you, my readers, and all the booksellers and librarians who have championed my novels and other authors' books as well. Thank you for making all of our lives a little more beautiful.

Thank you!

ABOUT THE AUTHOR

Meg Tilly may be best known for her acclaimed Golden Globe-winning performance in the movie *Agnes of God.* Other screen credits include *The Big Chill, Valmont,* and, more recently, *Bomb Girls* and the Netflix movie *War Machine,* starring Brad Pitt. After publishing six standout young adult and literary women's fiction novels, the award-winning author/actress decided to write the kind of books she loves to read: romance novels. Tilly has three grown children and resides with her husband in the Pacific Northwest. She is currently at work writing the third Solace Island novel.

The employees of Thorndike Press hope you have enjoyed this Large Print book. All our Thorndike, Wheeler, and Kennebec Large Print titles are designed for easy reading, and all our books are made to last. Other Thorndike Press Large Print books are available at your library, through selected bookstores, or directly from us.

